THE EAGLE DANCER

To Jim
With Best Wishes –
[signature]

The Eagle Dancer

By Neel Elliott

Red Mountain Publishing
Birmingham, Alabama

Printed in the United States by
Red Mountain Publishing
Birmingham, AL

Text and Cover design by Leslie Cummins
Painting on cover, entitled "He Sees Her," by Rocky Hawkins of Santa Fe,
        New Mexico
Author photo by Amanda Davis

ISBN: 0-9649279-1-8

This work is a work of fiction. Names, characters, places and incidents are either the product of the author's imagination or they are used fictitiously.

PRINTED ON
RECYCLED PAPER

Distributed by Southern Publishers Group
1-800-628-0903

Written for
LAURA, CONLEY AND MAGGIE ELLIOTT

There were many friends who volunteered to help the author with this work. Several were kind enough to endure earlier drafts. These included Philip Jackson, Kate Nielson, Nina Botsford, Ginga Mylius, Pat Trammell, Allan Causey, Vicki Gunter, Walter Gresham, Terry Vermilye, Melissa Strange, Walker Jones, Susan Warnock, Nancy White, Bubba Smith, Brandon McIntosh, Ben Tyson, Norean Overton, James Abele, and Bert O'Neal. Their comments encouraged the author to keep working to the end.

My parents, Bud and Ann, my brothers, Steve and Dan, my mother-in-law, Louise Conley, my housekeeper, Clarice Smiley, my cousin, Amanda Davis, and my great aunt, Emily Neel were supportive and encouraging, all along the way.

Special contributions were made by Julia Mae Taylor, Michelle Segrest, Mabry Rogers, Temple Tutwiler, Lawrence Katz, Ellen Smith, Steve Parker, Leslie Cummins, and Rocky Hawkins. These people helped the author turn a draft into a book.

This book was also written in remembrance of Rex Conley, Ches, Sr., Ches, Jr., and Lon Hogshead, Maggie Young, Joe Neel and Mur Ware. Also to be remembered are Floppy, Dixie, Prince, Greta, Lucky, Toothbrush and Hairbrush.

This work of fiction is further dedicated to Yoda, Sadie, Panda, and Hope.

PROLOGUE

The verdict was guilty. The sentence was death. The execution of the man who tried to change the world was shown on television, live on CNN. Most viewers turned the channel, unable to look. But many witnessed his final moments, and heard his last words, before his body succumbed to the lethal injection.

The day after his funeral, a full-page ad appeared in *The L.A. Times*, *The New York Times*, *The Washington Post*, and *The International Herald Tribune*. The prisoner's last words were printed over a riveting photograph. It had been taken when he was a young man, long before he became ensnared by the people and the circumstances that killed him.

BOOK ONE

Mac's Treasure:
The Constantine Papers

CHAPTER 1

The Solstice

In Flagstaff, Arizona, sunsets were religious experiences. When the weather was warm, many of the locals gathered on the wooden decks of a mountainside bar called The Landslide. It was a little rowdy, but the chatter quieted to a whisper when the sun touched the horizon. The crowd drank their beers and margaritas in reverence, watching as the sun retired for the evening. Once it disappeared, the congregation broke the silence with a standing ovation. It was a show of appreciation.

Dr. Nigel "Mac" McFarland was a stranger at The Landslide, but even so, he felt a sense of kinship to the cheering crowd. He raised his third beer of the afternoon and offered a toast to the Sun Father known by the Hopi Indians as Tawa. Those within earshot of Mac echoed the name, and drank their libations, hoping Tawa would rise again in the morning and give a repeat performance.

As a thirty-seven year-old, part-time archeologist and full-time anthropology teacher, Mac knew a little bit about Native American religion and mythology; but he was in Flagstaff to learn a little more. The Hopi Tribal Council had invited Mac to Arizona to excavate a site on their reservation. He accepted the invitation because the Hopi tribe was believed to be one of the first to inhabit this continent. The tribe was also one of the most reclusive, rejecting the European version of western civilization. For centuries, the Hopi had preserved their culture, mostly by restricting the access of outside influence peddlers.

But this summer, Mac was going to have an opportunity to observe first hand those protected traditions which were collectively known as the Hopi Way. So he might understand his subject more fully, Mac had requested the assistance of a Hopi guide and interpreter. The Tribal Chairman had volunteered a young man of twenty-eight years named Julio Masito.

Across the table from Mac was his wife, Betsy, and their new acquaintance, Julio. He was a tall and muscular young man with earth-toned skin. His jet black hair fell below his shoulders. His dark eyes reflected supreme confidence, balanced by his spirit that conveyed humility. Betsy and Julio had been talking for several minutes, while Mac ordered another round of beer and listened.

"This is a beautiful place, Julio. I'll bet you come here a lot, don't you?"

"Pretty often. Mostly to watch the sunsets. But in the winter when the ski slopes are open, this is a good place to get some lunch."

"I'll bet it is. I didn't even realize that you could ski in Arizona."

"The peak behind us is over 12,600 feet high. We get almost a hundred inches of snow each year in Flagstaff, and up on the mountain we get a lot more."

"That's amazing. I always pictured the desert or the Grand Canyon when I thought of Arizona. I didn't realize how diverse the climate and terrain is. It's kinda hard not to fall in love with this place."

"The Hopi say these surroundings are sacred."

"Well it's hard to disagree. Tell me a little about your tribe."

"Only about 12,000 Hopi remain in the Fourth World. For the most part, we stay together on the reservation. But a few years ago I decided I wanted to go to college..."

"Mac told me you are a student at Northern Arizona University."

"I just finished my junior year."

"Ready to go home?"

Julio nodded his head and said, "It's been a while."

When Mac heard this, he suspected that Julio was a little more than homesick. It had to be tough to be one of only a few from his tribe on a campus of 15,000 students. By now, Julio had been exposed to the constant pang of greed, the incessant drumbeat of the media, and the relentless pace of life that characterized America. It was possible, Mac thought to himself, that Julio's view of the world was completely out of sync with the views of contemporary American society, yet he seemed to have adapted well to both worlds.

Curiosity finally forced Mac to jump into the conversation with a loaded question. "Now that you've lived on and off the reservation, Julio, tell me, what's the difference between the Hopi Way and the American way?"

"That's hard to answer over a beer. There are so many differences...tomorrow, you'll start to see," Julio deferred.

"Then here's to tomorrow," Mac cheered, raising his mug once again. "Maybe by the end of this summer, if I dig deep enough, I'll discover the Hopi Way."

Julio touched his mug to Mac's and repeated, "Here's to tomorrow."

ᗡᗡᗡ

The next morning, Mac parked his jeep in front of Julio's garage apartment, and jumped out to help with his bags. After loading the luggage, Mac ordered his eighty-five pound, black labrador named Crow, to move over on the back seat to make room for another traveler. The dog was a child-substitute for Mac and Betsy, and tagged along with them almost everywhere they went.

Their destination was the capitol village of the Hopi, a town called New Oraibi. It was located about a hundred miles from

Flagstaff, at the foot of Third Mesa in the middle of the reservation.

When they arrived, they were met by several Council leaders who escorted them to meet the Tribal Chairman. The Chairman was sitting at the head of a large table in an adobe building that served as chambers for the Council. Mac, Betsy and the Council leaders all took their seats around the table as Julio made the introductions.

The meeting lasted only twenty minutes, but it was enough time for the Chairman to cover procedural matters. He assigned one of the Councilmen to oversee Mac's project, and report on its progress each week at the Council meetings. The Chairman announced that a dig site had been selected on top of Third Mesa, near the ancient village of Old Oraibi. From what Mac had heard about the site, he expected to unearth the remains of centuries-old housing that he hoped would contain the relics of previous generations.

Once business was concluded, the Chairman ignited a ceremonial pipe that had been packed with tobacco, and puffed vigorously until his lungs were full. He then passed it over to Mac, who drew in the smoke, symbolizing his acceptance of the hospitality of the Hopi tribe.

When the meeting adjourned, the three of them walked across the plaza to return to the jeep. Julio directed Mac and Betsy's attention to two larger-than-life figures, dancing to the sound of turtle shell rattles in a circle of children. The dancers were dressed as kachinas, imitating Hopi spirits that were half-man, half-animal or half-bird. Julio told Mac and Betsy that on this day, the day of the summer solstice, these kachinas began dancing at dawn. They would dance all day, until the entire tribe joined in during a special ceremony at sunset. It was called the Niman Ceremony, held each year on this longest day, which marked the beginning of harvest.

The sound of the rattles caused Mac to recall the only other time he had been on the Hopi Reservation. It had been several years before at another celebration called the Powamu Ceremony. This was a perennial "spring rites" festival centered around planting and fertility. It was also a time when Hopi children of age were initiated into the Hopi Way, Mac's first exposure to the expression. He remembered how spectacular it had been to witness the ceremony. The climax of the Powamu Ceremony had been the Bean Dance, the final ritual that took place in the kivas or underground chambers of the Hopi. The kivas had been part of Hopi religious ceremony for hundreds of years, chambers that symbolized the womb of Mother Earth, and the emergence of humanity into a new dominion on the planet's surface. The Hopi referred to this dominion as the Fourth World.

In a rare and privileged moment, Mac had been invited to participate in this secretive liturgy. At first, he felt unwelcome since he was the only pahana or white man in the kiva. But soon he felt a sense of connection, as the Hopi inhabitants shared with him a special bean stew, the Hopi sacrament of communion. During the ceremony, kachinas entered the kiva. There, in the warmth of the sacred womb of Mother Earth, the Bean Dance began. That had been Mac's first encounter with kachinas, an encounter that he would never forget.

Mac was awakened from his flashback by the sound of Crow's tail banging loudly against the jeep's interior. The brushstrokes had smeared slobber and dander across one of the windows in the style of a twentieth century abstract painting. Mac couldn't blame Julio for taking a deep breath before climbing into the back seat with Crow, but the effort was all in vain. Crow started licking Julio's face as soon as he sat down.

Mac followed Julio's directions out of New Oraibi along a bumpy and winding dirt road that eventually traversed a steep face to the top of Third Mesa. Their accommodations for the summer were located just outside of Old Oraibi, a village now in ruin. On arrival, Crow leapt out of the jeep and immediately marked his new territory, throwing dirt fifteen feet beyond the mesa's edge with his hind legs in an inexplicable show of maleness, creating a small duststorm that slowly descended six hundred feet to the valley floor below.

Feeling stiff from the journey, Mac stepped out and stretched his limbs, reaching out towards the expanse that lay between the mesa top and the horizon. Then he unlatched the tailgate of the wagon and unloaded the luggage, one piece at a time. They carried what they could into the McFarland's new home for the summer. It was a spectacular cliff dwelling built directly into the cliff-wall of the mesa. After taking care of the luggage, Julio led Mac and Betsy a short distance away to a spring-fed creek that would serve as their fresh water supply. Trekking over the rugged ground, Mac felt his adrenaline surge as it did each time he began something new.

When they returned, Mac asked Julio if he wanted to take the jeep back into New Oraibi. He refused, saying that he preferred to hike down an old trail that he hadn't travelled since going off to school. But before he left them, he invited Mac and Betsy to attend the climax of the Niman Ceremony that evening. It was an invitation they enthusiastically accepted.

Left to themselves, the McFarlands unpacked their belongings. They positioned their bedding to take full advantage of the magnificent view. It was so inspirational, they couldn't suppress the sexual energy that embraced them both. The two lovers spent the balance of the afternoon in their new bed, in their new home, literally on the edge of a new world.

At 6:00 p.m., Mac started a fire and opened a new bottle of wine to share with his beloved wife. He cooked their dinner over the open flame, while in the background a faint sound of beating drums could be heard from the village below. The percussions promised that this would be a night of enchantment, full of mysticism, full of magic. The dinner was delicious, but once finished, Mac and Betsy jumped in the jeep and descended the mesa, backtracking their way into New Oraibi.

Not wanting to disturb the celebration in any way, they parked a block away and took their place on the perimeter. The plaza was crowded with Indians of all ages, adorned in costumes, masks and body paints. In the center of the crowd was a bonfire of corn bundles that burned furiously, sending sparks dancing skyward. The clouds in the west that had earlier filtered the sun's rays had now parted, and the sun stood alone in all of its radiant power, beneath a ceiling of scattered cotton balls. The sky was beginning to show strata of color in a God-filled arrangement. A lone star appeared.

Mac watched with great interest as the tribal leaders took center stage, dancing about the bonfire with turtle shell rattles, harmonizing with the beat of the drums. It was a prayer, liturgy in its purest form, conducted at the altar of the setting sun. The fireball of glory was dispersing its radiance across a field of clouds — gold and silver, yellow, red and blue. The entire spectrum of light was displayed in this moment when the Hopi honored the sun.

While the event was clearly religious in content, the atmosphere was almost carnival. Mac scanned the crowd looking for Julio, but everyone's face was painted or covered by a mask or headdress of some sort. Wanting to record the moment, Mac finally found his subject among the feather-clad legions of kachinas, dancing around the bonfire.

Julio was having a vision. He saw himself as an eagle, soaring with outstretched wings, high above the Fourth World. The eagle flew so high that he heard the Great Spirit speaking. When he returned home, he delivered a divine message to the inhabitants of the Fourth World. But he was too weak to complete his mission.

So that he might regain his strength, the eagle flew low in search of food. He preyed upon poisonous snakes, nourishing when eaten, but deadly when mishandled. Each time he faced the vipers, the eagle knew it might be his last. But he was determined to carry on, until all heard the message.

Mac saw Julio emerge from his dream state. He focused the lens of his camera, framing Julio in a sensational pose as he danced around the circle. The sky had darkened, but the bonfire was burning brightly, shining light on the mesa wall that rose up behind the village. The glow created an aura about the eagle dancer that made him appear divine.

CHAPTER 2

The Seduction

It was a cool, fall afternoon in Northshore, Indiana and the Lions of Jesuit University were about to play a football game across the campus from Mac's office. He was peering out his open window toward the stadium and reaching for the kachina doll that sat upon his credenza. Julio had carved the dancing figure out of the root of a cottonwood tree. It was hand-painted and decorated with eagle feathers, resembling Julio's appearance the night of the summer solstice celebration. On the day Mac and Betsy left Arizona, Julio gave it to Mac as a going away present.

Lost in retrospect, the shrill ring of the telephone almost caused Mac to drop the gift that he held in his hand. He answered the phone in a deep, raspy tone barely recognizable even to himself.

"Hello."

"May I speak to Mac, please?" a female voice inquired.

"It's me, Vanessa. I know it doesn't sound like me, but it's me."

"It is I," she corrected. "It must have been those cigarettes and tequila, don't you think?"

"Yeah, I guess so. But tequila or not, that wasn't me you met last night. That was Mr. Hyde who behaved so badly."

"I don't care if you're Jekell or Hyde, so long as you do everything you promised."

Mac rubbed his face in his hands, not knowing what to say next. He knew that his need for discovery had on occasion gotten him into trouble. In days past, he had sneaked across guarded borders. He had taken uncountable risks along the way. Yet he always seemed to have a knack for escape from jeopardy. But this time he was worried. He tried to compose himself, remembering the drunken commitment he had made to meet her during the game on Saturday. Now he would be asked to finish what he started.

"Vanessa, I'm sorry about last night..."

"Don't say another word. I'll be there in five minutes. I know where your building is, just tell me how to find your office."

"All right, all right. The door on the side of the building is open. Come on up to the second floor, Room 221."

After hanging up the phone, Mac thought how stupid it had been to suggest that they meet in his office, but that seemed to be part of the fantasy they had conjured the night before. It was true that most of the school buildings would be deserted during the game, and so he foolishly thought it would be the perfect time to indulge his imagination. Mac looked down at his desk, eyeing the two tickets that would go unused that Saturday afternoon.

He stood up from his chair and struggled to the men's room, where he fumbled for the light switch. Leaning over the sink, he splashed cold water into his face and took a couple of aspirin, hoping to revive himself from his state of self-pity. He brushed his teeth three times and rinsed his breath, trying to exorcise the nicotine and mescal demons that had taken up residence in his mouth. Looking in the mirror, he saw traces of guilt and pain etched in his face. He returned again to the cold water, hoping to wash these traces away.

He scrubbed and scrubbed until he was certain that he could do no better. Then he toweled off and stood for the second time before the mirror to review his appearance. The look had changed, reflecting the thrill of anticipation. His adrenaline was pumping again. He felt ready for whatever challenge might come his way, even if it meant crossing the line. Vanessa, he convinced himself, was pure sport. He could read about the football game in the newspaper.

When Mac returned to his office, he sat down in his chair and again stared blankly toward the stadium. His thoughts wandered only a short distance away to the bar where he had been hours earlier, having a beer with Dr. Ivan Berkowitz, Mac's most devoted friend in Northshore. Professionally, Ivan was an Associate Professor of Geophysics, although he had graduate degrees in both astrophysics and geochemistry. His raw I.Q. was scary. He was a Russian-born Jew who came to the United States as an immigrant, financed by Operation Exodus. He and his wife, Katrina, had been resettled in Northshore, Indiana, by the Hebrew Immigration Assistance Society. There in Northshore, Ivan ironically landed a teaching job at the most parochial Catholic school of all, Jesuit University.

Mac liked Ivan from the first time they met, admiring his courage to stick out like a sore thumb in the almost homogenous environment at J.U. The two became fast friends, both dedicated to Friday-afternoon cocktails. Afterwards, they typically met their wives at a near-by Mexican restaurant. But last night had been different. Betsy and Katrina had joined two other faculty-member wives on a shopping spree in Chicago, leaving the boys to fend for themselves.

After several rounds at the bar and the usual catch-up talk about whatever went on during the week, Ivan and Mac took turns commenting on the female population. Mac remembered gawking at an especially attractive young woman, when his stare was interrupted by a tug and a voice that said, "Dr. McFarland?"

"Yes," he answered at a distinct disadvantage. "I'm sorry but..."

"I'm Vanessa, Vanessa Reilly. My roommate is taking one of your anthropology courses."

"Please call me Mac. Let me introduce you to my friend, Ivan, Dr. Ivan Berkowitz."

"Vanessa, nice to meet you," Ivan said.

"It's a pleasure to meet you both," Vanessa replied. "And this is my friend, Susan Phelps."

The two boys focused on the nubile faces smiling back at them. For the next twenty minutes, uninterrupted conversation flowed between Mac and Vanessa, but if sworn-in to testify, he couldn't have recalled a single word spoken. It was only when she asked him if he liked garter belts that his far-away eyes focused tightly on her. Looking down at her narrow waist and long legs, he acted on impulse, touching her thighs through her mini-skirt, confirming that the tease was no bluff.

Mac excused himself to go to the men's room and when he returned, tequila shots were in progress. Vanessa handed him his glass as he stepped back into the circle. He raised it up and offered a toast to the luck of the Lions. As soon as he set the empty glass back on the bar, she gently pushed a juicy lime slice into his mouth. He sat down next to her, wondering where these overtures might lead.

It was a vain effort to pull Ivan and Susan into their conversation, their chemistry clearly no match for the spontaneous combustion taking place between Mac and Vanessa. Rather than join in, Ivan rose to his feet to say good-night. He gave Susan and Vanessa a friendly handshake and then turned to Mac who stood and said, "Ivan, I don't think I can go to the game tomorrow. Sorry to cancel."

Ivan winked at Mac on the way out and asked him to call on Sunday.

After Ivan left, Vanessa searched her purse for the leather case that housed her cigarettes. While she was still looking, Mac reached for her lighter that had been sitting by her drink on the bar and lit her cigarette, reviving a social grace that had been dormant for years. When he, the non-smoker, took the cigarette that she offered him, he knew that he had surrendered his principles to her undaunted sexuality. But because she had come with Susan, and Susan was ready to leave, Vanessa had to tell Mac that they should see each other soon, alone. Mac seized the moment by suggesting that she visit him Saturday in his office, whispering in her ear promises that would be played out on game day.

⚊⚊⚊

When Vanessa knocked lightly on the door, Mac snapped out of his coma and opened it, not speaking a word but pulling her in, kissing her deeply. She raised up on her toes and gave herself to him, pushing her tongue far into his mouth and then circling his lips. He had to let go to gasp for air, shocked by the intensity and passion of this first kiss.

Across campus, the game must have gotten underway, for the crowd noise suddenly made it almost useless for them to speak. Instead, he locked the door and led her to the couch, anxious to make her comfortable, but impatient to taste her kisses and more. There on the couch, he remembered her teasing from the night before, and couldn't help reaching again for her thighs, this time looking into her eyes for a reaction. Vanessa pushed his hands away and stood up. She turned to face him, slowly pulling her skirt up just enough to show the top of her stockings, suspended by the silky ribbons of her garter belt. Her legs seemed a mile long. The excitement weakened him. She was taking control, exercising her power, casting her spell.

With her skirt hiked-up, she pushed his knees apart and knelt between them. She called the plays all afternoon like a Heisman quarterback, perfect timing, perfect control. Only her backing-off from time to time allowed him to continue. And as often as the Jesuit Lions scored, Vanessa screamed out her pleasure, muted only by the throng next door. It was a game neither would ever forget.

⚊⚊⚊

On Sunday, Mac kept his promise and called Ivan. They had been running mates for several years, but recently had started riding cross-country bikes, a new weekend tradition. When Ivan picked up the phone, he immediately demanded, "All right, Mac, let's hear it. Let's hear the whole truth and nothing but the truth, from the beginning to the end!"

"Why don't we go biking, and when you get out ahead of me, I'll dribble out bits and pieces to slow you down," Mac answered.

At the end of forty miles of strenuous pumping and sweating, they were laughing hard after Mac had shared Saturday's sporting news with his friend. Mac knew that Ivan was too disciplined to cross the line of infidelity. Mac also knew that Ivan was trustworthy, almost to a flaw. Both of them knew that what had been spoken that day was pure graveyard talk. As they put their bikes away to go inside for a refreshing drink, Ivan asked Mac one last question.

"Well, do you think you'll ever see her again?"

Mac replied, "Nope," and nothing more was said.

CHAPTER 3

The Invitation

Mac kept to his routine for the rest of the fall, teaching a full load of classes while trying to make plans for the coming summer. When his plans finally firmed up, he picked up the phone and called Ivan.

"Hey, it's me. What's going on?"

"Same old stuff, nothing new. How about this nasty weather?"

"I heard it's supposed to get worse before it gets better. I hate this shit. It drives me crazy."

"Yeah, me, too."

"Well, how about we go eat some Mexican food, drink tequila and tell some lies? I've got some good news for you."

"Is that your first lie?"

"Nope. I really do have some good news."

"Great! Let me call Katrina to make sure it's O.K. Unless you hear from me, we'll see you at 7:30."

"Good. See ya there."

Mac and Betsy sat at their usual table with a large half-empty pitcher of frozen margaritas sitting squarely between them. Across the way, two salted glasses decorated with green limes and straws stood empty waiting for Ivan and Katrina's arrival. The basket of tortilla chips was practically empty. Broken corners were scattered half-way across the table, with droppings of picante sauce marking trails from hand to mouth.

As Ivan and Katrina nudged their way past the crowd standing at the door, Mac poured their drinks and flagged a busboy to bring more chips. He stood to kiss Katrina and greet Ivan when they arrived at the table. After everybody took their seats, Ivan asked Mac to go ahead and announce the news, whatever it was.

"O.K., O.K.," Mac began with a big smile. "I'll give you a hint. Answer this right and this pitcher of margaritas is on me. What's your favorite bird on Thanksgiving?"

"Turkey?" Ivan and Katrina blurted out in unison.

"Yep. All right, next question for a free dinner. What city was the capitol of the Eastern Empire when the Romans ruled the world?"

"Constantinople!" Ivan said with the enthusiasm of a game show contestant.

"Correct! And now, it's time for double jeopardy! I will ask you one final question. If you answer this one correctly, then I'll buy your wife's dinner, too. Here it is. What is the name of this famous city today?"

Ivan smiled, knowing that it was Mac's turn to pick up the tab anyway. "ISTANBUL."

"That's it. You're a winner and the recipient of two free dinners, all expenses paid, at your favorite Mexican restaurant! This coming summer, that's where I'll be...Istanbul, Turkey! My sponsor has come through with the money!"

Mac refilled everyone's glasses until the pitcher ran dry, and then raised his glass to propose a toast, "Here's to Istanbul and the resurrection of the Lost Empire!"

Everyone clicked their glasses together, laughing at themselves for being so corny. That is, all but Betsy. Mac had already broken the news to her that she would have to stay home alone this summer, while he chiseled his way back in time. At least she would have the company of Crow, Mac consoled. And who knew, maybe this would be the summer that would bring fame and fortune. Based upon her expressions and her body language, she wasn't very comforted by these words.

Ivan noticed her unease and asked, "Betsy, you going with him?"

"Not this time. They don't allow women to work in the Middle East, and it would be too expensive to just carry me along. Mac is leaving me at home to take care of Crow."

Her frustration was apparent in her tone, so Mac steered the conversation in a new direction, "I'm thinking about calling up Julio Masito, the Hopi Indian who worked with me last summer. It'll be a good opportunity for him to see some of the world."

ʏʏʏ

The weather was so bad, Mac decided to work all weekend on details related to the project in Turkey. One of the last tasks he had to accomplish was finding some help, an assistant who would go with him. It was time to call Julio. In one hand he picked up the kachina of the eagle dancer from his credenza, and with the other hand he picked up the phone..

"Hey, Julio! It's Mac."

"Mac, it's good to hear from you! How have you been?"

"Well, we've had some nasty weather for almost a week now, and I'm getting cabin fever. It's colder than a North Pole nunnery. We've got freezing rain, and the wind is blowing at about thirty miles an hour. When these storms move down off Lake Michigan, it's not much fun in Northshore. What's it like in Flagstaff?"

"Here it's snowing again, but in Phoenix, it's eighty-five degrees. Our weather is nuts. The ski slopes above The Landslide have been open for a month now."

"You're kidding."

"We already have a sixty-inch base on the mountain."

"Wow! I didn't know you skied, Julio."

"Not very often, but I love it."

"Well, maybe one day, I'll come join you. It sounds like fun. Tell me, how's school going?"

"Super. It's been going really well. I think I'm learning to enjoy it more every year. The only problem is, this is my last year and I'm running out of time."

"That's right. You're a senior this year. Have you made any plans?"

"Not exactly. I put an application in to graduate school, but I haven't heard from them yet."

"There at Northern Arizona State?"

"No, actually at Georgetown University in Washington, D.C., their Graduate School of Foreign Service."

"Really, Julio. That's fantastic. What possessed you to go for a career in diplomacy?"

"I don't know exactly. I just want to get out and see the world I guess, kinda like you."

Mac was flattered that he had possibly influenced Julio to pursue such a noble role in life. Mac finally came to the point of his phone call.

"Listen, Julio. The reason I called was to follow up on what I said at the end of last summer, about the two of us working together again on a summer job. You probably didn't take that very seriously, but I meant every word."

"That would be great, Mac. Are you coming back this summer?"

"No, not to Arizona. How does Istanbul, Turkey sound?"

"Istanbul?"

"Yeah. I've got a job for both of us. It's gonna be a little different though, let me warn you."

"What are you gonna be looking for over there?"

"Roman Empire stuff. So, do you want to go with me?"

"To Istanbul? Are you serious?"

"Dead serious. Do you wanna go?"

"Uh...Mac, I'm embarrassed to tell you this, but I've never traveled outside of Arizona before."

"Hold it. Hold it right there. I'm gonna send you some information, and then you think about it. I'll call you back in a week or ten days. Think positive, my friend, think positive."

Mac hoped that Julio would say yes to the invitation, but now only time would tell. When Mac hung up the phone, he set Julio's gift, the Hopi kachina, back in its place on his credenza. He had a package of information to get in the mail.

Ten days later, Mac dialed Julio's number again, optimistic that his invitation would be accepted. "Julio..."

"Hey Mac!" Julio answered before Mac could identify himself.

"Did you get the stuff I sent you?"

"Yes sir."

"So what do you think?"

"It's looks great! I've got only one problem."

"What's that?"

"Well, since the last time we talked, I've been accepted at Georgetown."

"That's fantastic, Julio! Congratulations!"

"Thanks, Mac. Thanks a lot. The only thing is...school begins just a few days after we are scheduled to return. That won't give me enough time at home before I have to be in Washington."

"We can fix that! What if I move the trip forward by a week or so? Will that help? And, how about if I pay for your airfare from Phoenix to Washington when you get back, just a little bonus for helping me out."

Julio was ecstatic. "Really?" he asked.

"Yep. If that'll help, I think I can swing it."

"Well, yes, sir, that would solve everything! You see, my mother is the one having a hard time with me leaving for Washington. She's afraid she'll never see me again. If I could spend a little time with her and my sister before I go, well, that would make all the difference in the world."

"All right then, I'll make it happen."

"Thanks-a-million!"

"You're welcome."

"So, the trip is on?"

"Yep, the trip is on," Mac answered. "I'll call you again soon to tell you more about it." When Mac hung up the phone, he could just picture Julio jumping for joy.

CHAPTER 4

The Sponsor

Wanting to hear all about his first flight ever, Mac met Julio at his gate when he arrived at O'Hare International Airport. The two of them were scheduled to visit with Mr. Joseph Baldone, the sole sponsor of the project, before traveling on to Istanbul. Mac tried to brief Julio on Baldone during their cab ride into town.

"Yeah, he's one rich son-of-a-bitch. Got millions. Enough to buy himself a seat on the Board of Trustees at Jesuit University," Mac said cynically. Mac could tell Julio wasn't really listening. His attention was held captive by the skyline of Chicago.

As the cab pulled into the hotel where they would be staying, a bellman opened their door and said, "Welcome to The Drake, gentlemen." He attended to their luggage, gave Mac several claim stubs and directed them to the lobby.

Mac led Julio across the ornate room to the registration desk. The coffered ceilings were highlighted by gold-painted molding. Crystal chandeliers brightened the antique furnishings that were arranged on thick oriental rugs. Mac noticed the impression that the opulent decor made on Julio, who had never before seen such a showcase.

When Mac checked-in for the two of them, the registrar placed a message on the counter. The message read:

"Dr. McFarland:
     I have made dinner reservations for us in The Palm at 7:30 p.m. this evening. I look forward to seeing both you and your young associate. Welcome to the Windy City.
                                        Joseph Baldone"

At exactly 7:30, the twosome appeared before the maître d' in their jackets and ties and asked for Mr. Baldone. Mac had cleaned up nicely, although he preferred to maintain an element of disarray. Julio unintentionally appeared like a male fashion model, with his long hair pulled back into a stylish pony tail.

The maître d' escorted them to the table where Mr. Baldone was already seated with a distinguished black gentleman, whom Mac failed to recognize. Both men stood as Mac approached the table. Mr. Baldone was only five foot six or seven, and he appeared to be nearly sixty years of age with dark, thinning hair, gray sideburns and a pudgy build. He looked like he had enjoyed the last twenty years of his life in a style that only the very wealthy could afford.

Mac was the first to extend his hand and introduce himself. He then introduced Julio to Mr. Baldone, who in turn introduced his own guest, Dr. Myers Watson, the head curator for the Chicago Museum of Art. After all took their seats, Mr. Baldone poured four glasses of champagne from a bottle that had been chilled in ice at the table side. He lifted his own glass to propose a toast of welcome, then a second toast to the coming summer, and a third to the success of the Istanbul project. Everybody joined in, cheering the exotic adventure that lay ahead.

As soon as the waiter had taken everyone's drink orders, Mr. Baldone began, "Julio, how was your flight from Phoenix?"

"Everything went fine, sir. The weather was beautiful. It was a perfect day to fly."

"It was your first flight, I've been told."

"Yes, sir," Julio replied with some embarrassment.

"I'm very glad you came along with Dr. McFarland. He's going to need some help in Istanbul, probably more than he imagines."

"I'm glad to be included, sir," Julio answered humbly.

Mac saw this as an opportune time to jump into the conversation and added, "And I'm glad he's along, too. Julio and I worked together last summer in Arizona."

"So I hear, so I hear," Mr. Baldone said sagely.

In Mac's mind, Baldone was trying to control the conversation from the first word. He's a 'Little Napoleon', Mac thought to himself.

Baldone continued, "So, are your accommodations satisfactory at The Drake?"

Mac interpreted the question as a statement. Mr. Baldone wanted to make sure that everyone at the table understood that it was his money being spent and that he had plenty of it.

"Yes, they couldn't be nicer," Mac responded.

"Good, I'm glad to hear it."

"Well, let's get down to business and discuss the task at hand. Why don't I begin by telling you about the site that has been selected."

For the next twenty minutes, Mr. Baldone discussed the history of the site, its physical attributes and his plans for its excavation. After listening to him speak, Mac was convinced that Mr. Baldone had never in his life participated in an excavation of any kind, although Baldone talked as though he had personally unearthed Pompeii.

According to his story, a friend of his who owned an international construction company was hired to construct a multi-story office building in Istanbul. During the site testing and preparation phase of the project, core samples indicated potential load bearing problems, and so further testing was required. Larger core samples were drilled that revealed prior construction to a depth of thirty feet below the ground's surface. The study concluded that multiple structures had been built over the centuries, one on top of the other. The construction site, of course, had to be rejected due to potential settling problems.

"My friend knew that I had an interest in collecting Roman-period art, and so he mentioned the characteristics of the site to me at a social function, of all places. I told him to contact the owner and to make him an offer. The owner was thrilled to accept my offer, and that is how I gained control of this location."

When dinner was served, Mr. Baldone had to rest his monologue. Mac and Julio were relieved to see the waiter appear, weary of Baldone's self-aggrandizing style. While Mr. Baldone chewed his twelve-ounce filet mignon, Dr. Myers Watson took his turn at the lectern.

"Tomorrow, I am going to take the two of you on a tour of the Chicago Museum of Art. We'll send a driver over in the morning at nine o'clock. He'll pick you up in front of the hotel. The museum, of course, is my pride and joy. One of the most interesting of our exhibits is the Baldone Exhibit, and we will spend a good deal of time reviewing the collection, to acquaint you with Mr. Baldone's special interests. After the tour, we will break for lunch, and then meet Mr. Baldone in his office at the Hancock Tower for a final briefing. Your flight departs tomorrow evening at six o'clock from O'Hare. It's the red-eye to London, I believe. From there, you will take a connecting flight to Istanbul."

Mac acknowledged the schedule, but didn't participate much in the conversation. He thought it best to just listen and keep his mouth shut. Julio completely kept to himself, quiet as a church mouse. Mac suspected that Julio was slightly intimidated by the whole scene.

When dinner was over and the two of them walked back to their rooms, Mac told Julio not to worry. "Tomorrow night we'll be outa here. We'll be thousands of miles away from those two assholes."

☙

The next morning, Mac and Julio met in the lobby for coffee, and at the appointed time they stepped outside, where they were greeted by the bellman. The bellman addressed each of them by name, obviously informed by the driver of a white stretch limousine that was waiting in front of the hotel. Mac gave the bellman a couple of dollars and ducked into the back seat. Julio followed close behind. Once they were in, the driver said, "Good morning, gentlemen," before closing the privacy window and driving away toward the museum.

On arrival, they were met by Dr. Watson, who welcomed them warmly. They climbed the marble stairs and began the tour by walking directly to the Baldone Exhibit. Mac knew that Julio's knowledge of Roman-period art was non-existent, so Mac wasn't surprised that Julio remained quiet during the tour, probably afraid that even a question might expose his ignorance. It didn't really matter, because Dr. Watson was in his lecturing mode anyway. Occasionally, Mac would engage him in some esoteric conversation about various pieces, but even that was difficult. Dr. Watson was far more garrulous when not in the presence of Mr. Baldone. Mac attributed Watson's change in personality to the fact that they were in Watson's domain now. This was his turf.

After completing their review of the exhibit, Dr. Watson suggested that Julio be taken to see the museum's Native American collection. Watson then escorted Mac to the basement, where pieces that were being restored or preserved for display at a later date were held in storage. They agreed to meet Julio in thirty minutes in front of the museum, when they would all go get some lunch.

Mac and Dr. Watson descended to the bottom floor and walked into a dimly lighted area that was so vast that it reminded Mac of a warehouse. They walked down countless rows before arriving at the storage area reserved for the Baldone collection. Piece after piece of Roman art was uncovered, some with stories from Dr. Watson, and others without.

While preparing for the meeting with Mr. Baldone, Mac had researched most of the public works on display upstairs, but these unfamiliar pieces stirred his curiosity. Now it was he who was becoming garrulous and inquisitive, that is until Dr. Watson uncovered one Roman sculpture that shocked Mac into silence. Trying to recover, Mac injected some innocuous small talk, while Dr.

Watson draped the covering back over the piece. But Mac's nerves were now on edge. He knew that this sculpture had been stolen several years ago from a collection in Damascus. With great paranoia, Mac looked for a hint of recognition in Dr. Watson's eyes, but detected none.

After regaining his composure, Mac turned away from the subject of the collections and focused his inquiries on Mr. Baldone.

"Tell me again Myers, how long have you known Joseph Baldone?"

"Well, let's see. I have served as the curator for this museum for the last five years. I didn't personally know Mr. Baldone before that time, although he was known to me by reputation within the art community as one of Chicago's most generous art patrons."

This response was interesting to Mac, but it did not really tell him what he needed to know. Dr. Watson seemed unaware that his museum was harboring stolen goods. Afraid to push any further, Mac looked at his watch and suggested that they return to the surface to meet Julio for lunch.

When they walked out into the bright sunlight, Julio was waiting with the limousine driver. Dr. Watson instructed the driver to take them to a restaurant frequented only by locals where a light lunch could be served up in short order. Eager to learn more about Baldone, Mac began again with his questions to Dr. Watson.

"How long has Mr. Baldone been collecting?"

"All in all, I'd say he has been assembling Roman art for the past ten or fifteen years. I've been told that initially everything was purchased from the auctioneers at Sotheby's and Christie's. Money never seemed to stand in Mr. Baldone's way. I've also been told that he became almost fanatical in his desire to become known within the art community, which as you know can be quite provincial. He got their attention when, years ago, he personally financed a dig that turned up a number of pieces now on exhibit, plus several of those that I showed you in the basement.

"Why Roman art?"

"I'm not 100% positive, but if I were guessing I'd say that he has a strong interest in his heritage, and certainly the Roman period would be a high water mark in Italian history. Mr. Baldone doesn't do anything in a small way. His interest in the Romans borders on zeal. He has strong connections in both Rome and in the Vatican."

"Well, Julio and I feel fortunate to have this opportunity, and we hope to bring back the spoils of another successful dig to add to Mr. Baldone's collection and your exhibition."

After lunch, Mac and Julio were dropped off to check out of the hotel, and then were taken to the John Hancock Tower, along with Dr. Watson. The limo driver had been instructed to escort Julio to the top of the tower, so he could marvel at the spectacular view. Dr. Watson and Mac would conclude their final briefing with Mr. Baldone.

The four of them boarded a high-speed elevator that served the upper section of the tower. As the elevator raced skyward, Mac's ears popped twice. Then his stomach ascended into his throat as the elevator braked rather abruptly. Mac and Dr. Watson stepped out on the eighty-second floor. Before the doors closed, Mac told Julio that he would meet him in the street-level lobby near the entrance to the tower as soon as the meeting was over.

The elevator lobby on the eighty-second floor had dark, hardwood floors with inlaid, green, Italian marble chips. The walls were mahogany-paneled. Recessed ceiling lights focused upon original oil paintings, many by the Italian masters. Behind the receptionist, there was an impressive spiral staircase with brass railings and white marble steps softened by an ornate red Persian rug. Beyond the staircase was Lake Michigan, blue and endless like an ocean.

Mac stepped up to the glass and looked down. It gave him a mild case of vertigo, so he backed away a few feet. It was a windy day on Lake Michigan. Mac's thoughts were captured by the peristaltic rhythm of the lake's waves, appearing only as lines moving toward the shore. Within moments, Mac became hypnotized, but he was awakened by the stern voice of Mr. Baldone's secretary, who coldly escorted the two gentlemen back into Mr. Baldone's office.

"I hope you've enjoyed your stay in Chicago," Mr. Baldone said as he stood behind his desk and greeted Mac with a handshake.

"Our stay could not have been any better, thank you."

"Myers tells me that you found the tour of the museum to be interesting, and you might know more about the exhibit pieces than even he."

"Well, I don't..."

"Your modesty is unbecoming, Dr. McFarland."

"Well, I certainly am impressed with your collection."

"I understand that you were particularly interested in one of the sculptures in the basement."

Mac was stunned. He was at a complete loss for words. Apparently, Watson had noticed his suspicion and reported it to Baldone. Mac ducked the question entirely, but the transition to safer ground was awkward. He sensed that the entire summer project in Istanbul would be in jeopardy if he answered honestly.

"Yes, some of those basement pieces were so impressive, I'm surprised that they are not all upstairs on display."

It was just enough to steer Baldone away from his quest. Now it was time to follow quickly with a question of his own to close the door behind the treacherous subject. "Mr. Baldone, if you were to issue to us a mission statement prior to our departure, what would it say?"

"Your mission, Dr. McFarland, is simply to investigate the site — to find Roman treasures deposited in Istanbul when Constantinople was the eastern capitol of the Roman Empire. If you find them, then turn them over to your Turkish guide. He will take care of the other details. And by the way, Dr. McFarland, if you don't find them, then we will buy them through our connections in the Middle East. Baldone-sponsored excavations are successful, Dr. McFarland."

With that, Joseph Baldone pushed his chair away from his desk, stood and extended his hand toward Mac. He looked Mac directly in the eye, not releasing his handshake and said, "Any further questions, Dr. McFarland? You should ask them now, or forever hold your peace."

"No, sir." Mac replied, feeling very uncomfortable. Once freed from Baldone's grip, Mac turned and said good-bye to Dr. Watson, never looking back at the intense stare of Baldone.

After Mac departed, Watson and Baldone continued their conversation.

"Well, Myers, did he recognize it or not?"

"Yes sir. I'm sure he did, sir."

"How did he respond?"

"He'll be fine, Mr. Baldone. And even if he blows the whistle, the stolen sculpture will be a thousand miles from here by midnight."

"Do you think he passed the test, Myers?"

"If he gets on the plane, sir, he passes the test. And if later on he becomes a problem for us, he'll never come home from Istanbul. And if he does return, he'll be too involved to ever say a word."

"O.K., Dr. Watson. Let's send them on to Turkey."

As the chauffeur drove Mac and Julio to the airport, Mac pretended all was well.

CHAPTER 5

The Discovery

Not until they boarded the flight did Mac realize that he and Julio had first class transatlantic seats, his on the aisle and Julio's on the window. Once they were airborne and reached altitude, cocktails were served, then dinner, then more cocktails and finally a movie. It wasn't particularly entertaining, and by the time the credits rolled, almost the entire first class section had dozed off. Sleeping soundly through the announcements, Mac was awakened only when their tires crashed down on the runway. The 757 bounced before stabilizing under full flaps and retro-thrusting engines. Eager to get to the gate, the captain braked abruptly to make the nearest exit ramp, after a rude landing at London's Heathrow.

The pair gathered their carry-on bags, changed planes and continued their journey to Istanbul. They arrived at mid-afternoon, having lost nine hours to the change in time zones. When they disembarked, they were met at the gate by a friendly local with a noticeable smile and a sign that simply read, "Baldone Party."

The local introduced himself as Mustafa Alomar. He was a short man with a very stocky build, short hair and a beard so thick that a Persian rug could have been woven from the trimmings. With his big, gleaming smile that featured a sizeable gap between his two front teeth, Mustafa extended his meaty hand and welcomed Mac and Julio to Istanbul. In perfect English, Mustafa asked if he might carry their bags and assist them through customs. While waiting in line, they talked about the flight, the time zone changes, the weather and everything else, until they successfully worked their way past the document checkers and baggage handlers. Mustafa seemed to know most of the officials by name, speaking their dialect and making jokes that would never be shared with Mac and Julio.

The final leg of their journey was a simple car ride from the airport to their living quarters, at least for the next few months. The apartment was located in the commercial district of Galata on the banks of the Golden Horn, an inlet of the Bosporus Strait that ran through the city. Mac explained to Julio that Istanbul was the world's most cosmopolitan border town, because the Bosporus separated Europe from Asia.

Once they arrived, Mustafa helped Mac and Julio unpack their belongings, and then showed them to the balcony of the lavish apartment. Pulling the curtain back and stepping outside, Mac looked westward across the Golden Horn, with its ferry boats and commercial tankers crowding the waterway. Beyond the congested inlet, he could not help being awed by the domes and spires of Stamboul, the oldest section of the city.

Having lost so much time to travel, the day began to end almost as soon as it started. Dusk was approaching. The minarets of the mosques jutted skyward, like divine fingers pointing towards the majestic sunset. Mac pulled a half-pint of scotch from his jacket's inside pocket, scotch that he purchased at the duty-free shop at Heathrow. He took a tug on the bottle, rinsing his mouth with the swig before swallowing hard, thrilled by the anticipation of discovery and excited to be starting something new. For the sake of politeness, he offered the bottle to Julio, knowing that he didn't like scotch. He offered the same to Mustafa, hoping that he was a devout Muslim and didn't drink. When they both declined, Mac took one more tug before twisting the cap back on the bottle. Scotch had never tasted so good, he thought to himself.

At dawn the next morning, Mac was up making coffee, excited to get underway with the new project. He took his mug out on the balcony and watched the city slowly come to life. The misty fog lifted off the Golden Horn. The sounds ranged from low-pitched boat motors, to cars, dogs and roosters. In the distance, he could even hear chantings from those who began each day praying to Allah.

Minutes later, Julio appeared on the balcony, having found a hot cup of coffee for himself. Glad to have some company, Mac began with his pre-game speech, sounding like a high school football coach.

"Here we go...another foreign scavenger hunt. I've got a good feeling about this one, Julio...a real good feeling. Life may never be the same after this."

"I don't know what to say, Mac. I've got no idea what I'm doing."

"Well, today, you just enjoy yourself. Go sightseeing a little, but don't get into any trouble. God knows that's the last thing either of us needs in a place like this. I've got a little business to attend to at the Embassy. Call me there if you need me."

At 9:00 a.m., Mac heard Mustafa knock on the door, right on time. He was taking Mac to a scheduled meeting with the commercial attaché at the U.S. Embassy.

When the two of them arrived, Mac noticed that Mustafa knew everybody at the Embassy, making their visit go very smoothly. There was some paper work to fill out, so the project would be properly licensed and permitted. The Embassy officials told Mac that a license had already been obtained for site preparation work, and now they were applying for a construction license authorizing Mac to erect a commercial building on the site. Mustafa had earlier submitted architectural drawings of some fictitious building that would never be built. There was no mention during the meeting of archeological intentions, and Mac's paperwork listed him as a project manager/engineer.

This element of deception made it clear to Mac that Turkish officials would be kept unaware of their true objective, and that any discovery would go unreported. Whatever he found, Mustafa would likely smuggle out of Turkey into the U.S. and eventually to Baldone. The commercial attaché and Mustafa seemed to know exactly what they were doing, and Mac felt too committed to his summer plans to object or change course. He was reminded of his meeting with Dr. Watson and Mr. Baldone in Chicago.

Unable to challenge what was going on, Mac felt a little sick, not only for himself, but especially for Julio, who had no idea what this was all about. Julio was completely unaware that he would be an accomplice to this entire operation, if they succeeded in finding anything at all.

On the second day, Mac and Julio arrived on the site at 6:30 a.m.. The property had been scraped flat by the previous construction crew, the same crew that ultimately rejected and abandoned the site. The holes from the core samples that doomed the construction project were still marked by flagged stakes.

Mac was twisting the top off his thermos and pouring his third cup of coffee, when Mustafa drove up. He unloaded three Turkish laborers, who stood aside while Mac and Mustafa discussed how they would begin.

After working on the site for less than a week, Mac found a small sinkhole beneath the foundation that opened into a previously uncharted room. Accessing this room proved to be more difficult than initially thought. The project was delayed while they installed supporting timbers and roof bracing bolts, a safety precaution before proceeding any farther. During the delay, Mac drew sketches of what he thought might lie below.

The good news was that while this particular room was empty, it led to other rooms. During the third week on the site, Mac and Julio began to find relics, not from the Roman period, but ancient nevertheless. Mustafa was working very closely with Mac, and anything worth keeping was taken under his care, tagged and removed from the premises. Each day, as the dig progressed, their excitement for prospective discoveries heightened.

In the fourth week, Mac and Julio broke below a second foundation, and were digging and chiseling their way into another historical period, showing some architectural signs of the late Roman era. When Mac told Mustafa the news, he seemed relieved, having shown some signs of stress during the preceding week from his frequent updates to Mr. Baldone.

Mac's excitement intensified. He became consumed by the project, using his spare time to read more about the history of the period that he was exploring. He was so wrapped up in his work that he rarely socialized at all. He slept little, reading late into the night about ancient treasures that had been found in the city. Almost daily he would send Julio back to the library to find more books on the subject. But the most time consuming element of the dig, other than time spent at the excavation site, was the time Mac spent making his daily journal entry into the diary that he had started the night that he announced to Ivan and Katrina that he was going to Istanbul.

On those rare occasions when he allowed himself some personal time, he would call Betsy, talking sometimes for an hour or more about all that was going on. He would always ask about Crow, and tell Betsy how much he loved her and missed her. She always told him that she missed him so much that she didn't really care if he found anything at all. She just wanted him to come home, unsure if she could endure the lonely summer any longer.

ᵀᵀᵀ

It was at the end of a particularly hot and dusty day, and well after quitting time, when Mac noticed something peculiar about the wall that he was unearthing. Julio and the other workers had already gone home for the day, leaving Mac behind to continue with his work and to inspect the day's results. It was the discoloration of the wall that seemed odd to Mac. This particular place that he was inspecting appeared to have been re-plastered, and he was more than curious to know what might lie behind it.

Equipped with hammer and chisel, he pounded and chipped his way through the wall, until he managed to create a small, quarter-sized hole, from which he could barely retrieve his chisel. Once it was dislodged, a blast of stale, dusty air whizzed through the hole, blowing dirt all over his sweaty face. The dust gusher subsided only when the pressure on the other side of the blow hole equalized.

Mac tried to peer through the hole into the darkness. There was not enough room to look through the hole and lift his gas lantern up at the same time. He put the lantern down and started pounding again on the hole, making it larger every time he struck the chisel. Within an hour, he had made the hole large enough to put his head, arm and shoulder through the hole, holding the lantern on the other side and seeing for the first time what he had only dreamed about until now. His adrenaline was surging.

Beyond the wall was a tunnel or catacomb leading away from the excavation site. The direction probably extended across the street that was fifteen or twenty feet overhead. Mac continued working on the wall until he crawled through to the other side. Holding his lantern up high, he walked through the catacomb, ducking occasionally to avoid overhanging rocks, feeling the chill of the air that had been trapped in this cavern for perhaps a thousand years.

Twenty feet into the passage way, Mac found a set of narrow, steep stairs that led even farther below the surface, a shaft so dark that it swallowed his lantern's light. Fear couldn't overrule his excitement as he ventured down the steps. Once he reached bottom, he realized that he was on a landing, and a second set of stairs continued down in the opposite direction, seemingly into the dungeons of hell. He couldn't tell if it was his nerves or the chill in the air that was causing him to shake, but he continued on into the dark abyss.

The farther he descended, the colder it became. He knew that his stay, no matter what he found, would be of short duration. Finally reaching the bottom, he crawled down a short corridor on his hands and knees before encountering a large stone that jutted down from the ceiling, blocking his pathway. Fortunately it did not quite reach the floor, leaving Mac just enough room to get down on his stomach and squeeze beneath it. When he passed the rock and came up to his knees and held his lantern before him, Mac was surprised to discover that he was no longer in the dark, narrow hallways of the catacomb. He was now in a large, circular room, and to his amazement, one that was not empty.

Whether it was the cold air or his adrenaline surge that would not allow him to draw a breath, he could not tell. He was awed by what was before him. The walls had been frescoed. There were sculptures, icons, ceramics, papyrus scrolls and parchments laid about on tables that stood end-to-end, circling the walls of the chamber. There were figurines of ivory, bronze and gold. There were chalices, patens, ciboriums and reliqueries, all embedded with sparkling jewels and bordered with illustrative enamels. The room was full of treasure. Everything imaginable was there, except perhaps the Holy Grail itself. At last, Mac's dream had come true.

Once he recovered from his shortness of breath, Mac sat down in the middle of the room. He was trying to regain his composure, trying to decide what to do next. Not two minutes went by before he was haunted by a thought, that of Baldone and Mustafa. They were sure to take over the claim and move him aside, now that the treasure had been found. This was the moment in his life that he had fantasized about more than any other, and now that it was reality, he feared that his sponsor would take it away.

Mac pondered the situation as long as his body temperature would allow. The frigid air in the chamber was forcing him to hurry his decision. The large stone that blocked the entrance to the room prohibited removal of almost anything except the writings. Mac decided then and there that the parchments and scrolls would be his alone. He would have to share the other treasurers with his search party and sponsors. That would be it. He would take his chances on deciphering the written word to establish his fame and glory in the academic world. He would let the museums have the rest. Yes, he could live with that compromise, and so could Baldone, particularly if he never knew about it.

The next two hours he spent carefully shuttling the handful of scrolls and parchments to the trunk of his car. Once all of the writings had been removed, he took off his tee shirt and gently rubbed the tables, hoping to erase any traces of betrayal that might be left behind. He decided to face the problem of smuggling later on, once his arms and legs had thawed. In the meantime, he decided that an old army foot-locker back at the apartment would have to suffice as temporary storage for the treasure that he claimed as his own.

Once he finished hiding the contraband, Mac sat down with his computer notebook and made an entry to his diary.

"Today I discovered what will surely prove to be the capstone of my career. It is too early to confirm this hypothecation, but I've never before had a stronger feeling about my work. The contents of the discovery I have made are astonishing, and will be cataloged over the course of the next few weeks. Regrettably, I must turn these treasures over to Mustafa Alomar tomorrow. I feel certain that Mustafa will deliver the discovery to Joseph Baldone and Myers Watson through illegal channels of transport, somehow circumventing the laws of the Turkish Government.

There were ten manuscripts in the chamber that I have retained for my own account. They will require years of work to translate. I have decided to take these manuscripts under my own care, afraid that their significance might never be learned if they are entrusted to my sponsor.

Let the record show that this decision is mine alone, and not that of my assistant, Julio Masito, who knows nothing about any of this. Tomorrow he, along with the others, will learn about the discovery, but Julio knows nothing about my suspicions concerning Alomar and Baldone, and he knows nothing about even the possibility of these treasures being illegally exported.

No one will be told about the manuscripts. They are to remain in in my sole possession, and they shall be my sole responsibility. It is unfortunate that it has to be this way."

CHAPTER 6

The Return

When their plane landed in Chicago, Mac, Julio and Mustafa were met by Baldone's limo driver and were taken to The Drake Hotel. At the registrar's desk, they were each given individualized itineraries, detailing their schedules in Chicago. They were also given garment bags, with a note attached. Apparently, a formal dinner had been planned to announce the success of the excavation to a private gathering of Baldone's friends and business associates. His secretary had taken the liberty to rent tuxedos for the three travelers.

The banquet was held in a large, private meeting room at the hotel. Mac, Julio and Mustafa were sitting at the head table and enjoying desert, when Joseph Baldone tapped his silverware on his glass to capture everyone's attention. He stood once the room quieted down and welcomed everyone to his party, issuing eloquent acknowledgments to the head table and to his guests. He then announced to the crowd the discovery made in Istanbul, and asked Dr. Nigel McFarland to please stand and be recognized.

Mac rose from his seat and introduced his partner, Julio, and asked him to stand as well so that he might share in the acclaim.

After the applause subsided, Baldone made one other introduction — Dr. Myers Watson. The crowd settled in for a thirty minute dissertation on the significance of the discovery and the plans for exhibition at the museum. Mustafa assisted Dr. Watson with a slide presentation that included pictures of the treasure as it had been found in the circular chamber deep within the sealed catacomb. It was all there, Mac mused, except for the scrolls and parchments. When Watson finished the presentation, the audience politely applauded, but showed signs of tiring from Baldone's self-promotion.

After it was over, Mac was approached by several of the guests interested in meeting the man responsible for the discovery. The first introduced himself as Dr. Jack Andrews.

"Congratulations, Dr. McFarland. It sounds like you had a wonderful trip."

"Thank you. It was very special."

Dr. Andrews noticed the number of people wanting to speak with Mac was growing, so he cut short the conversation he wanted to have with the honored archeologist. Under the circumstances, monopolizing Dr. McFarland's time and attention would have been rude. Dr. Andrews leaned towards Mac as though he didn't want anyone other than Mac to hear what he had to say.

"I used to teach at Jesuit. I led a Baldone expedition myself, years ago. Call me if ever you just want to talk. Maybe I'm the only guy who understands what its like to work for Joseph Baldone."

Then he said good-bye and walked off, leaving Mac encircled by Baldone's guests. Mac wondered what Dr. Andrews meant by his comments, but before he could give them any real thought, another hand was extended and a new face was introduced.

The next morning, Mac had a debriefing appointment at Baldone's office, and it went much better than Mac expected. Everybody seemed elated with the results of the dig. As he was leaving, Mac was handed an envelope by Mr. Baldone who said,

"Take this with you, Dr. McFarland. This is a token of my appreciation for a job well done. I'm sure we will have occasion to work together again. Please remain in touch, and have a safe journey home."

During his descent in the elevator, Mac opened the envelope and discovered a $50,000 bonus check. As he spun through the revolving door and exited the tower, he felt dizzied by his mixed emotions. On one hand, he wanted to rush home to show Betsy the largest check he had ever held in his hand; but on the other, he felt a huge sense of guilt for taking the check. All things considered, it was a great relief to simply walk away from his association with Baldone.

The white limosine was waiting outside the John Hancock Tower to take Mac back to the hotel. He hooked up with Julio and they checked-out at Baldone's expense, while a bellman assisted with their luggage. They piled into the limo and told the driver to head for O'Hare. Julio was in a hurry to catch his flight home.

When they arrived at the airport, Mac went inside with Julio and took him to the ticket counter. There, on the spot, Mac bought Julio a first class ticket to graduate school, departing from Phoenix in a week and arriving in Washington, D.C., non-stop. When he handed it to Julio, Mac sensed that the pace of Julio's life was about to accelerate. Looking around at the harried crowd of travelers, Mac worried that this white-water rush through time might capture Julio and never let him go.

Once they were at the gate, Mac shook Julio's hand and then hugged him to say good-bye. They parted as family would, saddened that destiny would take them down separate paths, but enriched by the time they spent together.

As Mac neared the limo, he also felt homesick. He was anxious to show Betsy his bonus check; and he was anxious to get back to Jesuit University, so he could begin to make a name for himself. Without realizing it, Mac was becoming obsessed by thoughts of deciphering the confiscated manuscripts...his share of the loot from Turkey...loot that no one but he even knew existed.

⟨⟨⟨

In the first few weeks after Mac returned home, he was thrilled to be home with Betsy. But before long, he let work consume all of his time. He noticed Betsy's frustration build.

"When you were in Turkey, half-way around the world, I understood being lonely. But now, I feel abandoned! Why in God's name can't you come home at night, at least before I go to bed? This is ridiculous, Mac!"

"Betsy, please, don't get so upset. I'm sorry. It's just that I'm working on a very important project, and it's impossible to get it done during normal hours when I'm teaching a full load. I know you're upset about it, but please be patient. I've got to keep working on this."

"Well, what is it, Mac? The cure for cancer, or what? What's so important that it stands in the way of our marriage? What's so important that you abandon the only people that care about you? You're so busy, we don't even see Ivan and Katrina anymore. I'd think if you didn't love me anymore, you'd at least keep seeing your best friend in the world."

Betsy had struck a low blow. "Betsy, come on, just try to understand! You know that the University is always putting pressure on its faculty to publish. It's expected of college teachers. It's required for tenured professors. I'm writing a book, darling. I'm writing a book about my trip to Istanbul. It just takes a lot of time, that's all."

"Oh, great! I just have to sit on the sidelines, while you write a book. That's just great!" she said in a rage.

Mac didn't respond, thinking that it was better to have Betsy mad at him, than to disclose the truth to her about the contraband scrolls that he was working on. The stealth project had taken on a life of its own, and had even been given a name, the Constantine Papers. The scrolls and parchments were a collection that spanned the early Christian era and were written in three different languages: Hebrew, Aramaic, and Latin. Having only the linguistic training required by his doctoral program, his working knowledge was deficient for the magnitude of the task at hand. Mac spent many wasted hours trying to improve his translation skills. But in the final analysis, he conceded that he had bitten off more than he could chew.

This frustration, together with his already crowded schedule, only added to his ineffectiveness. It wasn't long before the strain began to surface in his teaching, his marriage and in his friendship with Ivan. As an escape, he turned to the diversion that Vanessa offered. He viewed her as a pure burst of excitement, the lure of entertainment, fun without responsibility.

Finally, one afternoon Mac stopped Ivan in the Student Union Building and told him they needed to talk.

"You want to talk right now?" Ivan asked.

"No, not right now. We need a few hours to cover what I need to tell you. How about tomorrow night? We'll go get a few beers. Will that work?"

"Yeah, that'll work. I'll see you at the bar at six o'clock. How's that sound?"

"That's fine. I've got some heavy stuff to tell ya."

"O.K. I'll see you then."

"Bye."

The next evening, Mac walked into the bar at 6:20, hoping that his friend hadn't given up on him. There Ivan was, sitting in a booth with an almost empty mug in his hand.

"Hey, sorry I'm running late."

"That's O.K. There's plenty of scenery in here to keep me occupied."

"Lately, pretty scenery has been the last thing on my mind. I probably would have gotten up and left. Thanks for staying."

"Alright, enough bullshit. Now tell me, what's been going on? Whatever it is, it's not normal. That's for sure."

"So you've noticed, too? God, my life's been screwed-up lately."

"More like ever since you came back from Istanbul. What's the deal?"

"I think I'm just a little over my head right now, with work and everything else. Let me tell you a story, just between you and me. Then, maybe you'll understand what I'm going through. I need your advice."

Mac started to tell Ivan almost everything, except the part about Vanessa, remembering that he had told Ivan a year ago that his involvement with Vanessa was over. As far as Mac was concerned, that part of his life wasn't the problem anyway. It was the weight of the Constantine Papers. It was crushing him.

For the next hour, Mac told Ivan all about Istanbul, trying to explain why things weren't exactly the same as before.

"So that's why you're so stressed out?" Ivan interjected. "How's Betsy taking all of this?"

"She's fine," Mac lied. Then he added, "I haven't told her a thing about the Constantine Papers, and I don't want her to know. You're the only person who does know — just you and me."

After three more beers, Ivan decided that he knew how to solve all of Mac's problems.

"There's this guy here at J.U.," Ivan said, "named Dr. Willis Barker. He's a professor in the Religion Department. He can probably help out with the translation work."

"Do you know this guy very well?"

"No, not really. He was the past-president of the Newcomers Committee when Katrina and I moved to Northshore. But I've heard that he's supposed to be some kind of genius with ancient languages. I'd be glad to make an introduction, but you'll have to thrash around and decide for yourself if you think he's good or not, and if he can be trusted. That's all up to you."

"Let me think about it, old buddy. Just let me think about it for a while."

Ready to put their serious discussion behind them, they raised their mugs and smashed them together, pledging to have nothing but fun for the rest of the evening. On his way to the restroom, Mac saw Vanessa having a drink with her girlfriends at one of the tables in the back of the bar. She happened to see him as well. Mac gave Betsy a call, telling her he wasn't sure when he'd be getting home. Ivan finished his beer and said he'd had all the fun he could stand.

CHAPTER 7

The Confidant

Mac felt relieved to tell somebody about his dilemma; now at least he could confide in a friend. He was glad that it had been Ivan. Keeping all of the pressure contained within himself had taken its toll. It had been more stressful than he could comfortably endure. But having an outlet didn't necessarily make his job any easier. Mac continued working almost eighty hours a week, until he had finally just had enough. It was time to call his friend, again.

"Ivan, how's it going?"

"Great! The world of physics has never been more exciting."

"Why does that sound like a contradiction in terms to me?"

"Because you can't use your imagination, that's why."

"My imagination works fine, thank you. It's just not quite as huge as yours," Mac replied sarcastically. "Listen Ivan, I've decided to waive the white flag on the Constantine Papers. Maybe it's time to talk to Willis Barker. Do you still think that's a good idea?"

"Sure. I'll set something up if you want."

"All right, go ahead and give him a call. But, don't tell him anything about how I got these scrolls out of Turkey. In fact, don't tell him anything at all. Let me handle all of that. Just introduce us, if you don't mind. I might back-out if I get a bad feeling. I've gotta wade into this nice and slow. Maybe I'll put a toe in the water and decide I'm not going in."

"Don't worry. I can handle it. And after I put you two together, why don't we get back to our old routine. In fact, that's all you'll owe me if this thing works out."

"O. K. It's a deal."

At the appointed hour, Ivan led Mac into Barker's office and made the introduction, "Willis, I want you to meet this guy I was telling you about, my good friend, Mac McFarland. Mac, this is Willis Barker."

"Hello Dr. Barker. Nice to meet you," Mac said, clasping Barker's outstretched hand in a friendly shake.

"Just 'Willis'," Barker replied stiffly.

Mac's first impression was not particularly favorable. He sensed an unnatural, almost artificial style — one he had seen too many times before, especially in the academic world.

"Most people call me Mac."

Then Barker turned to Ivan and offered, "Can I get either one of you a soft drink?"

"Sure, I'll drink anything you got," Ivan said.

"Me, too," repeated Mac.

After making the introduction, Ivan continued to play the facilitator. But as soon as Ivan tried to explain why the meeting had been called, Mac took over the conversation. He began by telling Barker about his own background and accomplishments, which led up to the expedition to Turkey. Mac was nearing the point in the conversation when he had to decide how much he was going to tell Barker. But just before breaking ground on the subject of the Constantine Papers, Mac stopped. It was time to learn about his peer, Dr. Willis Barker.

For the next thirty minutes, Mac conducted an interview of

Barker, inquiring about his linguistic skills, and testing his specific knowledge about translating original documents written during the early Christian era. After hearing Barker's story, Mac's impression improved significantly, and he became convinced that Barker's linguistic skills would make a huge difference in the pace of the translation work.

Standing at the crossroads, Mac decided to go forward. He selectively told Dr. Barker about the expedition, the sponsorship of Joseph Baldone, and his discovery of the papyrus scrolls and parchments. When Mac finished telling the story, he invited Barker to ask a few questions.

"So, how, exactly, are you caring for these ancient manuscripts?"

Mac felt a little guilty for having let his personal ambition interfere with standard caretaking procedures, but he felt confident that minimal damage had actually occurred. He rationalized his unorthodox handling procedures by focusing on the negative effects that publicity of any kind might have on the project. But what Mac was most worried about was confidentiality.

"Willis, given the gross mishandling of the Dead Sea Scrolls and the Nag Hammadi Library, there is nothing more threatening to this project than premature publicity. If we decide to work together on this undertaking, confidentiality is my first and foremost concern. Nothing would derail our efforts more than letting the Constantine Papers be taken from us in a custody dispute. We have to agree — no, we have to swear our confidentiality.

"If you choose to become involved, it must be on a blind basis at all times, blind even to Mr. Baldone. Not even Baldone understands all of the technical requirements of this project, and I will not tell him about our alliance. The less Baldone is involved the better. Otherwise, our project will be leaked at some high-brow cocktail party in Chicago."

Mac, of course, failed to mention that Baldone knew nothing of the scrolls.

Willis was obviously intrigued by everything that Mac had

said. The Constantine Papers would be a fascinating project to work on, no doubt. He seemed a little perplexed about having to play a blind role in all of this, but it was Mac's baby and he'd just have to go along. The last thing Mac wanted to cover was compensation, the least of all motivating factors in his mind, but necessary nevertheless. Mac agreed to pay Barker the going rate for his time and services, thinking that his $50,000 bonus check would probably end up in Barker's pocket before it was all over. Mac's reward would have to come on the back end. He comforted himself, though, with the thought that one day, fame and fortune would come his way.

When the meeting concluded, Willis said that he looked forward to learning more about the Constantine Papers, and he would clear his calendar for their next meeting. He made his promise to maintain confidence, and agreed to be a blind partner unless directed otherwise by Mac. Ivan excused himself from any further participation in the project, asking them to call only if they needed an astrophysicist.

By the time the meeting was over, Mac felt much better than he expected. He was certain that Barker's involvement would speed things up, and he was comforted by Barker's assurances about keeping a lid on the project. They shook hands and agreed on a date to meet again, so that Barker could be shown the actual goods.

A few days later, Mac was sitting at his desk when he heard a knock on his office door. He pushed his research aside and looked at his watch, confirming that his appointment was right on time.

"Come on in, Willis," Mac hollered. "Make yourself as comfortable as possible, because you're about to see one of the most fascinating discoveries of modern times."

For the next several hours, Barker poured over the parchments without speaking a word. When fatigue finally forced him to stop, all he said to Mac was, "Looks like we got a lot of work to do, partner."

Willis and Mac secretly worked on the Constantine Papers over the next three years, combining historical research with linguistic analysis and comparative literature studies. They were both addicted to the work, although they responded to their findings in very different ways. Mac was amazed, fascinated and intrigued while Willis was skeptical, confounded, and defensive. The two argued with each other constantly, debating their separate conclusions, sometimes even bitterly. Their differences suggested that they might not have the same goals in mind once the Constantine Papers were made public. Mac hoped that their confidentiality agreement would prevail, but now he wondered if he had expected too much.

At stake were religious beliefs that had been thought by the masses within Christendom to be indisputable. The Constantine Papers called the Church's authority into question. To Mac, the Constantine Papers were a revelation. To Willis, they were a threat.

In all, there were ten separate manuscripts. Included among the ten were eight gospels — *Matthew, Mark, Luke,* and *John,* and four others...*The Gospel of Philip, The Secret Book of John, The Apocalypse of Peter,* and *The Gospel of Truth.* While the first four had later been canonized as part of *The New Testament,* these last four had not been included. They had, however, been found in the collection known as the Nag Hammadi Library, and had been identified by Biblical scholars as "Gnostic" writings. The Gnostics were early Christians who experienced Christianity through personal and secretive "gnosis" or knowledge of spiritual truth or divinity. This knowledge was typically obtained by education, careful self-examination, and a certain measure of asceticism. The Gnostics assigned little value to the physical world. As a whole, they were heavily influenced by Greek philosophy.

The ninth manuscript was a lengthy historical account regarding the ascension of the Proto-Catholic Church. The Proto-Catholics were the forerunners to what is now called the Roman Catholic Church.

The tenth was merely a short, personal letter...but very telling.

The most obvious conclusion one could draw from the Constantine Papers was that there were many complex and divergent opinions that influenced the early development of Christianity. For example, the author of *The Gospel of Philip* said that Jesus had been spiritually conceived by a paternal God and a maternal Holy Spirit, contradicting the more physical description of a Virgin Birth by Mary. On a purely physical level, the Gnostics thought it incredulous that Joseph played no part in Mary's pregnancy.

As a second example, the writer of *The Apocalypse of Peter* expected the world to come to a very quick end with the second coming of Christ, negating the need for an ecclesiastic order and an authoritative Church. The author even ridiculed as ludicrous and arrogant those Church leaders who claimed to receive their authority directly from God.

But perhaps the greatest contrast of all regarded opinion about the resurrection of Christ. None of the Gnostic texts endorsed a physical resurrection of the body of Jesus. Unlike the Proto-Catholics, the Gnostics uniformly believed that resurrection was purely a spiritual concept. They adhered more closely to Platonic philosophy, relegating the realm of the physical to almost an illusory status, while defining reality in spiritual and intellectual terms.

Even so, the most surprising and controversial findings within the Constantine Papers did not regard theology or philosophy. The real controversy pertained to the fact that the contents of the gospels of *Matthew, Mark, Luke* and *John* were noticeably shorter in length and vastly different in substance from those which had been canonized by the Church in 362 A.D. This non-conformity in the texts was cause for true alarm.

Mac knew that up until his discovery, Biblical scholars believed that *The Gospel of Mark* was the earliest written testimony about Jesus of Nazareth. The scholars presumed that *Mark* had been written about 70 A.D., or some forty years after the death of Jesus. However, the same gospels that Mac found in Istanbul appeared to be written much earlier, leading Mac to conclude that significant editorial liberties had been taken somewhere along the way. It seemed likely that the Church's authority had been embedded into the texts, particularly as it became more apparent to the early Christian community that Jesus wasn't coming back real soon. The Proto-Catholic Church became convinced that it would have to carry the torch or the light would burn out. It also assumed responsibility for unifying the diverse factions of early Christianity into one Church. In their view, the only way they could succeed was to claim that their authority was ordained by God through the doctrine of apostolic succession.

Willis, of course, argued otherwise, insisting that these nonconforming gospels were not authentic at all.

The many problems which confronted the two men were more plainly spelled out in the last two scrolls of the ten.

The historical record detailed the split between the Proto-Catholic Church and other Christian groups, including the Gnostics. From the beginning, the Proto-Catholics took a firm stand on the authority of the Church. According to their views, this authority was God-given, and therefore above all other authority, including that of the Roman Empire. Given that there was no true separation between religious and political thought during those times, the Romans would not tolerate this challenge. It didn't take long for martyrdom to become the ultimate test for Proto-Catholic believers.

During the first two centuries, the torture and killing of Christians became a form of entertainment to the citizens of the Roman Empire. Those believers, who were willing to die for their faith rather than pledge allegiance to the Roman government, captured the attention of the viewing public. Many who witnessed their persecution became compassionate and sympathetic for the martyrs. The backlash resulted in mass conversions to the new religion. Over time, this phenomenon took on international dimensions.

As Christianity spread, the Proto-Catholics, who were on center stage during the heavy persecution period, declared themselves to be the orthodox and true Church. They began to define orthodoxy. The Gnostics, on the other hand, denounced martyrdom as self-sacrificial lunacy, and believed the orthodox masses had missed the point of Christianity all together. To the Gnostics, Christianity concerned salvation of the spirit...not the body. But in the eyes of the Proto-Catholics, this Platonic heresy was unacceptable. As the Proto-Catholics gained wider acceptance, all other Christians were labeled "heretics."

By the turn of the fourth century, the Church began to consolidate its power by purging non-conforming views, and with the co-operation of the Romans. After years of unholy discord, the two powers began to forge an alliance centered on a compromised theology. Christian orthodoxy incorporated both Judeo and Hellenistic characteristics: first, Jesus the Jewish Messiah, crucified and defeated by the suppressing and oppressing strength of the Romans; and then, Jesus the Hellenistic Son of God, born of a virgin, a performer of miracles, charged with blasphemy and put to death by the Jews.

The most essential ingredient added to the historical account of Jesus was his triumph over death by his physical resurrection. Prior to the birth of Jesus, the concept of resurrection had surfaced in Egyptian religion and mythology. And by the first century, many Jewish Pharisees also embraced the concept. In the final analysis, an event of resurrection seemed to meld diverse cultures together, serving a functional purpose for the rulers of a very culturally diverse Roman Empire.

Before *Matthew, Mark, Luke,* and *John* were canonized, all of these influences were added to the manuscripts that Mac had discovered. Mac surmised that the Proto-Catholic Church had mutated itself sufficiently over the first 300 years of its history to gain the favor of the Emperor, meeting its goal when Constantine became a Christian in 313 A.D. and declared Christianity to be the official state religion of the Empire in 320 A.D.

By the end of the fourth century, the Proto-Catholic Church had dispersed its adversaries or at least driven them underground with a hardened policy of intolerance. The orthodoxy, that initially emerged during the widespread persecution of Proto-Catholic Christians in the second century, had become institutionalized. The Proto-Catholics declared that its goal of unification had been achieved, and they began to call themselves the universal Church. With its newly acquired status, the Church proclaimed that its doctrine, ritual, literature and clergy were divinely inspired and carried the authority of God. With such powerful authority now acknowledged by the Romans, the Church leadership began to dominate its followers by casting shadows of doubt over their souls. The Church dangled the carrot of salvation before them, and wielded the stick of damnation at their backs. Both were needed to control the flock and access their pocketbooks. The laity was offered a simple choice between heaven or hell. They were either sheep or goats, saved or damned, either with the Church...or against it.

According to the history, the Church's ascension to power and wealth was no different than most. It came at the expense and to the exclusion of others.

Mac was fascinated by the account, but Willis, of course, strongly disagreed with all of these postulations.

The last scroll was simply a short letter. The letter was written long after the gospels had been written. In fact, on the Gregorian calendar, it dated around 395 A.D. The letter said,

> "These are original gospels. The historical record contained herein is accurate. Under the order of Roman Emperor, Flavius Theodosius, Christians have recently burned the world's greatest library in Alexandria, Egypt. Searches directed by the Bishop of Alexandria, Athanasius, and others, have forced me to hide these manuscripts. I am certain that discovery of this collection would result in my untimely death. So that I, and this collection, might persevere, I am sealing off the catacomb, with deep regret.
> Marcellus"

In the end, the Constantine Papers sharply divided Mac and Willis. Their polarized views mirrored the antagonism that existed between rival religious factions during those first four centuries. Willis represented the Proto-Catholic position, while Mac gravitated toward non-orthodoxy. And much like the Gnostics of old, Mac had no interest in becoming anybody's martyr.

CHAPTER 8

The Backchannel

The translation work was essentially finished by mid-September, three years after they began. Mac's next hurdle was going public with the Constantine Papers. While he had skated around Baldone three years ago, when the scrolls were smuggled out of Turkey, now Mac simply had to face Baldone, to level with him point blank. Maybe he would understand. Maybe he would even help. Then again, dealing with Baldone could be like handling a rattlesnake. Mac played out in his mind all of the possible responses that might come his way. He rehearsed his game plan again and again, and decided it was time to get on with it. He made the dreaded phone call to Chicago.

As expected, Mac's phone call was screened by Baldone's secretary. She took a message saying that Mr. Baldone was tied up in a business meeting and would have to return the call. After not hearing a word for several days, Mac tried Baldone four or five more times, each time being stiff-armed by the secretary who took Mac's number, and said she would make sure Mr. Baldone got the message. Finally, Mac tried a different approach, telling the secretary that he simply wanted to arrange an appointment with Mr. Baldone. She quickly cross-checked his calendar for a few dates that might work, but said she would have to call back to confirm an appointment. Mac endured two cancellations before the day finally arrived. All of this trouble caused Mac to dread the meeting even more.

When the elevator door opened on the 82nd floor, once again Mac couldn't help noticing the elegant decor; but rather than feeling impressed, he felt ill. The picture glass windows behind the receptionist that had previously showcased the blue waters of Lake Michigan, appeared this time as a cold, gray wall of glass, a mirror image of the cloudy circumstances that prompted his visit.

As Mac was being escorted up the spiral stairs, his palms were sweating so badly that he wondered if Mr. Baldone would notice when they shook hands. But when he entered the office, it was Dr. Myers Watson who first stood and extended his hand to Mac, making the situation even more discouraging. Nevertheless, Mac decided to go on with his agenda, wasting no time in getting to the heart of the matter.

"Mr. Baldone, I don't want to take up much of your time today, but there is an important matter related to our dig in Istanbul that I need to discuss with you."

"Of course, Dr. McFarland, let me assure you that the results of that job were terrific. Right, Myers?" Mr. Baldone queried.

"Absolutely. The new pieces in the exhibit are extraordinary."

"Well, thank you both, gentlemen, but that is not exactly what I was referring to," Mac said. "I need to talk about a very sensitive issue that has come up regarding the dig. In fact, Mr. Baldone, this really should be a private conversation. No offense to you, Dr. Watson."

Baldone responded, "No, Dr. McFarland, you don't understand. Myers is informed on all matters pertaining to my interests in art. Whatever you and I need to discuss, Myers will participate."

Myers shifted in his chair, assuming a defensive posture. He seemed very uncomfortable, uncertain what might be said next.

"O.K. then Mr. Baldone. Here it is. Three years ago when I discovered the catacomb that housed the art work, which you now have, there was more found than what was sent back to you. There were a number of papyrus scrolls and parchments which I kept for myself."

"Yes, indeed, Dr. McFarland, the Constantine Papers," Mr. Baldone interrupted.

Mac was shocked. Baldone knew. How did he know?

Mr. Baldone continued, "I have known about this for the past two years, and have followed your progress rather closely through our mutual friend, Dr. Willis Barker."

Again, Mac was staggered.

"If you knew, Mr. Baldone, why didn't you say something?"

"The work had to be translated didn't it? I told Dr. Barker to say nothing to you, and to just keep on working until you finished. He was glad to agree, especially when I doubled his income. I knew that you and I would have to have this meeting. And now that you've completed the job, you realize what you must do. Hand the Constantine Papers over to Dr. Watson."

"I'm afraid that's not possible. If you've learned anything about the Constantine Papers at all, you know that the project has taken on a life of its own. No longer is it some cure for my ambition."

"Don't be hasty in your decision, Dr. McFarland. There is perhaps more at stake in this matter than you realize."

Mac couldn't tell if this was a veiled threat, so he inquired, "What do you mean by that?"

"What I mean, Dr. McFarland, is simply this: you might distinguish yourself more than you intended. There are, after all, others who will be interested in the Constantine Papers, don't you agree? After all, the Turks might feel cheated. You did pilfer these parchments, Dr. McFarland. Am I right? At least my treasures were bought and paid for.

"And what about the Church? The Church will feel that its very survival is at stake. When Darwin introduced the theory of evolution, it was the Garden of Eden that was threatened. Secular society has all but dismissed the Virgin Birth...and now, the Constantine Papers will call into question the very Resurrection. Do you think institutional Christianity can survive without the Resurrection, Dr. McFarland? I'm afraid many will think not."

"What's your point, Mr. Baldone?"

"The point is this. Have you ever heard of a 'jihad'? It is the Muslim expression for a holy war. This is what you will face from the Church. And Christians shouldn't be underestimated in their zeal, either. Don't forget the Crusades and the Inquisition. People have died throughout history over lesser issues than those raised by the Constantine Papers. My guess is that I am your easiest way out of this mess. I wouldn't want the Muslims or the Christians after me."

Mac felt Baldone was shadow boxing, demonstrating his quickness and agility.

"Mr. Baldone, I am asking again that you and I talk privately about this. I'm afraid Dr. Watson shouldn't hear what I am about to say."

"Don't worry yourself, Dr. McFarland," Mr. Baldone said confidently.

Mac drew a breath and raised his glare to meet Mr. Baldone's eyes before throwing his punch.

"From what I can tell, we should all be a little worried about this. But worried or not, you need to know that I'm willing to risk everything to stay in control of this project. The question is, what are you willing to risk? Are you willing to risk going to jail, Mr. Baldone, or worse? You see, I know that you have stolen art treasures before, like that sculpture from Damascus that Dr. Watson harbors in the basement of his fine museum. I'd guess that the Turks won't be too happy with you either, when the press learns that Turkish government officials were paid off so you could smuggle their art treasures. And one other thing, Mr. Baldone. It would be a shame if Mustafa's cover is somehow blown in all this confusion. The C.I.A. wouldn't appreciate that at all."

There was a long silence. Baldone seemed rattled.

Mac grew tired of the silence and continued.

"In fact, Mr. Baldone, if you don't mind, I'd appreciate it if you would take care of the Turk problem for me, so the Constantine Papers can come out of the closet and be made public. Then, I can go on with my work."

Mac had gone from defense to offense, committed to walk out with his head up or not walk out at all.

Baldone regained his composure before speaking.

"Well, Dr. McFarland, it seems you are willing to risk quite a bit indeed. By the way, how's your Indian friend?"

Mac was not prepared for this. Baldone was a rattlesnake, willing to bring an innocent into the equation. Mac responded with caution, measuring his words to assure that nothing was said about Julio's whereabouts.

"Julio was just a kid who knew nothing about this, nothing at all. Besides, I haven't seen or heard from him in three years now, and I don't have a clue where he is. But just for the record, if you draw him into this, you'll lose by default. I'll go down in flames before you involve him."

"Maybe so, Dr. McFarland, maybe so." Obviously, Baldone had touched a nerve. He backed away for whatever reason, but Mac knew his confrontation with Baldone wasn't over. Bringing Julio into the arena wasn't the only card Baldone could play. Since he was on the Board of Trustees at Jesuit University, Mac expected his career was in for a bumpy ride. It felt bad walking into Baldone's office, but worse walking out.

CHAPTER 9

The Order

Mac was back in Northshore for a week when he felt the first tremor from Baldone. It came by way of a phone call from Dean Franklin, the Dean of the School of Social and Behavioral Sciences.

The Dean started off, "Dr. McFarland, at the last Board of Trustees meeting, Mr. Joseph Baldone, one of our Trustees, mentioned to me that the two of you were involved in some kind of dispute. He didn't define what it was all about, but let me advise you, it's not very smart to be butting heads with one of our Trustees. I would strongly suggest that you mend those fences right away, before this conflict escalates any further."

It was a warning shot, nothing more, but it was enough to get Mac's attention. Baldone wasn't going to quit until he had what he wanted. It was time to find out more about this guy. Mac had to think for a while before figuring out who might be able to help. Myers Watson surely hadn't told him much, and any information he sought through Watson would be reported straight to Baldone.

Mac tried to remember Baldone's friends, those he had met in the past. He thought back to the dinner in Chicago that Baldone had hosted when Mac and Julio returned from Istanbul. There was one guy, Mac thought to himself, that he had met that night. The man said he had been a professor at J.U., and that he had worked for Baldone. Mac didn't remember the man's name, but he thought he might recognize it if he saw it on a short list somewhere.

Looking for a clue, Mac wandered into the department head's office back at school and struck up a conversation. He picked up an old picture off the coffee table, a group picture of the entire teaching staff of the Anthropology Department, taken long before Mac joined the group. Mac's boss volunteered, "That was taken in the good old days, back when I was about your age, just a young buck."

"Who was this guy on the back row?"

"Bring it closer. Let me see. Which guy were you asking about?"

"That guy."

"Oh yeah, that's Dr. Jack Andrews. He was a member of the faculty. Old Jack was one hell of a guy. Retired several years ago."

"What's his name, again?"

"Jack Andrews."

"Where's he now? Still alive?"

"Sure. Jack is strong as a horse, not quite what he used to be, but he'll outlive us both. He moved to Chicago, bought a fancy condo on the lake north of downtown. Expensive real estate, let me tell ya. More than a teacher could afford, that's for sure. He retired a few years early, just out of the blue. In fact, it was right after he got back from his Baldone trip to Damascus. Baldone must have treated him pretty well. I figured you might be the next to retire early. Baldone must not have liked you so much; you're still working. I remember being kind of jealous that you got tapped for his last trip. I wanted that job."

"Ha! Let me assure you, Baldone didn't come close to paving the way to my retirement." Mac set the picture back down on the coffee table and said, "Time to teach a class. Gotta go."

When he returned to his office later that afternoon, Mac made plans to drive into Chicago. He thought it would be best to drop in on Jack Andrews unannounced.

In the middle of the lobby of the high rise condominium building was a large security desk and a uniformed officer. Mac approached the desk and asked if their was a house phone he might use to contact one of the residents. The guard pointed to a bank of phones and told Mac that if he wanted to go upstairs, the resident would have to call the front desk first to give approval. Mac had been through this routine more than a few times before, but he gave the security guard the respect he was looking for by just saying, "Yes, sir."

Andrews answered on the second ring.

"Dr. Andrews, my name is Nigel McFarland. Most people call me Mac. I'm a teacher at Jesuit University, and I worked with Mr. Baldone on a dig in Turkey three years ago."

"Yes, of course, Dr. McFarland. I met you on your return. I remember you very well."

"I apologize for just showing up like this, but I need to talk with you, if that's at all possible. Do you mind?"

"Not at all. Now's as good a time as any. In fact, I've been wondering what has taken you so long. I expected to hear from you a while back. Let me call that poor excuse for a security guard, and I'll meet you when you get off the elevator."

Mac and Jack talked for hours, but dispensed with formalities within minutes. They bonded like distant relatives who were getting re-acquainted. They quickly learned that Baldone was their common cross to bear, and they were glad to rest their burden, if only for a few hours. Both knew they would have to shoulder the weight, once again, when their visit was over.

Nothing was held back. Jack spilled everything he knew about Baldone, while Mac quietly listened.

"Baldone started out as a fork lift driver in a cotton warehouse in Chicago, the son of a poor Italian immigrant. He was drafted in the late 1960s, and rather than become a foot soldier in Vietnam, he joined the Air Force, flunked out of pilot school and became a flight mechanic When he returned to Chicago, he went straight back to his old job at the cotton warehouse. He learned over time what he could about the cotton trade: how the game was played, who the players were, who made money, and who lost. Joseph Baldone was known around the yard as a quick study.

"Before long, his employer at the warehouse helped him get his next job with a large cotton merchant as a salesman. Traveling all over the country, Baldone made friends with both farmers, who grew the cotton, and executives in the textile mills, who spun it into fabric. Then, at the age of thirty-two, Joseph Baldone formed his own cotton merchant company with the backing of a wealthy, Memphis merchant who wanted a presence in Chicago.

"The new venture grew explosively with the financial backing of the Memphis investor.

"Then, one day the house of cards fell. Baldone was suspected of defrauding his banks by submitting falsified cotton warehouse receipts. The day before the banks were going in to audit the warehouse where the cotton was supposedly stored, the warehouse burned to the ground. It happened to be the same warehouse where Baldone started as a fork lift operator. The bales, of course, were never found.

"After it was all over, neither the banks nor the insurance companies could prove anything. The banks were paid off by insurance proceeds, but terminated all of their lines of credit right after the fire. Baldone, of course, had to get out of the cotton business, but he came out smelling like a rose. He kept the millions of dollars the banks had previously advanced against those false collateral documents. The insurance companies took it on the chin. That's how Baldone got started.

"Baldone has always had a smell for money, like a bloodhound. His next venture was ten times more lucrative. Baldone built a chain of topless bars in Florida that absolutely minted money. He sold out in the mid-eighties for tens of millions, more money than he could ever spend. The one thing he lacked, though, was respectability and recognition. In Chicago, nobody had ever heard of Baldone. He was just the rich son of a poor Italian immigrant. Baldone wanted to elevate the status of his family name. So, in the mid-eighties, he made a trip to the Vatican, and the next thing I know, he's on the Board of Trustees at Jesuit University. And, of course, now he's become an art collector.

"That's when I came to know him, the bane of my existence. He led me down the path of greed and I sold out for this condo. I hate the man. But I didn't have a choice. He would have had me killed. I've seen him do it."

"You're kidding?" Mac reacted.

"I'm afraid not."

The conversation kept going, but eventually time ran out. Jack and Mac parted as friends, having sympathy for one another. At the same time, they promised to keep everything they had discussed to themselves, picking up their crosses once again.

When Mac returned to Northshore, he knew he had to call Julio, not to alarm him, but to at least find out where he was and what he was doing. It had been more than three years since Mac had even spoken to his Hopi friend. He needed to re-establish the link, so if Baldone ever tried to involve Julio in any way, Mac would know it. He felt a twinge of guilt as he dialed the number, an admission that this call was long overdue.

"State Department — Mexico Desk. May I help you?"

"Julio!"

"Mac! Wow! How are you?"

"Fine, fine. I'm glad I found you. I started with the Admissions Office at Georgetown, and then had to call the Graduate School of Foreign Service, and got some foreign clerk who couldn't speak English. I finally called the Alumni Association, and they told me where you are. God, it's been a long time since we talked. I'm sorry for that."

"Me too. We've been too busy, I guess."

"Sad, but true. Why don't you go first and tell me everything you've done since I gave you that ticket to Washington."

"All right, but stop me if this gets boring. I'll just give you the highlights. I graduated from Georgetown at the top of my class, and got married in a private ceremony conducted by the Chief Justice."

"Got married! And you didn't invite me?"

"Let me explain. When I said private ceremony, I meant just Mary and me, that was it. Just the two of us."

"No family?"

"No, my family wouldn't understand. It is not possible for them to understand."

"The Chief Justice of the Supreme Court?"

"Yes, yes. His son was in my class at Georgetown, and we became friends. He set it up for me. It was the sort of thing that can only happen in Washington. My wife was impressed. That's all that mattered."

"Well, congratulations, Julio! I'll be damned if I'm going to disappear for another three years. I'll miss out on all the fun."

"Hey, it's my fault, too. And I know that you haven't missed out on all the fun, Mac. That wouldn't be like you."

"Well, maybe not all the fun. So, what'd you do after you got married?"

"It was time to go to work. So, as much as I hated doing it, I cut my hair off and landed a job in the Department of State, working the Mexico desk. That's pretty much it. What have you been doing all this time?"

"Mostly working. No exotic trips. Just working."

"Got anything planned?"

"Nope."

"When am I gonna see you again?"

"I don't know, off hand. Sometime, though. We need to bump into each other."

"Well, I'm sure glad you called. Let's not let three years pass before we talk again, Mac. That's not right."

"Now that I know where you are, I'll be calling more often. Let me make sure you have my number."

Not a word was spoken about Istanbul or Baldone or any of

the mess that Mac had gotten himself involved with. But the call had served a purpose. The link with Julio was re-established. They were connected again. Mac was glad he called.

※

A few days later, Mac felt the aftershocks from Baldone's next move. This time it was more than a tremor. It was more like a small quake. Dean Franklin's office called asking for Dr. McFarland and his boss, the head of the Anthropology Department, to meet with the Dean as soon as possible. The Dean's secretary directed the two gentlemen into the conference room, where sitting across the table was Dr. Willis Barker and the Dean of the Humanities College. The last to enter the conference room and close the door was Dean Franklin, who sat at the head of the table. He began the impromptu meeting with a compliment to Dr. Barker.

"Willis, congratulations on your promotion to department head. Overseeing the Religion Department is an important responsibility at this university, and I am glad to see it fall into such qualified hands."

Mac was completely amazed, baffled at this unexpected announcement. Mac suspected that Willis had sucked up to somebody, and then it began to sink in. Baldone had made this happen. Now, Barker was dangerous.

Dean Franklin continued and, in less than ten seconds, Mac knew that Barker had totally leaked the Constantine Papers to the Dean. It took Mac a full minute to realize that Barker was trying to steal them away. Mac stood up to unleash his rage, but before he could say a word, his own boss in the Anthropology Department pushed his chair back, stood up, and told Mac to please share with him what this was all about.

Dean Franklin calmly suggested that everybody just sit down and shut up. It was time for Mac to explain for eveybody's benefit. Mac tried to tell everybody what had been going on, but couldn't find a good excuse for having worked for three years on a project without telling his boss anything about it. Barker argued that the Constantine Papers were controversial and could be handled most responsibly under the supervision of the Religion Department. When it was clear that Dean Franklin was going to award jurisdiction of the project to Willis Barker and the Religion Department, Mac lost control, calling Barker a two-faced son-of-a-bitch. In the end, Dean Franklin instructed Mac to let go of the Constantine Papers.

He paused a moment before answering, "Dean, I don't want to be insubordinate, but I just can't do that. I realize that my whole career at Jesuit University is hanging in the balance. You'll probably fire me for this, but I can't give 'em up."

The Dean said tersely, "I'm very disappointed to hear that, Dr. McFarland. As I'm sure you are aware, this is a very serious matter. I'll take your comments under consideration, and let everyone in the room know of my final decision within a few days."

When Mac and his boss left the meeting, both men were trying to harness their turbulent emotions. It was a long and silent walk back across the quadrangle.

CHAPTER 10

The Confession

It didn't take Mac long to realize that much more was at stake than his career. He was swimming with alligators: Baldone, Barker, and now Dean Franklin. But following the meeting, Mac realized that these men were the least of his problems. Losing his job was trivial compared to losing Betsy, his faithful wife whom he had all but neglected during the past few years.

When he arrived home, Betsy asked how his day had gone, although Mac sensed she had long ago lost interest in hearing his answers. The question itself was rhetorical, one of pure habit and typically so was the answer, but not on this day. Mac hugged her, not letting go, afraid that she would see the tears in his eyes. He did not speak a word to her of what went on that day in the Dean's office. Telling her the truth about how his day had gone would only stand in the way of telling her how much he loved her, and how they should slip away on a vacation to spend time with just each other.

What surprised him most was how she responded, as though

she were numb, unable to take his words at face value. Instead of squeezing her husband tight and saying, "That's a great idea! Let's just go," she pushed him away and saw the tears in his eyes.

"What's wrong, Mac?"

"I don't know, Betsy. It feels like I'm lost or something...like I've been traveling down the wrong road for the last couple of years. I've suddenly realized that I've invested way too much time and effort in my career and not enough in our marriage."

Looking into her eyes, he realized for the first time how badly damaged their relationship was. He apologized for being a poor husband, and he asked her forgiveness for leaving her to so much loneliness. He promised he would change, but she didn't seem to believe him and acted as if his words were too little, too late. Mac and Betsy said little else to each other that evening, and they went to bed feeling empty, hoping that the morning light might reveal some sign of life in their marriage.

Sleeping poorly, the next morning started like the night before had ended. The conversation was stale, and there wasn't even a hint of passion between them. The marriage seemed all but dead. In that moment of desperation, Mac made a promise to himself that he would end his extra-curricular relationship with Vanessa, the next time he saw her.

It was for that reason, and that reason alone, that Mac accepted Vanessa's invitation to rendezvous at The University Suites Hotel. He knew that this time would be his last. He was going to tell her that he couldn't see her again...not ever.

When he knocked on the door to their room, she opened it and pulled him straight across the threshold into her clutches, before he could say a word. She moaned loudly as she buried her tongue into his mouth, just like the first time they were alone together. It was always so intense when he was with her.

She moved her hands all over him while he gasped for breath, and began fumbling with the buttons that ran all the way down the front of her slinky cotton dress. He abandoned the buttons more than once, while he felt her breasts, and then raised her dress up over her buttocks, before returning to the buttons, impatient to see her naked. While she was famous for her sexy lingerie, this time she drove him even more crazy, for she didn't have on any at all.

Before he could finish undressing her, she had skillfully and without much commotion, gotten into his jeans. Once she unzipped them, she dropped to her knees and tugged until they fell about his ankles. Then she sprinted into the bedroom, casting her dress aside along the way, laughing at his stranded condition. He declared her the winner of this lusty race, as he hobbled awkwardly after her, sitting on the corner of the bed to remove his laced-up shoes.

That night they took turns giving and taking until neither could do anything but surrender to fatigue. Vanessa's hair was wet and stringy from her sweaty gyrations, while Mac's chest and stomach were scratched deeply from the nails that dug into his flesh when she climaxed. When he got out of the shower and looked in the mirror, he grimaced at the marks, guessing that they would heal in three or four days, soon enough to avoid the infrequent attentions of Betsy.

Almost recovered from his sexual fatigue, he started to tease Vanessa, hoping to talk her into bed once again before hitting the road. She turned to give him a hug and kiss before saying, "Mac, one of the reasons I wanted to see you tonight was to tell you in person that I am starting to see someone else. You always said you wanted to know."

Mac felt totally disgusted for not having addressed the subject himself. He had left his excuse for even seeing her at the doorstep. This lusty little college girl had robbed him of the chance to be strong...to be honorable. He felt nothing but impotence, guilt and shame. But then again, he was somewhat relieved that he didn't have to deal with a messy break-up, so all he said was, "I understand. Thanks for telling me."

While they were dressing, not too much more was said between them. Mac thought she probably interpreted his silence as being broken-hearted over her announcement. In truth, Mac wasn't broken-hearted over Vanessa at all. He was simply ashamed of himself.

The next day, Mac thought hard about calling Ivan, but he stopped before dialing the number. After sharing with him the news about the Constantine Papers three years ago, Mac hadn't followed through on his promise to return to their old routines. By neglect, Mac had simply let their friendship lapse. If he called Ivan now, Mac thought to himself, Ivan would rightly conclude that Mac was in some kind of trouble.

In addition to long term neglect, there was another reason Mac hesitated to call Ivan. Mac remembered telling Ivan, after his first night with Vanessa, that it was just a one night stand. Now he couldn't bring himself to admit to Ivan that he had lied. Mac was afraid that his best friend might become judgmental, and in his weakened state of mind, Mac couldn't handle the weight of con-demnation — even if he deserved it. Having nowhere else to turn, he decided to purge himself by making a confession to his priest.

As simple as it seemed, going to confession was undoubtedly one of the most begrudging decisions Mac had ever made. First of all, he hadn't been to church in well over a year; secondly, he hadn't gone to confession in over ten years; and last but not least, his work on the Constantine Papers had raised more than a few questions about the foundations of Roman Catholicism, making Mac potentially one of the Church's greatest adversaries. Yet ironi-cally, in this time of despair, no one needed the Church more than he.

Mac recognized the paradox and was content to live with it, even though it brought anxiety and confusion into his life. He decided to limit the scope of his confession to those matters that might help him heal his relationship with Betsy. It wasn't his soul he wanted to save, it was his marriage.

᭜᭜᭜

Wanting to be early so that he would not be seen waiting to take his turn, Mac kneeled in the dimly lit confessional and waited in complete silence, until he heard the priest enter the other side and get situated. The screen window slid open, and Mac began his Act of Contrition by saying the familiar words:

"Forgive me, Father, for I have sinned."

A voice unrecognized by Mac replied, "How long has it been since your last confession?"

"Ten years," he muttered.

"Well, where shall we begin?"

"Father, I've come to confess all my sins, but one in a particular. It is the sin of adultery, and the multitude of sins that go along with it."

"Yes, go on."

"There's nobody on Earth that I love more than my wife, although she doesn't realize it. There's no way she could; I haven't shown her. I only hope it isn't too late to change things. I'm ready to repent, Father, and turn my marriage around."

"Yes, I understand. How long have you been married?" the voice queried.

"Well, my wife and I have been married for eight years. During the first five years, we were very happy, and our marriage was wonderful. But the last three years have been tough for both of us. I have had to work too hard, and for whatever reason, I've let this affair distance me from her. Now I'm afraid the damage has taken its toll on both of us."

"Does your wife know anything about this?"

"No, I don't think so. I certainly haven't said anything to her. The only way she could know is if Vanessa...I mean the other woman...told her. But that won't happen."

"Have you told the other woman your affair is over?"

"Absolutely. In fact she told me she's already starting to see some other guy. Believe me, it's definitely over."

"Do you repent of your sin?"

"Yes, Father, I am deeply remorseful and repent."

"Then say fifty Hail Marys, twenty Our Fathers and the Rosary every Friday for the next six Fridays," said the voice in an almost ominous tone.

"Yes, Father," Mac responded, not feeling any better than he did before he confessed. On the contrary, he felt much worse.

Then the screen window slid shut. Mac remained there for a moment longer in the dark. When he left the confessional, he replayed the conversation in his mind over and over again, wondering why he had said so much. He let the floodgate open a little bit more than he wanted to, probably because he had been unable to tell anybody about it for so long. No doubt about it, he should have been more reserved. Bothered by it all, he wondered as he walked to his car if the clergyman recognized him or knew who he was. Now, all he could do was hope not.

⋎⋎⋎

Less than a week later, Mac was walking into the Student Union Building, where he picked up a campus newspaper. There in the headlines, he was stunned to find his name:

"McFARLAND ACCUSED OF SEXUAL HARASSMENT"

He quickly folded the paper under his arm, and with a flushed face, he headed out the door and went straight for his car. Once inside, he read the entire article. The paper had quoted his accuser, Ms Vanessa Reilly, who said:

> "Recently I broke off a three-year affair with Professor McFarland. He will not stop calling me, and now that I am enrolled in his class, he has threatened to fail me if I don't offer him sexual favors. I have tried to resolve this problem privately, but he continues to harass me. My only resort is to file a sexual harassment complaint and resolve this conflict in a court of law."

Mac's heart bounced off the ground. He knew that Baldone had beaten him. Mac knew that this wound was fatal, not only fatal to his career, but fatal to his marriage. He failed to show up for his classes that morning. In fact, he just drove around for a while in a daze, before pulling over to a phone booth and to retrieve his voice-mail messages. Yes, Dean Franklin had called him, and wanted to see him as soon as possible.

Ignoring his message from the Dean, Mac drove home to see Betsy. This would be the worst moment of his life, because he knew that innocent or guilty, his marriage would not survive. He knew there would be no forgiveness, only condemnation. There would be no salvation, only damnation. In Mac's opinion, the Church had sentenced him to hell on Earth.

CHAPTER 11

The Penalty

When he told Betsy, she was stoic at first. She didn't wait around for all of the gory details before asking, "Do you love her?"

Merely asking the question brought her to the brink of emotional collapse. Mac swore that he did not love his accuser and told Betsy that everything said in the article was false. But the dam had broken and out poured her heart, what was left of it. Mac confessed that he had seen the other woman a few times, but he did not dare inflict any more damage upon her than she had already sustained. When Betsy heard his confession, she couldn't even speak, her throat swollen from her giant sobs and irregular breathing. It seemed like she might not draw another breath. Within minutes, her eyes appeared sunken into her skull, and her nose became red and tender. After finally composing herself, she told him to get out. She would not look him in the eyes.

"And don't you ever go near that bitch again!"

"Betsy, before I leave, I gotta ask you one question. Do you think we can save our marriage?" Mac asked almost pitifully.

"Just get out!" was all Betsy could say.

After packing his suitcase, Mac made one more apology, "I know I have made a terrible mistake. There's no way I can undo what I have done, or I would. If you never forgive me, then remember that you are the only woman I have ever loved. I knew when I married you that if our marriage didn't last, it would be my fault. I'm sorry, Betsy. I blew it for us."

Then he walked out the door.

Mac had no idea where he was going, but he knew he couldn't avoid Dean Franklin any longer, so he drove back to campus. When he walked upstairs to his office, people looked at him, but no one spoke a word. Only his secretary showed any sign of support, standing to ask if she could bring him some coffee, while handing him a fistful of messages as he walked by her desk. He politely declined her offer, but took the messages into his office and closed the door.

On a normal day, he might have had two or three phone messages from friends, students or those who had returned his calls. But nothing was normal that day. The phone had been ringing off the hook all morning. On top of the stack was the Dean's message. He placed it aside, while he thumbed through the others, mostly messages from newspaper and TV reporters wanting an interview. The only other message in the stack that he recognized was a call from Ivan, and he pulled that one out also and placed it aside.

Mac didn't need to return the Dean's message. It simply said, "Dean Franklin would like to see you immediately." As he crossed the quadrangle in route to the Dean's office, he noticed that students he had never seen before were looking at him as though he were a convicted serial killer. He tried to hold his paranoia in check.

The meeting with Dean Franklin went pretty much like Mac expected. First, the Dean said that he was very disappointed to read the article in the campus paper. Then, the Dean said that he had fully intended to talk with Mac privately before this went public. And last, the Dean said that he could only imagine how much pressure this must place on Mac both at home and at work.

After making these sympathetic gestures, the Dean went on.

"Dr. McFarland, as I'm sure you are painfully aware, these are extremely involved and complicated circumstances. Monsignor Bates, the Church's representative on the Board of Trustees, apparently was approached by Ms Reilly. She wanted counseling from the Church, and the Monsignor has since asked the Chancellor for your resignation. Under the circumstances, I have no option other than placing you on indefinite suspension until the matter is cleared up. And furthermore, Dr. McFarland, I have made a final determination regarding the Constantine Papers. You must immediately give over the project to Dr. Barker and the Religion Department. If this other matter is resolved in your favor, then you will be allowed to resume your work on the project under the supervision of Dr. Barker."

Mac didn't protest or defend himself to Franklin. He simply asked a question,

"Dean, is my indefinite suspension with pay or without pay?"

Franklin replied, "Dr. McFarland, that all depends on you. Let me ask a question. Will you co-operate and give over the project to Dr. Barker?"

Mac paused, but only for a second. "I told you, I can't do that."

"Then you leave me with no choice on the matter, and I regret this very much. Your employment with the university is terminated."

Mac looked at Dean Franklin so intensely that he could not do anything but look away. Mac said nothing more and left. He returned directly to his office to gather his personal belongings and to make one more phone call, this one to Ivan.

"Ivan, this is Mac. I guess you've heard by now?"

"Mac," Ivan answered, "I'm so sorry..."

"Before we get into all of that, I need you to do me a favor. I'm at my office, and I can't talk about this stuff here. Betsy has asked me to leave the house, and Dean Franklin just fired me. Is there any way you and Katrina could let me stay in that little bedroom you've fixed up down in the basement?"

"Mac, my God, I can't believe what I'm hearing. I hate that all of this has happened to you. Sure you can stay in our basement. Absolutely. Let me tell Katrina, and I'll make sure it is cleaned up for you. Don't you worry about having a place to stay. You are welcomed at our house always."

▼▼▼

Over bottles of scotch and vodka, Mac and Ivan rehashed most of what had led up to the day's events. Katrina had long since gone to bed, realizing that there was no way she could stand between them. She knew that they would overindulge, imbibe until there was no more. The day had been filled with so much pain that getting drunk had to be the objective.

Before the night was over, Mac convinced Ivan that Vanessa had not made these accusations on her own. Mac speculated that his confession in church had somehow been leaked, and had possibly led his adversaries to Vanessa. No one else, he insisted, had any idea that he had been involved with her during the past three years. And besides, the last time he had been with her, she had been as fun-loving and as passionate as ever, even though they had agreed to go their separate ways.

Mac slurred, "These sexual harassment charges are total bullshit, made up by those bastards that want to get their hands on the Constantine Papers."

"You know, Mac, trying to talk to Vanessa at this point would probably only make matters worse. She's already been had by whoever set you up. Approaching her would probably back-fire on you. Next thing you know you'd be accused of being a stalker or something worse."

"Well, what if I went back to the church, and talked to that unholy priest. Maybe that son of a bitch'll tell me something. Goddammit, it's his turn to confess."

When Mac returned to the confessional, he knelt once again and waited for the screen window to slide open. Not wanting to raise any suspicion and hoping to recognize the voice of the priest, Mac began by saying:

"Forgive me, Father, for I have sinned."

"How long has it been since your last confession?" the familiar voice answered.

"Only a week ago, Father. Do you remember my voice?" he asked.

"Well, I am afraid not. But please, don't be offended. I see or listen to so many in a week's time that..."

"No problem, Father, no problem. I'll try to refresh your memory, and then we can go from there. You see, I was the guy that was having marital problems, and I confessed an affair that I had been having. Oddly enough, knowledge of this affair reached my employer the next week and resulted in my termination. Highly coincidental, since no one other than you had any knowledge about this affair. Do you remember me now?" Mac pressed.

Mac could hear the priest shift in his seat.

"Yes, I do remember you now. While I apologize for your circumstances at work, let me assure you that all confessions received by the Church are totally confidential."

Mac shifted himself, "Well, is that so? Let me ask you a question. Do you know Dr. Willis Barker? Do you know Dean Franklin?"

"Well yes, of course, I know these gentlemen, but what are you driving at anyway, Dr. McFarland?"

Hearing his own name surprised Mac, for he was sure that he had not given it.

"What I am driving at is simply this. Dean Franklin knew all the details that I confessed to you less than a week ago, and quite a bit more."

"But what about the girl...the newspapers...?"

"I never harassed that girl in my life. Somebody got to her."

The voice stopped the charade, knowing that the confessor was not going to back down.

"Dr. McFarland, all I can tell you is this. You are considered to be very dangerous to the Church. There are rumors associating your name with some new discovery referred to as the Constantine Papers. If you feel threatened, apparently so does the Church. I am very sorry it has come to this. But let me advise you, do not pretend that going public with the Constantine Papers is an option. It is not," the voice warned.

This time it was Mac who said, "You, Father, must say fifty Hail Marys, twenty Our Fathers and the Rosary every Friday for the next six Fridays. And even after that, Father, you, like me, will still be unforgiven."

༾

Mac was depressed and frightened when he pulled away from the church, overwhelmed by his sense of helplessness. He returned to what felt like a dungeon, his little room in Ivan's basement. There was nothing to do really but to sit down with his computer notebook that he had brought from home and update his diary, the same one that he had started when Baldone agreed to sponsor his trip to Istanbul. He composed his thoughts and finished his update.

Then Mac took four diskettes and with the help of his modem, he downloaded all of his translation work and his diary from his hard drive back at his old office at the university. After his copies were secure, he then removed the diskettes and erased all the files in his hard disc memory back at school, leaving nothing behind on the Constantine Papers. Everything was on the diskettes.

Not trusting a soul except for Ivan, Mac decided to stash the diskettes in a book locker at the university. It was a temporary fix until he could rent a safe deposit box or something more suitable, but it worked for now. He opened the door, placed the diskettes inside, inserted his fifty cents, and removed the numbered key. That was it for now. It was all he could do late on a Friday afternoon. He would wait until Monday before going to the bank to get a safe deposit box.

When Mac returned to Ivan's home, he went into the kitchen to get himself a bite to eat. He figured that Ivan and Katrina would be home soon, but he was famished, having eaten nothing all day. Just as he was putting the jar of peanut butter back into the cupboard, he heard the doorbell ring. He suspected it might be a delivery man of some sort, but he really had no idea.

The man at the door was middle-aged, who introduced himself as an out-of-town friend of Ivan's. He said that it had been years since he had seen or heard from his friend, and that unexpected business had coincidentally required him to come to Northshore. Mac didn't catch the name of the stranger, but he invited the gentleman in, and told him to make himself at home. After taking the stranger's coat and escorting him into the den, Mac asked if he could fix drinks for the two of them while they waited, adding with a smile, "For some reason I always get thirsty at this hour."

As Mac walked toward the kitchen, he asked over his shoulder, "What can I fix for you?"

"I'll have whatever you're drinking."

"That'll be a scotch, if that's all right?"

"That'll be perfect."

"Ivan'll join us pretty soon. He's a vodka drinker. Won't touch anything else."

"Some things never change," the stranger said. Then he repeated, "some things never change."

BOOK TWO

Ivan's Prize:

The Binding Force

CHAPTER 12

The Note

Typically, Ivan liked to leave the office a little early on Friday's; but on that afternoon, he had been detained. Even so, he got home before Katrina. Mac's car was parked out front, so when he opened the door in the hallway that led to the basement, he hollered, "Mac, come on upstairs. Let's have a few cocktails before Katrina gets home."

Ivan stood at the top of the stairs waiting for an answer, but he didn't hear a sound. "That's odd," he thought to himself.

Ivan gave up and walked on to the kitchen, where he made himself a stiff vodka, so stiff it made him remember the Motherland. After looking through the junk mail that had piled up on the counter, he walked back into the den and turned on the TV. He couldn't focus on anything, because he knew that earlier that day, Mac had gone back to the church to confront the priest. Ivan couldn't wait to find out how that went.

Disappointed, he decided to write Mac a note telling him to come upstairs to visit, no matter how late it was when he got in.

Ivan walked downstairs to post it some place where it couldn't be missed; but when he rounded the corner and turned on the light, horror exploded his senses. He screamed a primordial scream, a noise shouted from hell, but heard in heaven. His best friend's brains were splattered across the wall above the headboard of the bed. Ivan saw his own shotgun lying on the floor, having discharged in what used to be Mac's mouth.

"Oh, God, no! Please no, not this!" He reached down to hold Mac in his arms, hoping that some sign of life might be left. But it was an irrational hope. Mac was gone. Ivan let his friend go and rushed toward the bathroom, but didn't make it before he threw up. When he turned on the light and looked in the mirror, Ivan's eyes deceived him. He saw Mac the first time he looked, and then it was himself mortally wounded, causing Ivan to throw up again.

Having no idea what to do next, he went back upstairs and walked into his den to collect his thoughts. Feeling weak, Ivan collapsed into his chair, shocked by the horror. He had to call the police, but he had a basic mistrust of police from his days in the Soviet Union. Blood was smeared on his clothes. The lethal weapon was his shotgun. He worried that the police might suspect his involvement in some way. He was afraid that the police would probably question his whereabouts in detail, so he began to recall each place he had been that day, and those persons who could confirm his innocence. He wrote down their names on a piece of paper and stuck it in his desk, just in case he ever needed it. Once he was sure that he could handle the police's inevitable interrogation, he made the phone call to report the death.

After hanging up the phone, he called Katrina to see if she had left her office. No one answered. He knew she must be on her way home.

When the police arrived, Ivan met them at the front door, and told them to go down the stairs. Ivan followed them, knowing that nothing could prepare them for the gruesome scene. Soon Ivan heard other footsteps coming down the stairs, as a team of homicide detectives and a coroner arrived to assess the tragedy. Police procedure required the area to be treated as a crime scene until the preliminary cause of death was determined. The coroner estimated the approximate time of death, and then the detectives began their interrogation of Ivan. He answered all of their questions, and gave them the names of those who could confirm his whereabouts on that afternoon and early evening.

The line of questioning then focused on Mac. "Dr. Berkowitz, how long have you known the deceased?"

"I have known Dr. McFarland for years, ever since I began working at Jesuit University."

"How many years is that?"

"Almost ten years."

The detective went on to inquire about Mac's personal life, his marriage, and his job. The interview was interrupted by another detective who blurted out that the next door neighbor had heard a loud blast around 5:00 p.m., but dismissed it as something other than a shotgun blast because gun violence just didn't go on in that neighborhood.

Ivan knew that when Katrina arrived and saw the blue and red lights flashing in the driveway, she would panic. She would probably think that Ivan had suffered a heart attack or gotten injured in some way. Just as he expected, Katrina was frantic when she burst through the door and saw her husband standing there in the kitchen, giving his statement to the police. She seemed to be scared to death. He broke off his interview with the police officer and took her into the den, sitting next to her and holding her before telling her the news that Mac was dead.

For ten minutes, Katrina cried in Ivan's arms. They were interrupted by a homicide detective who stuck his head in the den and asked Ivan if he could use the phone. Ivan offered him the phone next to the sofa where he was sitting, and led Katrina back into the kitchen so the detective could have some privacy. Shortly afterwards, Ivan heard the detective call a meeting in the den with the coroner and the other police, presumably to discuss their findings on the case.

While the others held their meeting, Ivan and Katrina stayed in the kitchen and talked about Betsy. How could they tell her?

The fact that Mac and Betsy had separated would probably make the news even worse for her, since all hope of reconciliation was now dashed forever. Ivan knew she would be devastated.

Their conversation was interrupted by the chief homicide detective, who announced that the death had been officially ruled a suicide. He asked Ivan to remain in town for the next few days, in case any additional questions came up. Then, the detective instructed the paramedics and ambulance team to remove the body, and asked the fire department guys to please stay around long enough to clean up. Finally, he turned to Ivan and said, "I'll give notification to the next of kin. That would be Mrs. Elizabeth Ann McFarland, right?"

"That's correct, but that won't be necessary, detective. Under the circumstances, I think I had better do that. Mac was my best friend in life. He was staying with us as our guest. Probably I should tell her."

"O.K., fine, you tell her. And give her these personal effects: her husband's wallet, watch, wedding ring and other stuff."

"Yes, sir," Ivan promised.

ᛊᛊᛊ

Ivan and Katrina were right about Betsy. The news almost destroyed her. Both Ivan and Katrina tried to console her, but, unable to bring Mac back from the dead, they couldn't comfort her. Ivan volunteered to stay at Betsy's all night, afraid that in her state of shock, she might even harm herself. The night was gut-wrenching and sleepless. It was probably the worst night of Ivan's life. It had to be the worst of Betsy's.

The next morning, Betsy looked like she had died herself, drawn and ashen from the night before. Ivan gave her the envelope that contained Mac's possession's. Betsy wasn't functioning normally, so Ivan opened the envelope on the kitchen table and poured out its contents. He quickly counted the inventory: a watch, a wallet, a wedding ring, some car keys, some pocket change, and a numbered key to a book locker at the Student Union. Ivan recognized the key right off the bat. He called out to Betsy

86

each item that he'd found in the envelope, but all she seemed interested in was the wedding ring. She slid the ring on and off every finger on both hands, fixated on the symbol she had once given Mac.

It was obvious that Betsy was in no state of mind to do much of anything, even though much had to be done. Ivan stopped by his house to pick up Katrina and asked her to help out with all of the funeral arrangements and to keep an eye on Betsy. After dropping her off at Betsy's, Ivan then took the book locker key back to campus to see what Mac might have left behind.

It was easy finding the locker. Ivan turned the key and opened the door, not knowing what to expect. Peering into the darkness of the box, he first thought it was empty, but that would be odd. Why would anybody spend fifty cents to lock a box with nothing in it? He stuck his hand into the recesses of the locker, feeling along the bottom until he bumped into an edge that slid all the way back into the corner. He guessed that it might be a three and half inch diskette. In the other corner, he found another, and then two more in the middle, but that's all there was. He took the four diskettes with him, and left the numbered key in its place.

By the time Ivan returned to Betsy's, Katrina was busy on the phone making calls to Betsy's friends, telling them the shocking news. She handed Ivan the brief press announcement for Ivan to proof-read before calling the newspaper. After Ivan nodded his head in approval, he handed the announcement back to Katrina who read it over the phone line to the reporter responsible for obituaries:

> "Dr. Nigel Clancey McFarland died at the age of 41. A memorial service will be held on Monday, November 2, at 10:30 a.m. at the All Saints Chapel to be followed by a burial service at graveside at 11:00 a.m. at the Heritage Cemetery. He was a professor of anthropology at Jesuit University and is survived by his wife, Mrs. Elizabeth Ann McFarland. The family has asked that in lieu of flowers, contributions be sent to the Native American College Fund."

When Betsy heard it, she started crying again, so distraught that she could not control her emotions. Katrina hung up the phone and told Ivan to go back home and rest. She would take care of Betsy, and help her receive visitors later in the day. Ivan hugged and kissed both women before he left them.

Once home, Ivan went into the kitchen, needing badly to make himself some coffee. He took his steaming, hot cup with him down the hall into his small office. There, he sat down in front of his PC, booted the system and loaded one of the diskettes into the A drive. Then he took a deep breath and a sip of his coffee, hoping this review would help him understand what could have bothered his friend so much that he took his own life.

Ivan scrolled through the files, recognizing immediately that part of Mac's translation work on the Constantine Papers was on the diskette. Not really wanting to get into the subject at the moment, he ejected the first diskette and inserted the second, and then the third, both of which were more of the same. The fourth diskette turned out to be different. It was Mac's diary, entitled the Istanbul Project, just what Ivan was looking for. The first entry of the diary began on the same day Mac announced his trip to Istanbul, the day Mac, Betsy, Ivan and Katrina had raised their margarita glasses at their favorite Mexican restaurant, celebrating Mac's good news. It seemed so long ago.

Knowing that he would have plenty of time to read all of it, Ivan rifled through three years of journal entries to the very end, the entry made on the last day of Mac's life. According to the diary, Mac had indeed gone back that day to visit the church, meeting again with the priest in the confessional. Almost every word spoken was keyed in the diary. Ivan became so absorbed that he let his coffee get cold.

Near the end, after the priest had said, "You are considered to be dangerous to the Church," Ivan's stomach started to turn. Mac summarized his interpretation of the meeting in the last paragraph by saying,

> "All of this paranoia on the part of the Church is getting out of hand. They are so powerful that they are destroying me. I don't think I can contain these people. I cannot limit the extent to which they are

willing to go to eliminate the threat. They have already destroyed me. They have destroyed Betsy. I am worried now for anyone who even knows about the Constantine Papers. I am even worried about Julio, who doesn't know a thing about any of this. As innocent as he is, my adversaries know that he is dear to me. Now, I fear that even he could be endangered by his mere association with the Istanbul Project."

Mac signed off by saying,

"Were it not for my love for Betsy, and my hope that we will survive, I would surely fall into the abyss."

Ivan thought this last line was very strange for someone who was about to take his own life. He wondered if Mac and Betsy had fought or something after this entry had been made.

Ivan re-read the whole thing, more slowly this time, analyzing every word. He couldn't let go of Mac's haunting words of warning.

"I am worried now for anyone who even knows about the Constantine Papers."

That included Ivan.

CHAPTER 13

The Funeral

After putting the diskettes in a safe place, Ivan decided that the next thing he needed to do was make some phone calls. Betsy had asked him to be a pallbearer, and she also wanted Ivan to call five others: Mac's three cousins, Betsy's brother, and one other to make six. After talking it over with Ivan, she followed his suggestion and decided Julio would be the best choice. Ivan agreed to call them all, but his first was to Julio.

"May I speak to Julio, please."

"Just a moment," a charming, female voice replied.

Ivan assumed it must be Julio's wife. Mac had mentioned in his diary that Julio had gotten married.

"Julio, this is Dr. Ivan Berkowitz at Jesuit University. How are you?"

"I've been feeling kinda sick the last day or so. I'm sure I'll get over it, though. I remember Mac talking about you, always telling stories about the two of you. I've been thinking about him lately," Julio said.

"Well, regrettably, I have some very bad news to tell you. Our friend, Mac, is dead. He died Friday evening."

Julio swallowed hard, so hard that Ivan could hear it over the phone.

Ivan continued, "The police have ruled his death a suicide. His funeral is Monday and Betsy wanted you to be a pallbearer. I know your friendship meant a lot to him. You were very special to him," Ivan finished.

"Mac is dead?"

"I hate to say it, but yes," Ivan repeated.

"A suicide?"

"That's what the police have said, but we need to talk."

Julio then told Dr. Berkowitz, "Should I come in Sunday night?"

"Yes. That'd be good. I'll pick you up at O'Hare. You're welcome to stay with Katrina and me, if you don't mind sleeping on a sofa-bed."

"I don't mind at all. Thanks for offering," Julio said.

"All right then. Call me back with your flight information, and I'll see you Sunday night."

"Yeah, O.K." There was a pause of silence and Julio added, "I still can't believe Mac's dead."

"I'm having a hard time with it too, Julio. I don't want to believe it either."

When Julio called back to confirm his plans, Ivan told him that he would pick him up outside the baggage claim area in his easily identifiable Volkswagon van, with bumper stickers substituting for a fresh paint job. Ivan's vehicle was a form of personal expression, more than a mode of transportation. The rolling billboard counterbalanced his introverted personality. The bumper stickers were mostly political in nature, especially when he first started putting them on the van. But after a while, it didn't really matter what the decals said.

Ivan learned that Julio, too, was easy to recognize: six foot three, jet black hair, jet black eyes and earth-toned skin. Out of a hundred or so people gathered around the bag carousel, Julio stood out like a Sequoia in a pine forest. Ivan greeted him with a handshake and took his bag. They climbed into the van and started off for Northshore, speaking sparingly at first.

The silence was nothing more than reflection on the macabre circumstances. They made an effort to rise above their depression by exchanging stories about Mac. Then Ivan asked Julio to tell all about himself so the two of them could get better acquainted. Ivan learned that Julio was now 32 years old, his wife's name was Mary, and they were expecting their first child. The two of them lived in a garage apartment behind an estate-sized home in Old Towne, Virginia, just across the Potomac from D.C. proper. As bad as the traffic was in Washington, Julio said it was a short commute to the State Department. He added that he enjoyed living in D.C., but he sometimes missed his family and friends in Arizona.

Along the way, Ivan pulled over to a coffee shop to tell Julio what he had learned about Mac, his life and his death. Near the end of the story, he told Julio about the diskettes. They finished up their coffee and continued on to the house. As the two were walking to the back door, Ivan warned, "I'm afraid it's gonna be a late night around here." When they stepped inside, he shouted, "Hi, Katrina. We're home."

Katrina came around the corner and gave Ivan a little kiss before being introduced to Julio.

"Kat, this is Julio...and Julio, this is my wife, Katrina."

"It's nice to finally meet you, Julio," Katrina said, extending her hand to greet him. "I'm just so sorry you had to come visit us on this occasion."

"Thank you, Ms Berkowitz. Thank you for having me," replied Julio.

"I apologize for not having a bedroom for you to stay in, Julio. I hope you won't mind sleeping on the sofa-bed in the den," Katrina said.

"That'll be fine. You should see how small my house is. You could almost fit it into your kitchen. We're expecting our first child soon, so it won't be long before we'll have to move into something larger."

"Well, I just hope you'll be comfortable while you're here."

"I'm sure I will be. Don't worry about me for a minute. I'll be just fine."

They all went into the den and visited for an hour or so, until Katrina excused herself to go to bed. Then, Ivan led Julio down the hall to what used to be the second bedroom on the main floor, a bedroom that Ivan had converted into his little office, right after they moved into the house. Ivan reached inside his desk drawer to retrieve the four diskettes. He had labeled the first three the Constantine Papers, Part One, Two and Three. The fourth diskette was Mac's diary, which he labeled the Istanbul Project. Ivan turned on the monitor, booted his operating unit and inserted the Istanbul Project into the A drive. He opened the last file on the diskette and scrolled forward to Mac's last words. When Julio saw his own name mentioned, he looked at Ivan with an expression of disbelief. Julio had never heard of the Constantine Papers.

Ivan told Julio that he could read all night, if he wanted to, and if he had any problems operating the computer, to call at any hour. Ivan then told Julio that the Istanbul Project would probably raise more questions than give answers, but he did know one thing for sure — all they were going to get was on those diskettes. He wished Julio a goodnight, leaving him to search for clues that might explain the loss of his friend.

The next morning, Ivan shook Julio's shoulder to wake him up, reminding him that the pallbearers were to meet at the funeral home at 10:15. Ivan asked, "Did you sleep well?"

"What time is it?"

"It's 9:00."

"About four hours, I guess. Four hours of nightmares."

"That's what I was afraid of, but you had to see it."

"Yeah."

"Nobody on this planet knows about those diskettes but you and me. I'm afraid going to the police wouldn't do any good. It would only broaden the circle of people who know, and put more people at risk. I don't want Katrina to know anything about this. And I honestly don't think Betsy knows about it. We should leave it that way."

"I agree. This would scare Mary to death."

"Right. Now listen, you and I have to stay in touch, just in case anything ever comes up about this. Hopefully, it never will. Are you with me?"

"Yes sir. I couldn't agree more."

꿍

At the funeral home, Julio and Ivan were introduced to Mac's three cousins and Betsy's brother. Everyone's conversation revolved mostly around Betsy. All were concerned about how she was enduring the pain.

During the chapel service, Ivan gave a short eulogy, reminiscing about Mac's boldness and sense of humor. Ivan also talked about his good-natured humanity. He said that when Katrina and he first arrived in Northshore, Mac was among the first to befriend the two Jewish immigrants in this predominately Catholic community. Ivan finished by saying, "Mac lived his life fully, sometimes beyond measure. He enjoyed life so much, he sometimes had a difficult time saying 'no' to whatever experience came his way. He had the courage to try anything. He never intended to harm a soul. Like all of us, he was imperfect; but he was the best friend I've ever had. Now he has laid down his life. I will grieve his death and mourn his absence; but in remembrance, I will celebrate his passion for living, always. Amen."

Betsy wept.

When the service moved to graveside, the small crowd lined up to sign the guest book. Many watched tearfully, as the pallbearers carried the closed casket from the hearse to the grave. It was a very somber procession. In looking at the faces of those in attendance, Ivan noticed that everyone seemed confused in their bereavement, not understanding how Mac could have taken his own life. It was bleakest of all when the widow, Betsy McFarland, stepped out of her car, and moved under the tent. When she took her seat in front of the coffin, Ivan felt his own tears well up, and spill down his cheek. He fought to regain his composure. Moments later, Monsignor Bates asked the guests to gather in more closely, so that the service could begin.

When it was over, Ivan noticed that the Monsignor did not give his blessing to Mac. In Catholic tradition, such a blessing could be optionally withheld in the circumstance of suicide; and so it was that day. Monsignor Bates concluded the service with a prayer for the soul of Nigel McFarland, and a prayer of warning for those who might be tempted to follow in his footsteps.

Ivan looked over at Betsy to see if she noticed the omission. She seemed lost, angry, and bitter. Monsignor Bates leaned over to say a few words to console her. Ivan overheard him say, "Betsy, please come visit me at the church. We will try to help you through this."

She replied softly, "I'd rather visit Mac in hell, if that's where he'll be."

Everyone in earshot seemed surprised by her bitter remark. The Monsignor took his hand from her shoulder, and walked away, acting as though Betsy had given no reply at all.

<hr/>

After the crowd had gone home, Ivan and Julio stayed behind. Ivan was having a difficult time telling Mac good-bye. He watched silently as Julio, in accordance with the Hopi Way, asked Taiowa, the Great Spirit and Supreme Creator, to unite the Sun Father, Tawa, and the Earth Mother, Tuwa Katsi, in a Song of Creation, and to guide Mac's spirit, now on its journey back to the womb of Mother Earth.

CHAPTER 14

The Will

For the next few weeks, Ivan and Katrina spent a lot of time with Betsy, helping her pull herself together. They tried to entice her out of her home, but it was the only refuge she knew. Ivan noticed she had lost a little weight, but he was more worried about her financial situation; the bills kept rolling in. Ivan's first call was to Mac's life insurance agent, who only apologized before saying that the policy did not pay out in the event of suicide. The second call was placed to Mac's attorney, who had drafted his will. Ivan scheduled an appointment to have it read to Betsy, hoping that the reading of the will would initiate the probate process.

Years ago, Mac had asked Ivan to serve as Executor of his estate should the circumstance ever arise. As a friend, and in his official capacity as Executor, Ivan accompanied Betsy to the attorney's office. Ivan brought his copy of the will with him to follow along and to make notes in the margins if the attorney's comments or instructions needed to be remembered. The reading itself seemed uneventful, at least until the lawyer neared the end of the document. The lawyer began reading from text that was not in Ivan's copy.

"Hold it, please. Let me interrupt you for a second. This section you are reading from is not in my version."

"That's correct, Dr. Berkowitz. You have the original, unamended copy of the will, as it was written several years ago. Dr. McFarland amended his will — quite recently, in fact. If you would like, I can have a copy of this page passed out, so that you can follow the changes. They are very slight, actually."

"No, please continue. You're pretty near the end, aren't you? We'll get copies after you're through. Sorry to interrupt."

"That's all right. Please feel free to ask questions at any time. That's what this meeting is all about. Now, let's see, we were reading from section 5.03, paragraph (a), clause (ii) on page six. 'With respect to my work on the project known as the Constantine Papers, I bequeath the original texts and all copies thereof to the custody of the Roman Catholic Church, together with all translation work pertaining thereto'."

"Excuse me, again," Ivan interjected. "When did you say this amendment was written?"

"I believe it was less than a week before..."

Betsy began to cry at the inference. Ivan looked askance at the attorney. He felt certain that someone had tampered with the will, but he wasn't going to raise the question now. He took advantage of Betsy's deteriorating emotional state, and asked for a recess while she regained her composure. Ivan offered to walk her down the hall and show her to the ladies room.

Once they were alone, Ivan asked her a question, "Betsy, did Mac ever say anything to you about the Constantine Papers? Have you even heard of the Constantine Papers?"

"No, he never said a word to me."

"Well, the lid is off now. the Constantine Papers is what Mac had been working on so hard for the last three years. What did he tell you he had been working on?"

"He said he had been writing a book about his trip to Istanbul."

"Well, that's sort of true, I guess. When you're ready, let's go back in that conference room and get this over with. Let's not ask any more questions about the amended will right now. I think there's a lot more to this than we know, but now is not the time or place to discuss it. Let's wait until we get out of here."

When they returned to the meeting, the attorney continued with the reading. There were no other surprises. Mac had left all other worldly possessions to her, even though it wasn't much.

In fact, when they added up the value of the estate, she began to cry again. She told Ivan she was nervous about surviving. How was she ever going to pay her bills? She couldn't even afford Mac's funeral costs, much less the mortgage.

When she settled down, the attorney handed out a few other documents that had to be signed to facilitate the probation process. They spent the next ten minutes discussing the mechanics of probation. It was obvious the attorney wanted her to sign the paperwork on the spot, but Ivan intervened.

"If you don't mind, counselor, we would like to take any documents that need to be signed, and a copy of the amended will, home with us, so they can be reviewed more carefully."

The attorney seemed surprised by the request, but he obliged Ivan, barking out orders to his secretary to make two sets of copies of everything for Dr. Berkowitz and Mrs. McFarland to take with them.

As a last measure, the attorney placed a call to Monsignor Bates on the conference room speaker phone. The Monsignor was notified of the purpose of the call, and he was informed of all present in the conference room for the reading. The attorney then told the Monsignor that Dr. Nigel McFarland had included the Church as a beneficiary in his will, and that the Constantine Papers would belong to the Church as soon as the will was probated.

Monsignor Bates expressed his gratitude on behalf of the Church. His tone seemed inappropriately cheerful. He did not even bother to ask how Betsy was getting along. Ivan wondered if the Monsignor was relishing in his victory.

༚༚༚

After the meeting adjourned, Ivan escorted Betsy out of the office building. He wasn't sure how much he should tell her about the Constantine Papers, but he had to tell her something. What happened back there in the attorney's office just didn't make any sense. Mac had been scared to death of the Church. Mac's diary confirmed that. There was just no way Mac amended his will to leave the Church a dime, much less the Constantine Papers. But what could be done about it? Ivan was afraid that taking his suspicions to the police would only place Betsy and himself in harm's way. He decided the next best thing to do was to set up a meeting with Monsignor Bates. Let him explain it all to Betsy. After all, at the funeral he had invited Betsy to come see him. As Executor of the will, Ivan would just go along.

Once inside his van, Ivan borrowed Betsy's mobile phone and called the church. The Monsignor was still there. He welcomed the call, and invited the two of them right over.

༚༚༚

"Ah, Mrs. McFarland, it is so nice to see you out, and looking so good. Please, you and Dr. Berkowitz come on in, and have a seat. We can visit for a while."

"Thank you, Monsignor," she patronized, wanting the conversation to at least get started on the right foot.

The Monsignor began, "Well, Betsy, are you recovering? Feeling any better? I know you have grieved terribly. I hope time is starting to heal your spirit."

"Yes, Monsignor, as they say time heals all wounds, but I don't know. I just don't know," Betsy said, appearing to be near another emotional break down.

"Well, well now, you must be patient Betsy," he prescribed.

Ivan knew that Betsy wouldn't be able to withstand much more of the Monsignor's insincere counseling, so he tried to transition the conversation to business.

"Monsignor, if you don't mind, please tell us what you know

about the Constantine Papers. But before you get started, you should know that we are slightly disadvantaged. We don't know a thing about these papers. Mac never mentioned the Constantine Papers to either of us. So first, tell us what they are."

Ivan looked over at Betsy and gave her a discreet wink, signaling to her that he was going to feign ignorance.

The Monsignor paused before answering, aware that the subject and mood of the conversation had taken a sharp turn.

"The Constantine Papers," he repeated. "Yes, well, to be honest with you, I don't know much at all, but the Church is very grateful that Mac thought of us in his will. We look forward to learning more about this gift, when it is delivered to us."

"Monsignor, I don't mean to be rude, but do you know anything about them?" Ivan asked.

"Well, yes, I know a little bit. Apparently, Dr. McFarland discovered several ancient manuscripts when he was in Turkey. During his translation work, Dr. McFarland recognized that the manuscripts pertained to matters that concern the Church. He was gracious enough to leave them to us in his will. It's as simple as that."

Betsy spoke up, "Monsignor Bates, Mac never told me about these manuscripts, but God knows, I've had to listen to him complain about the Church over the past few years, almost as though you were at odds. He worried that the Church might interfere with his work, because he said it was very controversial. Did you ever talk to him about this?"

Monsignor Bates leaned back in his chair and brought his hands up in front of his chest, pressing his fingers together. "Yes, Betsy, we talked. Mac sought reconciliation with the Church. In fact, twice within the last month, he came to confession, hoping to put behind him those things that separated him from both the Church...and you, I'm afraid."

Ivan could imagine the hair on the back of Betsy's neck standing up. She was incensed.

"Monsignor, this reconciliation might have taken place with the Church, but it wasn't shared with me. It sounds like I've got a lot to learn about my deceased husband, certainly before the will is settled."

Betsy stood up to leave, and Ivan followed her signal. He extended his hand to the Monsignor, feeling the light grip of his thin-skinned, cold, narrow fingers. Then Betsy took the Monsignor's hand and said in an almost hostile tone, "Time might heal my wounds, Monsignor, but probably not."

Ivan noticed that she pulled away from him sooner than he had let go, leaving his empty hand still extended. It was an awkward departure.

Only a few days later, Ivan received a phone call at home from Betsy.

"Hello," Ivan answered.

"Hey, it's me...Betsy. The Monsignor wants to meet with us again."

"Did he say what he wanted to meet about?"

"No, not really. But he did say we should meet privately. I told him you were helping me through all of this, and if it had anything to do with Mac's will, then you needed to be there. You were the Executor. He didn't seem to have a problem with that. So, should we meet with him?"

"Yeah. Why not? Let's just see what he wants to talk about. Maybe he knows more about the Constantine Papers."

"Ivan, I know you told me not to talk to anybody about the Constantine Papers, but I couldn't help myself, so I called a few people."

"You what?"

"Don't worry about it. Nobody knows anything. I called Mac's boss at school. He said he never heard of them. Then I called Joseph Baldone's office in Chicago. Baldone's the guy who sponsored the trip to Istanbul. They told me he was out of the country, and wouldn't be back for a while. So, the bottom line is: I haven't learned a thing."

"Damn, Betsy, I mean it...don't call anybody else about this.

Until we figure out who and what we're dealing with here, this whole thing worries me. Promise me you won't go do that again. You have to promise."

"I'm sorry. I promise, I won't do it again."

"All right, then. I apologize for getting on to you like that, but I'm only trying to protect the two of us. Somehow, we'll figure this out...together. Let's start off by hearing what Bates has to say."

The three agreed to meet on neutral ground at the fountain in one of the city parks. It was a windy afternoon and only a few people were standing near the fountain, probably afraid that the spray might get them wet, Ivan thought. On the windward side, Ivan and Betsy found the Monsignor.

"Betsy, thank you for taking the time to meet with me. Ivan, thank you, too. Shall we take a walk?" Monsignor Bates began.

"Sure," she replied.

"Like I told you on the phone, I've learned a great deal more since we last talked, and I think you'll both find what I have to say very interesting. By the way, Betsy, I understand that your life insurance agent was unable to help you under the circumstances. I'm very sorry to hear that. I'm sure this entire ordeal has put you under some pressure...financially speaking."

Ivan could tell that Betsy was caught off-guard by the remark. She didn't even respond.

"Well, anyway," the Monsignor continued, "let me get to the point. The Church understands the situation you are in, and wants to do everything in its power to make you feel comfortable with the terms of the will. We feel that the Constantine Papers are quite valuable to the Church, that true or false, they make up a part of Church history. Understanding your situation, we want you to be treated fairly as well. We do not want to bicker with you over the disposition of these manuscripts. They might be of value to the Church, but surely they are of no value to anyone else. The Church is willing to make a one million dollar financial settlement with you, just to keep our differences from escalating or getting in the public eye. The one million dollars certainly should take care of your personal financial needs, probably forever. Would you be interested?"

This time Ivan was caught off-guard. Monsignor Bates fell silent, looking for a response of any kind to the offer he had just made. As best Ivan could tell, she revealed nothing. She had a poker face like no one Ivan had ever seen, leaving Bates in total suspense. After walking for what seemed to be a half-block in total silence, she finally responded to his offer in a brutally blunt tone.

"When Mac died, I lost what I can never have back. Your money won't make any difference. Now, it's your turn to answer a question. Why are the Constantine Papers so important that you would offer me such a large payoff just to avoid a contested will?"

Betsy didn't wait around to hear the Monsignor's answer. She took Ivan by the arm and led him into the grass, vectoring straight toward Ivan's car, leaving the Monsignor standing by himself on the sidewalk.

The Monsignor yelled after them, "We are only trying to help you, Betsy. There are certain financial realities."

Ivan was stunned by the entire scene he had just witnessed.

᯽᯽᯽

A week later, Ivan was at home, trying to unwind after a frustrating day at work. He was listening to Katrina complain about her day when the phone rang.

"Hello," he answered. All he could hear was sobbing. He knew it was Betsy.

After a brief pause, Ivan continued, "Calm down, Betsy, just calm yourself down. You need to take it easy. I'll be right over."

The call was all Ivan needed to crown his day. After hanging up, he said to Katrina, "Let me go see what's bothering her, sweetheart. I'll be back in just a little while."

When Ivan arrived at Betsy's, she opened the front door and

TH E EAGLE DANCER

let him in. She looked awful, with red cheeks and swollen eyes. Ivan walked into her den and found a seat before asking, "Tell me what's the matter, Betsy?"

"It's these bills, Ivan. There's just no way I can pay them all. What am I going to do? This afternoon, I got a letter from the credit card company cancelling my card. I owe so much money, I'll never pay it all off."

"Can you cover your mortgage?"

"Barely, but there's nothing left to pay these other bills. I've either got to sell my house, or find a higher paying job, or something."

"Have you thought anymore about the Monsignor's offer?"

"Yes, and I feel guilty every time I think about it, but I don't really know why."

"Betsy, the Constantine Papers don't mean anything to you, other than you know they meant a lot to Mac. The sentimental value won't make you financially secure. Maybe you should reconsider. A million dollars is a lot of money. And let me tell you, taking the Church's money doesn't mean you love Mac one bit less. You can't view this as selling out. This is all about surviving, that's all."

CHAPTER 15

The Scientist

For years, Ivan remained deeply suspicious about the circumstances that surrounded Mac's suicide, but he was afraid to do anything about it. The warning that Mac had issued in his diary to "anyone who even knew of the Constantine Papers" continued to reverberate in the back of Ivan's mind. He felt cowardly for not challenging more directly Barker and Bates and the attorney who amended Mac's will, but then again, this had never really been his fight in the first place.

In the meantime, the Church was providing Betsy with financial assistance, adding to Ivan's reluctance to rock the boat. He certainly didn't want to jeopardize her financial security, anymore than he did his own. But as rational as his decision to remain silent was, he wasn't proud of it. Ivan had come to realize that for better or worse, he and Betsy had jointly shoved their suspicions into the closet.

Hard work was Ivan's best distraction. His superior intellect and diligence made him a stand-out among his peers, and as a result, his career steadily progressed. Two years after Mac's death, Ivan became the department head of the Physics Department, and two years after that, at the age of 45, he was chosen to be the Dean of the School of Natural Sciences and Mathematics. The recognition was gratifying, but Ivan was a scientist, not an administrator. He wanted more from his career than a nice salary and promotions every few years.

What he wanted was a quantum breakthrough in his research...research he had been working on for over ten years. The breakthrough he imagined would catapult his career far beyond his current sphere of influence, to an entirely new level. And he felt confident that he was close to achieving it.

Ivan's focus in research had been on two opposite, but related theories. The first was the theory of chaos and the second, the theory of self-organization. These theories had been proclaimed years ago, but it was their relationship to one another that captured his imagination. He had been searching for the trigger mechanism that might cause a system to either collapse into chaos or to seek higher order. If he could identify, isolate and manipulate that mechanism, then his aspirations would be achieved. He labeled the mechanism "the binding force."

When he began his research on the subject, he was simply confirming existing formulas that dealt with random theory. But now he was far beyond his beginnings, leading a team with combined talents in physics, mathematics, geochemistry and virology. The team, under Ivan's leadership, was far along in its efforts to understand the creative or destructive properties of particle systems that could result in either balance or imbalance, health or sickness, order or chaos.

The applications of his research ranged from forecasting the reactions and responses of viruses in a micro-cellular setting to understanding more fully the workings of the universe. The technical aspects of his work reached far beyond the general public's knowledge or understanding, and even farther beyond the scope of casual conversation. But the philosophical implications were vast, whether the general public knew it or not. And in Ivan's mind, one day they would know. It was only a matter of time.

A year later, Ivan published his work in a book entitled *The Binding Force*. The book illustrated why physical systems, which have been energized away from stability, tend to regain it; and conversely, why physical systems, which have been deprived of energy, tend to lose their binding properties, and consequently tilt toward collapse. At one end of the spectrum were the creative or evolutionary forces where order ruled. At the other end were the destructive or degenerative forces where chaos ruled. In the very center of his research, Ivan was trying to define "the binding force", the fulcrum of this universal balance.

Although the book was not widely read, it served as a catalyst for spirited conversations within the academic community. The book concluded that the physical universe did not necessarily have a beginning point as measured by linear time. The controversial extrapolation that such a universe would not need a Creator is what fueled the debate. And while the feud between science and religion started long before *The Binding Force* was ever imagined, the fight seemed to have escalated to a new level. It was like stoking a smoldering fire that suddenly burst into flames once again.

The scientists, led by Ivan, ironically assigned almost religious significance to this binding force theory, arguing that the universe could, under certain conditions, self-organize out of chaos, threatening the traditional religious view that God, separate from creation, was the divine architect and Creator. Ivan suggested that the universe did not have to have a beginning or an end. It was simply governed by an infinite number of big bangs and big crunches, speculation that only invited a stiff rebuttal from the Church.

The religious community was again on the defensive, as perhaps it was when Charles Darwin first published *Origin of the Species*. The Church officially refused to recognize the book, which added to its popularity. Furthermore, the Church decreed that

The Binding Force had no jurisdiction over matters pertaining to the Church and certainly none regarding the creation. Their official statement was terse in every way: brief, rigid and judgmental.

The Church's response was exactly what Ivan expected, even what he wanted.

CHAPTER 16

The Debate

It didn't take long for the debate to become more than spirited. Pretty soon it started spreading like wildfire across college campuses, but nowhere was it burning more out of control than where it started, on the campus of Jesuit University. Locally, *The Binding Force* had attracted an enormous amount of attention, putting Ivan in the spotlight. Those who disagreed with the book or renounced it were in need of a spokesman. It was no surprise that into the spotlight, opposing Dr. Berkowitz, stepped Dr. Willis Barker.

Over the past few years, while Dr. Berkowitz had been promoted to Dean of the School of Natural Sciences and Mathematics, Dr. Barker had achieved his own status. He had become the Dean of the Humanities College. The stage was set for a heavyweight bout in this university community. Both men knew it was coming. They just didn't know when or where. But neither expected the fight to begin as it did, with a call from the campus newspaper.

The student government routinely lined up extracurricular activities on campus. Typically, these were a mixture of speakers, cultural events, and musical concerts that served to broaden the horizons of campus life. Many of those who catered to the college campus circuit made a very good living doing it. Speakers had ranged from former Presidents of the United States, to foreign dignitaries, to revolutionaries, to authors, to performers in the arts, to ex-convicts, to stand-up comedians, and even to TV talk-show hosts.

But this time, the student government apparently wanted to hear a public debate from within its own faculty. The invitation was issued from the campus newspaper, a powerful invitation that neither opponent could refuse.

The debate was scheduled outdoors, on the broad steps of the library. It was an elegant building, distinguished by its classical architecture. Ivy crept up its brick facade. The library stood on the edge of the campus quadrangle, a beautiful open square lined by old university buildings and large oak trees. At the center of the quad was a majestic fountain that spouted water thirty feet skyward. The fountain was surrounded by sidewalks that vectored in all directions. The quad was always a fun place to be, emitting that college ambiance where freedom of expression and freedom of thought were reinforced, not penalized.

The President of the Student Government Association was going to be the debate moderator. He began by reviewing the rules that would govern the contest. Basically, each opponent would be allowed a brief opening statement before the moderator began alternating questions to the debaters. After each question was answered, an opportunity followed for a brief rebuttal. The final question would be addressed separately to each debater, with no opportunity for rebuttal. Then, each opponent would give his closing statement.

After reviewing the rules, the moderator thanked the crowd for their attendance. Then, like a Las Vegas ring announcer, he said, "And now for the main event, ladies and gentlemen...let's get ready to RUUMMMBLE!!!" The crowd cheered loudly as the moderator introduced the contestants, Dr. Ivan Berkowitz and Dr. Willis Barker. The two gentlemen approached the moderator, shook hands, and returned to their respective podiums.

The S.G.A. President then turned to Dr. Berkowitz and called for his opening statement. Ivan, feeling slightly nervous for having to go first, stood tall and gathered his composure before speaking.

"Science should help shape our world view by either confirming or refuting an ever-evolving base of information that ultimately stands behind the presuppositions that govern our world view. Religion on the other hand, should help interpolate or extrapolate our metaphysical beliefs from that evolving base of information. As separate disciplines, science and religion should constantly work together to jointly underwrite our understanding of self, others, our surroundings, and the workings of the universe as a whole. The relationship between science and religion is most functional when it is characterized as a symbiotic coalition, but the relationship breaks down under adversarial circumstances, resulting in chaotic and often irrational mud-slinging. I hope that today's debate will illustrate the former case, and not the latter."

The crowd politely applauded Ivan's short statement, sensing that Dr. Berkowitz was hoping to find some common ground with his opponent, feeling him out perhaps, rather than starting a verbal brawl that could spark hostilities.

But next it was Dr. Barker's turn, and both Ivan and the crowd quickly realized that Barker had no interest in a diplomatic compromise. Dr. Barker began.

"God has revealed to us through Christ, His only begotten Son...through His written Word, The *Bible*...and through the Holy Catholic Church, a clear understanding of His nature, the nature of man, the nature of creation, and the way of salvation. The fellowship, communion, and instruction offered by the Holy Catholic Church helps its believers live purposeful lives. Science, while a useful professional discipline, should not attempt to define the domain of God in purely secular terms. Religion is defined by statements of ultimate faith, and not by scientific discovery."

Dr. Barker's statement was well-received, although not all in the audience cheered. This was a partisan crowd, and it seemed excited at the possibility of witnessing an academic duel, no holds barred. The moderator then took to his microphone, announcing that the questions would now begin, the first going to Dr. Berkowitz.

"Dr. Berkowitz, what in your opinion is the religious significance of *The Binding Force*?"

Still wanting to be conciliatory, Ivan leaned forward to give his answer.

"When I first began the research that ultimately led to the publishing of *The Binding Force*, I did not think that there was any particular religious significance at all. I was simply trying to increase my understanding of the balances and imbalances that I observed in various experiments conducted under laboratory conditions. After broadening my research team, and expanding the applications of the research, I began to comprehend the universal characteristics of the binding force. Only then did I sense the far-reaching religious implications. After completing my work on the subject, I have often wondered if the binding force might be one of the most essential and fundamental physical characteristics of God. I now believe that *The Binding Force* touches upon the most fundamental of religious issues, that is...the understanding of God's nature as witnessed by the workings of the universe."

Dr. Barker did not wait for the moderator to formally signal his opportunity for rebuttal. His voice was turned up a notch from Dr. Berkowitz, reflecting a more rigid stance.

"While Dr. Berkowitz certainly has the right to form his own opinion regarding the existence of God and what might be His essential characteristics, Dr. Berkowitz should not authoritatively hold his views up in defiance of his own Jewish heritage, nor should he challenge the authority of the Holy Catholic Church and those ordained by the Church, particularly at this parochial university."

The moderator stepped forward quickly at the end of Dr. Barker's rebuttal, letting the crowd know that the second question would be posed to Dr. Barker.

"Dr. Barker, can you please tell us why *The Binding Force* is officially unrecognized by the Roman Catholic Church?"

Dr. Barker seemed glad to continue.

"Yes, let me put this as plainly as I possibly can. As I just mentioned, it is a simple question of authority. The challenges that Dr. Berkowitz has championed can only be met with condemnation, rejection, and the Church's refusal to recognize his work. The many assumptions that Dr. Berkowitz has made, and the conclusions he has drawn, leave the reader with the feeling that there is no personal God, there is no Creator, there is no Judge, there is no beginning, there is no end. These challenges to the Church's views must be simply cast aside. They are challenges which have no basis even for argument. The Church has acted to limit the possible damaging influence this book might have and so it goes unrecognized, a consistent and commonly practiced judgement on the part of the Church."

The crowd had stopped applauding, feeling uncomfortable with the rejection Barker had thrown at Berkowitz. Even those sympathetic with Barker's position sensed the stiff arm he was giving his adversary. Most people felt awkward, not knowing just how to respond.

Dr. Berkowitz drew a deep breath and clinched firmly the sides of his podium before delivering his own rebuttal. He spoke more forcefully. He took an offensive position.

"You have accused me, Dr. Barker, of self-proclaiming the religious significance of my scientific findings. You have judged that I lack authority to influence others pertaining to religious matters. Let me respond by saying this. No institution in history has ever been more self-proclaiming than the Roman Catholic Church or more intolerant of others' perspectives. The Church's intolerance has ranged from the heinous and indiscriminate book burning in Alexandria, Egypt in 392 A.D., to the Crusades, to the Spanish Inquisition, to the Church's current intolerant positions on the marriage of priests, birth control and the second class treatment of women. I can only say that the Church's decision to ban my publication came as no surprise."

The gloves had come off. This time those partial to Dr.

Berkowitz roared as though the prize-fighter they had bet on had finally thrown a heavy punch, landing solidly on the chin of Dr. Barker. Those who were not cheering were grumbling, possibly on the verge of booing. In either case, the crowd had been sparked and so had Dr. Barker. He tried to defend himself and the Church, but was cut-off by the moderator, who again reminded both men that they could say whatever they wished in their summary closing statements.

The moderator then addressed Dr. Berkowitz with his third question. "Dr. Berkowitz, in your view, does the theory of self-organization explain creation?"

"Perhaps in certain respects, it does, for it is entirely possible that the creation process is inseparably linked to the relationship between chaos and order. We know that the dissipation of energy results in death and collapse, but perhaps death and collapse are in certain respects related to rebirth, a mysterious consolidation of energy, the essence of creation, governed by properties of the binding force.

"If this is the case, and my research indicates that it is, then it might be argued that creation is a continuous process, complementing the process of collapse. On the largest of scales, the universe is either in a state of expansion or a state of contraction. On a more local scale, our own solar system or galaxy might experience the same cycle, but within its own time frame. The cycle I am referring to would be a cycle of big bangs and big crunches, as opposed to the creation out of nothing scenario that is endorsed by the Church.

"My research says that creation is not a static, unilateral event that starts at the beginning of a linear time line. Some have asked me if time advances so long as the universe is in a state of expansion, and then reverses itself as the process of collapse takes place. Several years ago, Stephen Hawking endorsed the concept that the universe, now in a state of expansion as evidenced by an observance known in physics as red shift, eventually will reach its outer limits and transition to collapse, commonly referred to as the big crunch. Hawking's research indicated that the laws that govern entropy set the direction of time, and therefore, time does not reverse itself. He said, however, that all laws of science are suspended in that instant when the big crunch condenses to the point of singularity.

"I agree with his research, although I might take his conclusions one step further by saying that I have reason to believe that at the point of singularity, the big crunch transitions to the next big bang. Again, I agree with Hawking that all laws of science are suspended in that instant.

"But I also believe that time, together with all of the physical laws of science, would, in that instant, have completed one lap, and would start anew on the next, like the second hand of a watch that sweeps past twelve, and begins a new minute. I believe that the relationship between order and chaos is governed by the natural laws of science. I believe the natural laws of science must operate within the order of time. I believe that time is best described by a closed loop, yet a continuum, represented well by the symbol for infinity. The crossroads in the figure eight symbol would be that point of singularity in the transition.

"I have formulated a mathematical equation which illustrates the changing portions of self-destruction or self-organization as the universe accelerates toward extreme collapse, or decelerates as it approaches its outer limits. The equation accounts for the near equilibrium that occurs when expansion reaches its outer limit, energy is dissipated and the system converts or transitions to collapse upon itself. This collapse is nothing more than a mass retrieval system or consolidation of energy that begins slowly and accelerates toward maximum density until a big bang is repeated. A small-scale example of this process is illustrated by the collapse of stars, the formation of black holes, and the birth of super novas."

The crowd responded politely, mostly amazed by the power of this man's intellect, whether they understood him or not. Even those who supported Ivan didn't want to hear about the qualitative and quantitative details behind his research. But many seemed to be enchanted by the alternative concepts that Ivan described.

A poised Dr. Barker then offered his rebuttal in an equally calm tone, although somewhat smug and condescending.

"We have all heard it said before that everything can be explained by mathematics, but why is that so hard to fathom? If I may answer my own question, let me say that mathematics, with its eigenfunctions, its formulas, its slide-rules and its calculators, cannot address questions regarding the soul. Mathematics cannot address questions regarding ethics and morality; and most importantly, mathematics cannot offer salvation.

"If, in fact, you simply look at the world around you, you must conclude that there is a Great Designer, not some primordial soup that by happenstance became what this magnificent universe is. Let me answer the question regarding creation, for I can do so without speculation or hypothecation as my colleague, Dr. Berkowitz, puts forth. The *Bible* says, 'In the beginning, God created the heaven and the earth'."

Those who sided with Dr. Barker this time went berserk, roaring with applause, holding their index fingers up high as though they were number one, or perhaps it was a throw-back to the "one-way" campaign popular among Christian fundamentalists years ago. No matter, the crowd by now was noticeably divided and vocal on both sides, with Berkowitz's fan's mumbling among themselves, hoping their man would throw a heavy punch soon. But they would have to wait, because the fourth question was addressed to Dr. Barker.

"Dr. Barker, is the doctrine of a personal, separate, supreme Deity threatened by Dr. Berkowitz's postulations as presented in his book *The Binding Force*?"

Barker seemed a little hand-tied on this question, and the crowd sensed him reluctantly reciting a rehearsed party-line in his answer.

"Well, this question is difficult to answer because the Church simply refuses to recognize Dr. Berkowitz's work at all. Again, this is a jurisdictional issue that gets back to the question of Dr. Berkowitz's authority versus the authority of the Holy Catholic Church.

"But let me say this. While Dr. Berkowitz's theories might call into question the existence of a God who is supreme, omniscient, omnipotent, eternal and separate from all of creation, his theories in no way threaten the absolute truth that is held by the Church. Dr. Berkowitz's research seems to fall in line with secular relativism, secular rationalism, and secular materialism. He is, at best, putting forth a theory of theistic evolution. The Church, however, remains steadfast in its commitment to absolute truth. The absolute truth is not revealed through a science laboratory. It is revealed by God, to His people, through His Church."

The answer was interesting, but it was nothing more than a glancing blow, bouncing off the gloves of Dr. Berkowitz, whose fans were now hoping for a knock-out counter-punch. Dr. Berkowitz seemed rested and ready to launch an assault when he rebutted.

"Once again Dr. Barker has refused to allow me onto the same playing field as the Church. And for the record, let me make clear that my research and my writings were not intended for the purpose of attacking the Church. Rather, my purpose was simply that of discovery, the pursuit of an inquisitive mind. What I discovered was so profound to me that it changed my view of God entirely. No longer could I accept the traditional Judeo-Christian concept that has been perpetuated for thousands of years. We now know that Earth is not the center of the universe, with heaven above and hell below. This is simply not an accurate description. And so if my research leads me away from the existing egocentric, anthropomorphic imagery concerning God, then so be it. I am only trying to be honest with myself."

Berkowitz's people cheered loudly, probably louder than the situation warranted. While Ivan had landed a heavy body blow, he had not thrown a knock-out punch.

The moderator asked Dr. Berkowitz his next question.

"The moral argument for the existence of God is not addressed by the concept of the binding force. Can you tell me if your view deifies everything in a sense, including such nefarious characters as Adolph Hitler, for example?"

"This is an interesting question that I have asked myself over and over again, because you are right, the concept of the binding force encompasses everything in existence. It does not distinguish between good and evil characteristics. That leaves morality in the hands of society. I believe morality is a self-imposed standard of responsibility, not a God-given absolute standard. For the sake of argument, one might agree that the moral code for homo sapiens is meaningless to other life forms, because they do not share the same responsibility.

"Therefore, I think that the moral argument is merely another means of imposing anthropomorphic characteristics on our admittedly very limited understanding of God. I cannot delete Adolph Hitler from the binding force equation simply because he was devoid of ethics or morality. To me, Adolph Hitler's life was evidence that the universe possesses some powerfully self-destructive properties, properties that have to be counter-balanced by others who possess the power to create. The maintenance of this balance is what brings about a moral standard. It is based upon our instincts of survival. Our moral standard calls for responsible behavior, and gives us a sense of purpose. It gives us definition. But once again, it is a self-imposed standard that conforms to the needs of society."

Dr. Barker offered his rebuttal. "I have to strongly disagree with Dr. Berkowitz. The moral argument for the existence of God is one of the most compelling arguments put forth by scholars and theologians over the centuries. God is absolute goodness. There is no room for evil or self-destruction in the body of a perfect God. Secular society has tried to make a case for situation ethics over the years, but its just not true. God's standards are absolute, not relative. To me, this very point is where his entire argument fails."

The crowd seemed to be thinking deeply, unable to make much noise while they weighed the opposing views. The moderator then addressed his next question to Dr. Barker.

"Dr. Barker, how can a perfect God permit such suffering in the world?"

"This is a difficult question to answer, but, of course, the Adam and Eve story in Genesis explains original sin, and gives account for the imperfect world that we live in. We have chosen to sin; we have separated from God; but God has joined with us in our suffering; and through the crucifixion and resurrection of Christ, God has provided for us the Way, the Truth and the Life, if we simply accept that Christ is our Redeemer, Lord and Savior. The Jews, of course, have not accepted this, and they continue to take comfort in being "God's chosen people".

"Dr. Berkowitz, do you have a rebuttal?"

"Yes. The question about a perfectly good and loving God allowing evil and suffering in the world is worth spending some more time on. You see, not all suffering is the result of sin. Starving babies have not had a chance to accept Jesus as their personal Lord and Savior. Natural disasters affect believers and non-believers equally. I believe that our concept of a perfect God is itself a flawed concept. It gives rise to a dualistic theology, a god of good versus a god of evil. Judeo-Christian theologians do not like to admit this dualism, and they dismiss it by relegating the god of evil to a lower status than the god of good. Satan is merely an angel. But of course, in the end, Satan is dealt with on Judgement Day.

"I believe the eastern concept of yin/yang comes a little closer to reality in a dynamic world. Ultimately one side of the equation defines the other. You must have evil to know good, you must have darkness to define light, you must have suffering to define joy and you must have chaos to define order. The binding force theory accounts for birth and death, creation and destruction, expansion and collapse."

Everybody recognized that the debate was up for grabs. It had turned out to be one helluva fight and not a soul in the audience was disappointed.

The moderator then stepped up to his mike and said, "Gentlemen, I will now ask each of you the same question, without provision for rebuttal. This question will then be followed by your summary closing statements, which will first be given by Dr.

Barker, and then by Dr. Berkowitz. Now for the final question of the debate. Dr. Berkowitz, will you please share with the audience your personal definition of God?"

The audience became very quiet, aware that a strong answer to this question was essential for either man to finish well. Dr. Berkowitz took his turn.

"Unfortunately, I am not quite prepared or qualified to offer a concise definition if that is what you have asked for. But I can quote others, even Christian theologians, who have offered interesting descriptions, which have helped shape my own perceptions of God, even though I am Jewish by birth. First of all, I believe it was St. Anselm who said, 'God is that than which no greater can be conceived.' And the theologian Paul Tillich said, 'God is the ground of all being.' These descriptions come to mind as I try to reconcile my personal views concerning God with my ongoing research concerning the binding force.

"As I said before, my personal perceptions have, in fact, moved away from the traditional, Judeo-Christian interpretation. To me, the traditional view appears as a 'god created in man's image'. The anthropomorphic god I am referring to seems to have created man for his own entertainment. One must wonder what this god did before man was placed on the linear time line. I understand how this came about, because I believe that our very thoughts are limited by our personal experiences, and even by our linguistics, and so whatever we come up with in the way of a description can only be that, a mere description of a perception. It just so happens that as I learn more about the universe, and as my world view evolves, so does my perception of God."

You could still hear a pin drop when the moderator said, "And Dr. Barker, the same question. Will you please share your personal definition of God?"

"Yes, well first of all, let me thank Dr. Berkowitz for admitting that he is not qualified or prepared to answer the question. You see, that is my very point. Only God can give us the answer. We cannot find the answer for ourselves. But the answer is given in The *Bible*. God is our Father, our Judge, and our Creator. He is all-knowing, all-powerful, and eternal. God is personal, and He created man in His own image, so that we can know Him. God exists in the form of the Holy Trinity: Father, Son and Holy Spirit. By the grace of God, and through the death and resurrection of Christ, we can experience eternal salvation. You see, the question is not so hard to answer, if only you accept that which He has given to you through the protective and ministering hands of the Church, not through the self-reliant observations of science.

"For those of you who are interested in the questions and answers that have been discussed here today, I would strongly suggest that you read Pope John Paul II's book entitled *Crossing the Threshold of Hope*, published in 1994."

Silence ruled. The moderator said, "And now for your closing statement, Dr. Barker."

"Thank you. First, I would like to thank the university and the Student Government Association for hosting today's debate. It is important that each of you have the opportunity to freely choose the path that you will take in life. Secondly, let me thank my distinguished colleague, Dr. Ivan Berkowitz, who offers such a distinct contrast to the views of the Church, making the path offered by the Church one which is clearly marked, easily identified and one that can only be described as 'the high road' when considering the alternatives.

"My appeal to the audience to follow the Church is based upon God-given revelation and authority, not empirical laboratory research that, at best, reduces to mathematical conjecture once the researcher enters the realm of God. The Church offers a personal relationship with God, the Father Almighty, through Christ Our Lord and Savior, not some transempirical connection to your surroundings by way of the binding force."

Dr. Barker had finished strongly, a consistent argument from the start.

The moderator then interjected, "And now for your closing statement, Dr. Berkowitz."

"Yes, I, too, want to thank the university and the Student Government Association for scheduling this event. And I also want to thank Dr. Barker."

Ivan went on, "Sometimes the old adage about shooting the

messenger seems all too true. You see, I am only trying to discover that which is before me.

"Divine revelation is not confined to the realm of The *Bible* or the Church. We can observe divine revelation all around us. We must simply open our eyes and look. These religious claims by the Church which bestow exclusive God-given authority serve only to make us dependent, to blind us from looking at and discovering revelation for ourselves. I believe that all comprehension, beyond our basic instincts, is limited by our personal experiences, our linguistic restrictions, our ability to turn thoughts into words, and our ability to turn words into deeds.

"But even so, there is a notable difference between religious thinking and scientific reasoning. By its nature, religious thinking involves mythological concepts which only describe the metamorphosis of God in our own minds. On the other hand, scientific thinking typically involves empirical concepts which are proven to be true or false statistically. Both science and religion can sometimes become caught up in conjecture, or lose touch with reality as it is arguably perceived. And both science and religion can irrationally project hardened, dogmatic, exclusive positions which are still limited at best.

"With respect to this debate, I am hoping that science and religion can meet happily in the middle. *The Binding Force* leads me to believe that we are all transempirically connected, that God perhaps is not separate from creation, but rather one and the same with the universe. As I said earlier, my own views are evolving in tandem with my work. But in the final analysis, I cannot let the Church tell me to blindly follow its lead. I cannot retreat from discovery just to avoid conflict, controversy or change. I can only hope that humanity will ultimately gain a transcending sense of connection, represented by the binding force in each of us, individually, and in the world around us, collectively. Thank you very much."

At the end, the audience was hushed simply because they were both amazed and confounded. The silence was broken as the crowd joined together in applause, showing bipartisan respect and appreciation for both men. The moderator did not ask for any indication from the audience of who might be the winner. The students who heard the debate were the winners. They left the library steps with the feeling that they were free to form their own views, away from the tutelage of their families, removed from the pressure of conformity in the workplace, free to take or leave what had been offered that afternoon, on the edge of the campus quadrangle.

CHAPTER 17

The Demotion

In less than a week, Ivan received a phone call from the office of the Chancellor of the university, Dr. Preston Monague. The Chancellor wanted to see Ivan personally, so Ivan dropped everything he was working on and made his way to the Chancellor's office. He suspected with good reason that such a meeting could only be bad news.

Behind closed doors, Chancellor Monague wasted no time before issuing a verbal reprimand to Ivan for causing such controversy at Jesuit University. The Chancellor reminded Ivan that Jesuit University was not just any school. It was integrally affiliated with the Catholic Church. It was parochial in the strongest sense of the word. He instructed Ivan to tone down his controversial views, since he was a high-ranking representative of the university. In addition to these instructions, the Chancellor cut Ivan's expense account budget, telling him that the university would no longer reimburse him for travel expenses to speak about his research at other colleges and universities.

"Dr. Berkowitz, yesterday the Board of Trustees called an unscheduled meeting to discuss this whole situation. Officials from the Church participated in the meeting as well, and let me tell you, this is a very serious matter as far as they are concerned. The Trustees voted to require specific Board approval before the S.G.A. will be allowed to host future events. I was instructed to take whatever measures might be necessary to discourage any repeat performances. I hope these words of warning will suffice."

After leaving Chancellor Monague's office, Ivan was more than a little upset. He felt censored. He had been cut off from talking openly about his research. Without any peers to empathize with his woes, he braced for the inevitable onslaught of depression.

In defiance, Ivan continued on with his speaking engagements at other colleges and universities, even though his expenses were no longer reimbursed by J. U.. Soon, the host schools were paying Ivan a speaking fee, in addition to reimbursing his out of pocket costs. It did not take the administration at J.U. long to realize that their attempts to stifle Ivan were not working.

Over time, the tension between Ivan and the administration escalated. Finally, the Board of Trustees accepted the recommendation of Chancellor Monague to demote Dr. Berkowitz from his position as Dean. He was replaced by a spineless lieutenant named Kevin O'Leary, who couldn't hold a candle to Ivan in any endeavor other than appeasing the administration by playing campus politics.

Fortunately, Ivan retained his teaching job at Jesuit University, enduring the humiliation caused by the demotion. The administration's condescending attitude conveyed the unspoken message: We are doing you a favor by keeping a place for you.

Ivan learned one thing after his fall from grace. He learned to stop taking the sycophants so seriously. He realized that his detractors were enslaved by conformity, unable to set their own agendas in life. Once Ivan stopped trying to please them, he appeared more relaxed, happier and self-confident. He actually was relieved to get back to teaching, and in his classrooms he spoke honestly about his research, ignoring the saber-rattling by the administration. He got to the point where he ignored the administration altogether.

By word-of-mouth and on the editorial pages of the campus newspaper, Ivan's popularity spread among the students, causing enrollment in his classes to explode. Although the administration had kicked him around, the students began to elevate him to a new status, at least in their minds. Ivan Berkowitz was becoming somewhat of a local cult figure, a symbol, a rising star.

This newfound popularity was not appreciated by all. It disturbed no one more than Willis Barker who had enjoyed witnessing the demotion of Berkowitz. While Barker was becoming more and more agitated, Berkowitz was feeling stronger than ever, relieved of the meaningless administrative detail that flowed across a Dean's desk.

But Ivan had no idea that Barker was so bothered, until he approached Ivan at a faculty cocktail party and said, "Ivan, don't take your fame and glory too seriously. It might turn out to be more than you can handle. Remember what happened to Nigel McFarland."

Barker then turned to walk away.

Ivan's first reaction was shock. His second thought was to accuse Barker of having something to do with Mac's death. Ivan wisely bit his tongue. He caught up with Barker, spun him around and said, "Yes, I remember Mac, all right. Every day of my life."

Then he clicked his glass against Barker's and said, "Here's to Mac. We should both remember him."

🐾

That night, Ivan opened the closet door that had hidden his innermost feelings about Mac's death. Ivan had always believed that there would be a reckoning for the injustice that had befallen his friend. Maybe now was the time.

CHAPTER 18

The Investigator

When Ivan arrived home that evening, Katrina was busy cooking dinner. Ivan kissed her on both cheeks, mixed himself a strong Vodka, and then told Katrina what Barker had said at the faculty cocktail party.

"Kat, I think it's about time to find out who might be involved in all this. I never found out who got to Vanessa Reilly, that girl who accused Mac of harassment. And I still don't believe Mac committed suicide."

"It's been four years since Mac died, Ivan. What can you possibly do about it now?"

"I don't know. I was thinking about calling Howard Liebermann. Maybe he could help."

Ivan took his drink, and wandered down the hall to his little office. He picked up the telephone to call his old acquaintance, one that he had almost forgotten how to contact. Howard Liebermann had taken early retirement from the Hebrew Immigrant Assistance Society. He had been the former head of Operation Exodus, at the time when Ivan and Katrina were trying to leave Russia and come to the United States. He remembered distinctly Mr. Liebermann's instruction to call him personally, if they ever needed some help. Mr. Liebermann didn't say how he would help. He just said he would. There was something emphatic about the man that exuded confidence. Ivan decided it was time to find out if this confidence was justified of not.

When Mr. Liebermann answered, he recognized Ivan's Russian accent right away, arresting the paranoia that he would not be remembered at all. He imagined that Howard had to be between 50 and 55 years of age, and possessed the strength and stamina of a man half his years. Ivan was sure, however, that the conversation they needed to have couldn't be had on the phone. He arranged to meet Liebermann in Miami, Florida, where he lived in a high-rise condominium off Brickell Avenue, near Coconut Grove.

For some reason Ivan had always trusted Liebermann, mainly because he made good on his promise to get Ivan and Katrina out of Russia. But Ivan also knew that Liebermann was well-connected; he was a hired trouble-shooter with lots of gray hair; and while his gray hair stood for experience, more importantly, it stood for longevity. Ivan suspected that somewhere along the way, Liebermann might have been affiliated with an intelligence agency: the C.I.A., Mossad, the K.G.B. or somebody. Howard had never openly discussed it.

Before going to Miami, Ivan called Betsy McFarland to invite her to lunch. He wanted to tell her what was on his mind...to ask what might be on hers. He needed to know how she would respond if she knew he was going to delve so deeply into the past.

As they were leaving the restaurant, she hugged and kissed him, and shed a few tears before thanking him, telling him that she had been haunted by it all, too. She hated taking the Church's money. She hated herself for selling out Mac's passion. She wanted desperately to change direction, if only she could.

Finally, she begged Ivan to let her go with him to see Mr. Liebermann. Ivan resisted at first, trying to discourage her involvement. But when he saw how consumed she was, he said, "O.K., but let me warn you. The more I tell you, the more endangered you become, and as we both know, this can be deadly."

For the first time, Ivan told her about Mac's diskettes, and asked her if she still had a copy of Mac's will. Their best hope was that Mr. Liebermann might help them either solve the mystery, or at least counsel them on how to avoid falling prey to the wolf in sheep's clothing. The wolf had already claimed Ivan's best friend and Betsy's husband.

▼▼▼

Ivan asked Katrina to take them to the airport in Chicago. He had convinced Katrina that the two of them needed to make an effort to clear their consciences about Mac. And while Katrina seemed to understand, she was appeared a little unnerved that her husband was digging up old skeletons from the past.

When they arrived in Miami, it was almost sweltering outside, but a gentle breeze made the heat tolerable. Neither Ivan nor Betsy were accustomed to seeing short-sleeved shirts and palm trees, but it was a pleasant change from the long, cold winter in Northshore. They rented a car and took off searching for Brickell Avenue. Pastel-colored towers and palm-tree-lined streets were interspersed between blue water channels. Miami seemed to be a beautiful town where summer was eternal.

He looked at his watch to see what time it was. They had ten minutes to spare before they needed to be in the lobby of the Mayfair Hotel. Liebermann had insisted on the hotel, making it a rule never to hold a business meeting in his home. He chose the Mayfair for two reasons: first because it was convenient; and secondly, because it was one of the most beautiful hotels in Miami. It was a good place to meet for lunch, but Ivan and Betsy weren't planning to stay the night. Their return flight was scheduled to leave that afternoon, and Katrina was going to pick them up at O'Hare later that night.

129
▼▼▼

When they walked into the lobby, the first thing Ivan noticed was that Liebermann was not there. Ivan and Betsy found a comfortable place to sit down, but after fifteen minutes of waiting, impatience finally got the best of them. Ivan approached the front desk, and asked if perhaps he might have a message from a Mr. Howard Liebermann. As it turned out, there was a message that read more like an apology. The typed message said,

"To: Ivan Berkowitz
From: Howard Liebermann

Ivan, I've had an unexpected conflict that could not be avoided. Please try to meet me for dinner at Monty's Stonecrab House, there in the adjoining mall, at 7:30 this evening. I hope you will be there. I'm very sorry if this has inconvenienced you in any way. If you can stay, please check with the front desk. I have booked you a room at the hotel."

Ivan went back over to Betsy to break the bad news. Then, he returned to the front desk to inquire about accommodations. He was told that there were no additional vacancies, but fortunately Mr. Liebermann had reserved a deluxe suite for them. Ivan asked about the room rate and was told that while the room was $395 per night, the room had been comped by Mr. Liebermann. Ivan wasn't sure what comped meant, so he asked.

"The room has already been paid for, Dr. Berkowitz," the registration clerk replied.

That settled it in Ivan's mind, but he needed to consult with Betsy to see if she was agreeable. He was a little bit worried about explaining it all to Katrina, but he really had no choice. After all, Liebermann intended no harm. He didn't even know Betsy was coming along.

After registering at the front desk, the clerk signaled for a bellman to assist with their bags. Ivan quickly let the clerk know that they wouldn't be needing any assistance. Once given the room key, he and Betsy headed for the elevator.

The suite appeared to be a honeymooner's dream. The

bedroom had an elevated floor that featured a king-sized platform bed, mirrored walls, teal and pink wall coverings, a rich car-
pet underfoot, and a balcony with a hot tub overlooking a gigan-
tic tropical atrium. This would have been pure paradise for anyone other than Ivan and Betsy. In the living room, there was a big-
screened TV, leather upholstered lounge chairs, a sofa and a coffee table. The good news was that the sofa could be converted
into a bed, and so Ivan went ahead and asked the question.

"You won't mind if I take the sofa, will you?"

"Just this once, Ivan. I'll let you have it."

They both laughed at themselves and their predicament. But
before they could finish laughing, they heard a knock at the door.
Ivan peered through the peephole and saw a room service waiter.
He stood there with a food cart that carried a small fruit basket,
an ice-cold bottle of champagne, and two chilled champagne
glasses. Apparently, this was standard fare for arriving guests at
this extravagant hotel, but it was pure comedy for Ivan and Betsy.
Ivan opened the door and let him in and tipped the waiter a couple
of bucks in exchange for the two champagne glasses. Ivan closed
the door behind the waiter as he departed, laughing again at their
awkward circumstance.

Rather than uncork the bottle, crawl in the hot tub, drink the
champagne, rub their naked bodies all over each other, and then
jump into bed in a sexual frenzy, Ivan set the glasses down on the
coffee table, excused himself to the bedroom, and picked up the
phone to call Katrina.

"Hello," Katrina answered.

"Katrina, wow, I'm glad I got you," he started.

"So am I," she interrupted. "This morning Chancellor
Monague was looking for you. He called and said it was very
important that he speak with you."

Ivan's blood pressure skyrocketed.

"What did you tell him, darling? You didn't tell him where I
was, did you?"

This conversation wasn't going too well. Ivan hadn't told her
to conceal his whereabouts, because he didn't want her to worry

or know too much for her own safety. But she, of course, knew that he and Betsy were going to see Liebermann. Telling her that much seemed harmless enough.

"Yes, Ivan. I told him. I told him he might be able to reach you through Mr. Liebermann, and I gave him Mr. Liebermann's phone number. That was all right, wasn't it?"

Ivan's stomach turned.

"Yes, that's fine, but there is a little problem. We haven't met with Liebermann yet, and I don't even know how to get in touch with him. No one is answering his phone, and according to a message we got at the hotel where we were supposed to meet him, Betsy and I won't see him until dinner." Ivan grimaced. He had dropped the bomb.

What are you talking about, Ivan?"

"I told you, darling. Liebermann didn't make our meeting today, and he left a message that all he could do was meet us at dinner," he repeated.

"So, when are you coming home?" she asked.

"Tomorrow, on the earliest possible flight, darling. I'll have to call you again with new flight information. I'm staying at the Mayfair Hotel."

"Is Betsy staying, too?"

"Yes, Liebermann didn't even know Betsy was coming with me," Ivan began awkwardly. "When he found out he couldn't meet me as planned in the lobby of the hotel, he called to leave a message. The message asked if I could please stay. He reserved and paid for a room to compensate, I guess, for the inconvenience. The Mayfair had only one room available, so Betsy and I..."

"What?!"

"We are staying in the room that Mr. Liebermann paid for. There's not another room available in this hotel. The room we have is a suite, Katrina, actually two rooms. I am on the couch in a whole different room from Betsy. It's no big deal, I promise.."

"All right, all right. Don't worry about it. Just call me before your flight comes in."

"Thanks, darling. I'm sorry it worked out like this. I love you, and I'll see you tomorrow."

After saying good-bye, Ivan walked back into the other room where Betsy was, and suggested that they go shopping for incidentals, anything to get out of the room. They walked through the lobby doors and into the multi-storied mall. Surrounding the atrium were the most elegant and expensive boutiques Miami had to offer, which sold everything money could buy except what they needed.

♈♈♈

At 7:20 that evening, they again left the room, this time heading for Monty's Stonecrab House. It was a popular spot, with better than average cuisine and a fun atmosphere, but it was patronized mostly by tourists. The locals in search of good seafood more typically went to hole-in-the-wall night spots, places too small to cater to tourists, and too hard to find without a navigator. But Monty's was perfectly convenient and appropriate for the occasion, that of getting re-acquainted with Howard Liebermann.

When they arrived, Mr. Liebermann was standing next to the maitre'd, looking exactly as he did the last time Ivan had laid eyes on him. He was about six feet tall, with broad shoulders, a square jaw, and a bald head. His waist was narrow and his grip was strong. He had the beady eyes of a predator. He hadn't changed a bit.

After shaking hands, Mr. Liebermann gave Ivan a friendly pat on the shoulder and said, "The American way of life must suit you well, Ivan."

"Yes, Howard, we've been very fortunate. But before I tell you all about it, let me introduce you to a friend of mine. Howard, this is Betsy McFarland. And before you ask me anything, let me answer. No, she is not my new wife. She's not even a Jewish girl."

"It's so nice to meet you, Betsy," Liebermann said.

"Howard, I know I didn't mention to you that Betsy was coming with me, but at the last minute she decided to join me. You'll understand why later on, when we get a chance to talk."

"Well I'm glad you came along, Betsy. I look forward to getting acquainted." Then Liebermann added the trite expression,

133
♈♈♈

"Any friend of Ivan's is a friend of mine."

From Ivan's point of view, the ice had been broken. He felt a lot better knowing they had not been stood up twice.

Once they were seated at their table, Howard immediately apologized to both of them for his afternoon conflict, although he didn't volunteer any details about what had come up. He added how greatly relieved he was that they had chosen to stay, and meet with him for dinner. Ivan, of course, accepted his apology and thanked him for the room, although the awkwardness of traveling with Betsy and not Katrina was embarrassing to both of them. Even so, he complimented the hotel, and said he hadn't seen anything quite like it ever before.

Setting the apologies aside, Liebermann then asked Ivan to bring him up to date on everything: career, family, hobbies, the works. Betsy just sat there quietly while all of this went on, feeling slightly ignored by the two men. Ivan suspected she wasn't exactly thrilled that she had decided to come along.

But before she lost patience, they did get to the point. Ivan prefaced the discussion by telling Howard why Betsy had come with him. He told Howard all about the life and death of Dr. Nigel "Mac" McFarland. The three of them talked for more than an hour, starting with Istanbul, and progressing through Mac's alleged suicide. Ivan covered the waterfront, so Howard could sort through all that had happened.

Once Ivan finished talking about Mac's demise, Liebermann asked a question.

"So, Ivan, you haven't told me. Without intending any disrespect to Ms McFarland, why are you dredging up something that happened four years ago?"

"Howard, this whole thing has haunted Betsy and me ever since it happened. I buried my suspicions earlier for the sake of not rocking the boat, and for Betsy's sake. But lately, I've felt like I'm going up against the same opposition that Mac faced. Let me tell you what's happened to me."

They discussed Ivan's research and the resulting book he had published, *The Binding Force.* Ivan described the controversy that had been stirred up by the campus debate, and the demotion that ultimately followed. Last of all, he shared his run-in with Barker, the veiled threat, whether it was perceived or real. Ivan ended their discussion by leaning back in his chair, and asking Howard a question.

"O.K., you've heard it all now. Is there anything we can do about it? Can you help us solve the mystery surrounding Mac's death? Can you help me take on the Catholic Church?"

Liebermann responded, "I'll look into it Ivan. Maybe we can take on the Church, or maybe we can't. That's a pretty tall order. If we can't, then maybe I can at least steer you down a different path. In the meantime, at least until you hear from me, why don't you keep a low profile. Try not to stir the pot. You might think about curtailing your speaking engagements for a while, at least until you hear back from me. By the way, does anyone else know what's going on?"

"No, sir," Ivan quickly responded.

"That's good. Let's keep this whole subject very confidential."

"Yeah, that's for sure. Oh, by the way, Howard, did Chancellor Monague from Jesuit University call you today looking for me? His office called Katrina at home trying to get in touch. I think Katrina gave them your number."

"No, no, I'm afraid I didn't hear from anybody, but I'll let you know if you have any messages when I get home."

"Thanks, Howard."

By now, almost everyone else in the restaurant had gone home. Howard had long ago covered the check. He pushed his chair back to stand and said, "Ivan, aside from what you've told me here tonight, I'm glad you and Katrina are doing so well. And Betsy, I'm so sorry to learn about your husband and the circumstances surrounding his death. I hope that I can help you in some way cope with the hardship you have endured. Be patient, though. It might be a while before you hear from me; but hopefully, when you do, I'll have some answers for you both."

Ivan then reached into his coat pocket, and pulled out a long envelope that contained a copy of Mac's will and a copy of the four diskettes. He handed it to Liebermann.

"What's this?" Howard asked.

"It's a copy of Mac's will and a copy of the diskettes that we've been talking about."

"Good, I'll need this." Howard took the envelope and opened the front door to the restaurant for Betsy. Once outside the restaurant, Ivan shook hands with Liebermann, who repeated what he had said earlier.

"Don't forget, until you hear from me, say nothing to anyone. And Betsy, you keep taking the Church's money. I want everything to remain status quo until I contact you, O.K.?"

"O.K., Howard," they replied, almost in unison.

"Good. Now remember, nothing but the status quo," Howard repeated.

CHAPTER 19

The Prize

Following Liebermann's advice, Ivan cancelled many of his off-campus speaking engagements when he got back to Northshore. He tried to keep a fairly low profile to avoid antagonizing the Church during Liebermann's investigation. He never did find out why Chancellor Monague had been looking for him while he had been in Miami. Monague's secretary didn't have a clue, and Ivan's phone messages to the Chancellor were never returned. Truthfully, Ivan was relieved. He didn't enjoy talking to the Chancellor anyway.

As far as he could tell, Betsy was following Liebermann's orders, too. She continued to pick up her check twice a month from Monsignor Bates' office. But not all was working well. While Ivan and Betsy were doing their part to maintain the status quo, neither of them heard a word from Howard Liebermann for over a year. Ivan tried to call him numerous times, but either got his wife, who didn't know anything, or a voice message recorder. Howard never returned the calls. Justifiably, Ivan had some serious questions about Liebermann that couldn't be answered. All of it was driving Ivan crazy.

He thought: What happened to Howard? Why wasn't he returning my calls? Did I do something to make him mad? Did he find out something about me? Has he been found out and threatened himself?

These questions and more rattled around in Ivan's mind as he was losing patience. Finally, Betsy and he decided it was time for a new gameplan. The Liebermann plan didn't seem to be working. For starters, Ivan decided to take a more aggressive stance with his speaking engagements, but he quickly found out this wasn't as easy as turning on a light switch. He had turned down so many invitations that his opportunities had dwindled down to almost none. Ivan's morale was at an all-time low.

It was late in the day on a rainy afternoon when Ivan was rooting through his in-basket at the office. Things were so slow that he was actually cleaning up his desk when his phone rang. The caller was an international operator with a noticeable foreign accent, asking if she had reached Dr. Ivan Berkowitz. This was a person-to-person call. Once she had confirmed and instructed her party to go ahead with the call, a distinguished voice, again with a noticeable accent, introduced himself as Dr. Johan Klamer with the Swedish Academy of Science in Stockholm, Sweden.

After a few formalities, Dr. Klamer quickly got to the point of his call.

"Dr. Berkowitz, as you probably know, the Nobel Foundation was established by the late Alfred Bernard Nobel when he died in 1896. His will decreed that a foundation be established that would annually recognize and honor those who have made outstanding contributions to mankind in five categories: physics, chemistry, medicine, the humanities and peace. As a representative of the body responsible for awarding the prize for physics, and on behalf of the Board of Directors of the Nobel Foundation, I congratulate you for being this year's recipient of the Nobel Prize for outstanding achievement in the field of physics. This award was granted to you for your many accomplishments, not the least of which is your book, *The Binding Force*."

Ivan was in a state of shock and disbelief. At first he wondered if this was some prank call, but before he could challenge his caller, Dr. Klamer continued, "Today, by mid-morning, you should receive, hand-delivered by courier, first class airfare for two, departing next Saturday for Oslo, Norway. There, you and your wife will attend a reception in your honor on Monday, before receiving the Nobel Prize at a ceremony in Stockholm, Sweden, on Wednesday evening. Your return flight has been booked for the following Friday, but of course you are welcome to stay longer if you wish. All of your accommodations have been arranged, and a press conference has been scheduled at 2 p.m. this afternoon. You should expect a call from Chancellor Monague, who by now has been informed of your selection. I very much look forward to meeting both you and your wife. I shall see you in Oslo."

Ivan was elated almost to the point of tears. It was hitting him now, the truth. He had won the most distinguished honor in his field. Finally, his ambition had been achieved. In the short span of a phone call, he had risen from his lowest emotional depth to his highest peak! He had reached the top.

Before Ivan could thank Dr. Klamer, he saw his second line light-up, and wondered if it was the Chancellor. No one else picked up the line, so it rang incessantly until he had finished his call with Klamer.

"Ivan Berkowitz," he answered.

"Ivan," the Chancellor said warmly. "Congratulations! What a surprise! A Nobel Prize winner. I'm so impressed!"

Ivan winced, but accepted his pat-on-the-back.

Chancellor Monague went on, "Did this news surprise you as much as it did me?"

He had such a way with words. While of course it shocked Ivan, Monague didn't need to act like it was some kind of fluke or something. Ivan just said, "Yes, sir. It surprised me."

"I understand there is a press conference coming up at two o'clock here in my office. Why don't you come by about 1:30, so we can cover a few things before the show gets started."

"Yes, sir," Ivan said. "I'll see you at 1:30."

As soon as he hung up, both lines lit up. He didn't answer either one of them. He needed to get to another phone to call Katrina. She wouldn't believe him, but he had to tell her the good news anyway.

ᛣᛣᛣ

At 1:30, Ivan appeared before Monague's secretary to tell her the Chancellor was expecting him. Before he could speak, she stood and extended her cold hand to congratulate him and said, "The Chancellor will be right with you, Dr. Berkowitz." On most occasions, she wouldn't even look up from doing her fake nails when he walked in the room. This time, however, she batted her eyelashes at him, sat down and buzzed her boss.

Monague burst through the door followed closely by Ivan's replacement, Dean Kevin O'Leary. Both of them proceeded to make a scene as though Ivan had been and would forever be their best friend. When all the hoopla died down, the Chancellor invited Ivan and the Dean into his office and closed the door behind them.

Ivan took a seat, the one nearest to the door, and listened while Monague and O'Leary both got very serious. They lowered their voices and softened their tone to make an ultra-sincere appeal, but Ivan was no sucker. He knew them well enough to recognize that when they became so sincere, it was time to watch out. He only wished they would cut the bullshit and get to the point.

Monague was batting his eyelids almost as badly as his secretary had been by the time he said, "Ivan, achievements like this confirm to me that we are on the right track here at Jesuit U. Your administration, your colleagues, your students, your university, all of us are very proud of you and glad that you are one of us. As a token of our appreciation, and as a deserving reward for your grand achievement, Dean O'Leary and I want to offer you a five-year contract that doubles your salary, effective immediately."

Having made this offer, Chancellor Monague walked the contract and a pen over to Ivan and stood there expecting him to sign it. He didn't even read it. He simply folded the contract and put it in his pocket, telling them both that he appreciated the offer; he would review it and get back to them. He didn't say when.

Chancellor Monague stumbled back to his desk, not sure what to say next. He awkwardly changed the subject, turning his attention to the upcoming announcement and press conference. Chancellor Monague and Dean O'Leary had apparently dress-rehearsed the program already, and were now going to tell Ivan how it was going to go.

"Ivan," the Chancellor said. "First of all, Dean O'Leary is going to introduce you, and then present to you a Jesuit University honorary doctorate degree, in recognition of your achievement. Then, Dean O'Leary is going to introduce me, and I'll make a few remarks about the university in general, and you, Ivan, in particular."

He nodded his head, knowing that Monague's real function would be to control the press coverage. The Board must have been called to discuss the public relations impact this announcement might have on the university. Monsignor Bates, Ivan imagined, must have been stunned and outraged by the whole affair, but there wasn't much he could do about it now, other than threaten Chancellor Monague if he didn't excel at damage control.

Ivan continued to nod his head in compliance when Monague told him, "Don't worry Ivan. Just enjoy the ride. I'll handle these press guys. It'll be a piece of cake. Just smile in their cameras."

Just as Monague had said, everything went smoothly while Dean O'Leary made the introduction, and the presentation of the honorary degree to Ivan. When Monague took center stage, he told the crowded room that the university had always strongly supported its research programs. Ivan wasn't surprised. His political instincts had improved over the years, and even he had learned to occasionally follow the path of least resistance. He knew this was not the time to get upset over a few half-truths. After all, Katrina was in the room over in the corner, gleaming with joy, sharing her elation with Betsy, who had come to keep Katrina company.

When Monague concluded his remarks, he invited questions from the press, intending to handle all of the answers himself. But the first question came from an aggressive campus newspaper writer who stood up in a crowd of local TV and news journalists and asked, "Dr. Berkowitz...could you please tell the press if the research for which you have won the Nobel Prize poses contradictions for the Catholic Church?"

"Oh, my God!" whispered Chancellor Monague to himself. Then, he stepped forward to his microphone, held his hands up to quiet the crowd, and said, "Ladies and Gentlemen, please, please. Let's remember that today is a day of celebration over the recognition of one of our local citizens, one of our own faculty, one who has been selected among his peers to be honored. Today is not the time to delve into any controversial topics, whether there are grounds for controversy or not. Please show your respect to Dr. Berkowitz and the university by holding these questions for another day. Thank you ladies and gentlemen for your attendance and your attention. Thank you."

With that, Monague turned off his microphone and stepped away from the podium toward the reporters. The TV cameras were still rolling, watching his every move. Fortunately for Ivan, Katrina and Betsy moved quickly to cover him up with hugs and kisses. The press conference was over.

⟁

Saturday came before he could catch his breath. Katrina had shopped out their credit cards, getting ready for the trip. Ivan didn't own a tuxedo, and she didn't have a stitch of formal wear. By the time their new clothes had been altered, and their bags were packed, she was exhausted. Her first moment of rest came when they practically collapsed in their cushy first-class seats, bound for Scandinavia. They both ordered a Bloody Mary, interlocked arms, clicked their glasses together, and looked deeply into each others eyes.

Once they disembarked in Oslo, they were immediately taken in tow, with every hour of their day and night scheduled according to a lengthy itinerary. It was fascinating to see the sights and attend the social functions. There was never a dull moment. But the climax of their stay in Oslo was the formal reception dinner and dance that Monday night, where the five recipients of the five distinctive prizes were honored.

But this extravaganza paled in comparison to the ceremony in Stockholm. The presentation of the Nobel Prize to Dr. Ivan Berkowitz for his work as described in *The Binding Force* was nothing short of monumental. He received his gold medal and diploma in front of a standing ovation that brought chills, and then tears, to Katrina.

ㅉㅉ

When Ivan returned home, the celebration continued. He tried to get some work done, but couldn't. He went to the office on Saturday morning just to see who had called while he had been gone. The pile was so high, he decided to sort through them. Many were reporters wanting an interview. Others were invitations to speaking engagements, now at quadruple the money. But one caller in the bottom of the stack captured Ivan's attention more than any of the others. It was a call from Howard Liebermann. Ivan wanted Betsy to be with him when he returned that call. Both of them deserved to hear whatever Liebermann had to say.

CHAPTER 20

The Recruit

Betsy wasn't home when Ivan called, so he left a message for her to get back to him ASAP. In the meantime, Ivan finished returning his own messages, and then pulled out the contract that Chancellor Monague and Dean O'Leary had offered him. No doubt about it, doubling his income was generous, but what was in this contract? He had not seen one of these before, but it seemed appealing on the surface...five years of good pay and five years of job security. He had to turn on his desk lamp for extra light to avoid straining his eyes.

The first part of the contract was standard boilerplate: a preamble and recitals followed by a consideration clause. The small print was embodied in the terms and conditions section. For all Ivan knew, this could have been drafted by the Dean of the Law School. Somebody had done it fairly hurriedly, because Ivan noticed a couple of typos that surely would have been corrected in a form document. Maybe this contract was a one-of-a-kind variety. After all, he was the only Nobel Prize winner on the entire faculty.

Like most such documents, it was almost unintelligible for all of the legalese. The first paragraph of the terms and conditions section placed about a dozen duties on Ivan; the second gave the university all kinds of rights and interests; the third listed certain prohibitions and restrictions; and the last but not least gave the university the unilateral right to terminate the contract with 60 days notice or immediately upon specific breach of its terms and conditions.

"What kind of contract is this?" Ivan muttered to himself, as he pushed it away and leaned back in his chair. "Thank God I didn't sign this son-of-a-bitch in the Chancellor's office."

He re-read the contract again in its entirety, this time realizing that it was worse than he originally thought. Arguably, the university had given itself ownership rights in Ivan's publications retroactively to the date of his original employment.

"God almighty!" Ivan yelled.

Furthermore, the contract stated that as a representative of the university, he would have to represent the views of the University in all job-related matters, including off-campus speaking engagements, interviews with the media, and in future work-related publications. Any variance from this policy would require specific written consent from the Chancellor.

"Unbelievable!" he said to the four walls, shaking his head.

This was tantamount to a gag order when it came to his speaking engagements. And when it came to publishing, signing this contract would effectively allow the university to take away his personal interests and rights in his work. It was nothing short of thievery.

"Those BASTARDS!"

This contract wasn't going to be signed...not at any price. He picked up his phone and called Chancellor Monague's office number on impulse, forgetting it was Saturday. When the beep signaled the start of Monague's voice-mail recording, Ivan hung up, deciding that he'd better handle this matter in person. It could wait until Monday. It would have to.

Through a friend of Betsy's, Ivan learned that she was out of town for the weekend. He decided that if the two of them had waited for over a year, Liebermann could surely wait on them for a few days. Monday would be soon enough. In addition to teaching his normal schedule, Ivan predicted a short meeting with Chancellor Monague, and then getting together with Betsy to return Liebermann's call.

Dread caused the remainder of the weekend to move along slowly. When Monday finally arrived, Ivan called the Chancellor's office first thing to schedule an appointment. Monague's secretary told Ivan to drop by after lunch, which worked out fine, since he had three morning classes to teach. When 1:30 finally arrived, Ivan appeared for his meeting.

As expected, both parties exchanged a few niceties before getting down to business. Ivan thanked Monague for the increase in pay, but told him that the contract was unacceptable and would have to be re-drafted. When Monague asked specifically what changes he had in mind, Ivan avoided a lengthy exchange of ideas about the fine print, but just said, "...the whole thing."

With that, he dropped the unsigned contract back on the Chancellor's desk and started for the door. Just before he walked out, Ivan paused to ask a question, "Chancellor Monague, we never discussed the consequences if I didn't sign the contract. What happens next?"

The Chancellor stood up from his oversized leather chair and dislodged his bunched-up boxers before answering, "I don't know, Dr. Berkowitz. I just don't know. Your response has certainly caught me off-guard. I'll have to get back to you on this."

"Well, thank you Chancellor Monague. I'll wait to hear from you."

Once Ivan returned to his office, he called Betsy and invited her to come over. He told her it was time to call Liebermann. She seemed excited that Liebermann had called and anxious to hear what he had to say. Soon after she arrived, Ivan dialed the number on his speaker phone.

"Liebermann." Howard had always answered the phone with just a last name, that was it. He never said "hello", "good morning", or anything...just "Liebermann".

"Howard, this is Ivan Berkowitz and Betsy McFarland, returning your call. It's been a long while since we've talked," he said in an almost cold tone of voice, hinting his disappointment and displeasure that Liebermann had gone off the air for so long.

"I know, it's been a long while, and I'm sorry for that. Thanks for returning my call. By the way, Ivan, congratulations! I knew you were gonna be a star. I read in *The Miami Herald* all about your Nobel Prize. That's terrific! And Betsy, what do you think of this guy? Strong stuff, huh?"

"He's a very special man," Betsy answered without elaboration.

"Look," Howard said. "I know both of you are disappointed that we haven't spoken sooner. What's it been now, over a year? And I'm even sorrier about the news that I have to tell you. This whole mess is a lot bigger than we ever guessed, and it's scarier than your worst nightmare."

"What are you saying, Howard?" Ivan asked.

"What I'm saying is this. You had best just leave this whole business concerning Mac's death alone. Let the sleeping dog lie. I know this sounds harsh and cold. I know it's not what you want to hear, but you should both just let it go. I'm particularly sorry for you, Betsy. I am very sorry. Mac struck a nerve with some very powerful people, and it cost him his life, but you cannot pursue this any further. It is way over our heads, and it is very dangerous."

Ivan responded coarsely, "That's all you have to say, Howard? Leave it alone? You've waited for over a year just to say that? That's bullshit, Howard. That's pure bullshit."

"Please, Ivan, please hear me. This whole episode involving the Constantine Papers and Mac's death is more complicated than it might appear. There are a lot of players involved. It has a deadly plot. Please, just leave it alone. I'm begging both of you, PLEASE."

"Howard, why'd you call if only to say this?"

"Ivan, you're on centerstage now, a Nobel Prize winner. Your profile is much more elevated than its ever been. Don't be tempted to take this matter into your own hands. I was afraid that the two of you might grow impatient with me and try to go it alone. That wouldn't be a good idea. I promise."

"That sounds almost threatening. I've got the feeling that we won't ever hear from you again. Am I right?" Ivan asked.

"That all depends, Ivan. That all depends. I would love to help you in any way I can, but whatever we do in the future, it must take us farther away from this trouble, and not closer to it. Right now I can only tell you this. Suspect the worst. Do not push your adversaries into a corner. They will strike back. They will escalate to the maximum. They have already proven that."

"We understand, Howard. Thank you for the advice. You know where we are if you need us for any reason. Let's not sever the link between us," Ivan said. "At least not now anyway."

Betsy and Ivan hung up the phone and looked at each other in disbelief, now wishing that Liebermann had never called.

ππ

Ivan had never been so frustrated. Monague didn't call him back at all, leaving Ivan with the feeling that he had been blackballed by the Chancellor. It was odd to feel rejected by his employer, just as he reached the pinnacle in his profession. He knew all along that it had only been the momentum of his research that had given him the resolve to stay at Jesuit University for so many years. But now that his achievement had climaxed, he wasn't sure if he wanted to stay any longer. Ivan decided it was time to move on, but before searching for employment options, he first needed to find out if he had any. Regrettably, he thought to himself, it was time to call Liebermann, again.

Unlike his previous attempts, Ivan got Liebermann on the second try, relieved that he took the call. For the first twenty minutes of the conversation, Ivan poured out his soul to Howard, reviewing his bittersweet association with Jesuit University in detail. Howard knew all along where this was leading. When Ivan realized he was repeating himself, he finally quit lamenting and asked a question.

"Howard, you've known me for a long time. You know my predicament. You know how frustrated and unhappy I am. You know that I need to make a change, but can I?"

Liebermann pondered the question for a moment before answering.

"I understand your dilemma, more than you know, but that doesn't mean I can solve it for you. My guess is that if you simply transfer to another university, and continue your work in an outspoken manner, you will probably not escape the reach of your adversaries. My suggestion is that you change gears entirely, that you move out of the academic community altogether. You might enjoy a new challenge that takes you away from teaching and publishing. What do you think about that?"

This time Ivan paused, "Maybe you're right. I hadn't really thought of that. But I don't know where to start."

Howard replied, "I'm gonna have one of my old friends with NASA give you a call. Maybe he'll have some good ideas for a Nobel Prize winning astrophysicist. Let me talk it over with him, and then I'll have him call you. His name is Lt. General Oliver Wakeman. If he calls you, don't give him any details other than standard resume stuff. Nothing about what you and I have discussed. That's strictly to remain between us, O.K.?"

"Sure. That'll be fine. I'll wait to hear from him, and thanks for your help. Oh, one more thing, Howard. Is Wakeman a military man?"

"Yeah, you could say that. He is retired military, a highly decorated officer with a very distinguished career in the Air Force. But he has been with NASA for over fourteen years. He's a top-notch guy, Ivan. He can help you. Trust me."

"All right. Thanks again for the help, Howard. It's much appreciated."

<center>~~~</center>

When Wakeman called Ivan, he didn't act as though he were begrudgingly honoring a duty to return a favor for Liebermann. Lt. General Oliver Wakeman sounded excited and enthusiastic, like he had just received orders for a new mission. He flattered Ivan with compliments, praising his accomplishments and professional experience. Wakeman didn't conduct a laborious phone interview like Ivan expected. Rather, Wakeman said that he wanted to jump on a flight from Houston to Northshore to have dinner with Ivan. Then they could talk, eyeball to eyeball. That's the way the Lt. General liked to do things.

<center>~~~</center>

Ivan didn't know where to take Lt. General Wakeman, but being from Houston, Ivan guessed he liked Mexican food. Wakeman responded so favorably that Ivan concluded Wakeman was a Mexican food junkie, a common condition in Texas. It was perfect...a relaxed, informal setting that made both men comfortable.

Still, Ivan didn't know quite what to expect. He wasn't sure if he should lead the conversation or follow. Howard only said Wakeman might be good with some ideas, but in the first ten minutes after sitting down, Ivan knew that Wakeman wasn't there to bat around ideas about Ivan's future. Wakeman acted like he knew all about Ivan's future.

According to Wakeman, Dr. Ivan Berkowitz belonged at NASA. They had the perfect slot for him. In fact, Wakeman was so excited about it that he could barely choke down his burrito supreme. Perhaps the most telling observation Ivan made about Wakeman during dinner was his total disregard for the hot sauce that sat at the center of the table. It wasn't hot enough for him. He put the

150
<center>~~~</center>

cap back on the bottle and reached for the extra hot. He sprinkled it liberally over his burrito while Ivan cringed, knowing that a drop would make most grown men cry.

ϖϖ

Ivan's excitement that evening about the job opportunity at NASA was contagious. He went home that night and told Katrina that Wakeman was going to fly them down to Houston to visit the Johnson Space Center and NASA Headquarters. As he shared the news with her, their excitement built into passion for each other.

After many years of marriage, their lovemaking had evolved into ritual, and after exchanging climaxes, Katrina turned away from him, while he stroked her back in afterplay. It was an act of renewal. She stared blankly at the wall with glassy eyes, while Ivan involuntarily closed his own. They both felt a sense of contentment and gratification, evidenced by faint smiles, even though neither could see the other's face.

ϖϖ

They could not have picked a prettier spring day to visit Houston. The azaleas and dogwoods were in bloom everywhere. It was undoubtedly Houston's best season, masking the overbearing heat and humidity of summer. Ivan spent his day in-tow, following Lt. General Wakeman, while Wakeman's wife escorted Katrina to the malls, the clubs and the nicer residential areas. Just before sunset, Ivan and Katrina were left alone to enjoy the evening together at the Ritz-Carlton, sharing impressions and opinions formed during the day. They both agreed that Houston's skyline was it's pride and joy, with glitzy office towers dramatically rising above the flat terrain.

When Katrina asked Ivan to tell her all about NASA, he shared with her what he could. He told her that NASA, once the space exploration agency, had been transformed over the years through public debate and subsequent presidential policy. Now, it's charter was more tightly defined, more focused than it was during earlier years, primarily due to budgetary considerations. The agency consisted of only four divisions: one responsible for over-seeing orbital communications and traffic control, one for assessing and defending against the risk of asteroid and meteorite collision, one for implementing military projects that were strictly related to national security interests, and last but not least, one for monitoring the Earth's environmental condition.

The Environmental Division was responsible for measuring the ozone levels, tracking and forecasting global warming and cooling trends, tracking and forecasting major weather systems, and reporting on the general state of the planet. No longer was NASA launching lunar or inter-planetary missions. All funding for exploration had been terminated by Congress in the name of financial deficit reduction. The new focus of NASA was more introverted, more pragmatic, than the extroverted exploration programs initiated in the 1960s. NASA's new mission was to assure the preservation of the status quo.

And NASA wasn't the only space agency looking over the Earth's shoulder. There were now dozens of such agencies, all formed with national interests in mind, each one supposedly monitoring the heartbeat of the planet. Katrina was fascinated to hear Ivan tell her this background material about NASA, but what she really wanted to hear about was the job itself.

"Tell me about the job, sweetheart," she said impatiently.

Ivan kept talking to her, rambling at times, but wanting to tell her everything. According to his story, Lt. General Wakeman was trying to fill an executive division manager position which was vacated recently by the untimely death of its executive officer. This particular division governed the environmental responsibilities of NASA.

"Wakeman is considering me for the job. More accurately, he's recruiting me for the job."

"What timing! Wakeman's got no idea how frustrated you've become at J.U. The timing of this whole thing seems almost too good to be true."

"It's not a done deal yet. Let's hang in there and play this out. I think he's ready to make an offer, maybe tomorrow."

The match made perfect sense. Ivan's background in astro-physics and geochemistry was suited to the task. And more par-ticularly, his accomplished studies in chaos theory and the theory of self-organization made him the ideal candidate to bring a higher level of understanding to the issues that this job encompassed. Perhaps even more important to some was the Nobel Prize, which would bolster the esprit de corps and the prestige of the agency. And, it would promote the clout of the new President, who tech-nically would fill the position by presidential appointment. The President would be perceived as one who could summon the very finest resources America had to offer.

But beyond the obvious resume match-up and political ad-vantages, Ivan felt he would be personally challenged by his new position as executive division manager. In addition to the scien-tific and analytical demands, Ivan would lead the U.S. Task Force on Environmental Issues. This task force participated with del-egations from other national agencies in an environmental con-sortium, which reported to the United Nations Environmental Council. As head of the U.S. Task Force, Ivan would have a per-manent seat on this Council.

By the time he had finished telling everything he knew to Katrina, she was fast asleep. It had been a long day.

The next morning, just before leaving for the airport, the Lt. General extended his formal offer. It was a tremendous package, one that far exceeded Chancellor Monague's generosity. In addi-tion to an ample salary, the package covered moving expenses, benefits and club memberships, all if he accepted the offer. Ivan was thinking, "Isn't America great?" as he dialed Chancellor Monague's number to schedule another appointment. It was the last thing he had to do before getting back to Wakeman.

"Come on in, Ivan. Come on in and have a seat over there at the table," invited the Chancellor. "Let's give ourselves some room to spread out, so we can look at some of this paperwork you're fussing about."

"Thanks," Ivan replied, wasting as few words as possible.

When they got seated, the Chancellor opened a personnel file that Ivan could only assume was his own. It contained a lot of paperwork, but Monague only extracted the document on the top, not disclosing what else might lie underneath. Before the revised contract hit the table, Ivan pulled his own sheet of paper out of his satchel, and set it down in front of the Chancellor. It was a letter, short and to-the-point.

"Dear Chancellor Monague:
    Please let this letter serve as notice that I hereby resign my position with Jesuit University, effective two weeks from the date of this submission.
                            Sincerely,
                            Dr. Ivan Berkowitz"

Monague picked the letter up and read it slowly, like he had never seen one before. He collected the contract and returned it to the file before he said, "Quite frankly, I'm not surprised. It has been a difficult situation for both of us; but even so, your resignation is accepted with regret, Dr. Berkowitz. I wish you well and hope that you will have fond memories of the university. Dean O'Leary will assist you with any details related to your resignation."

Chancellor Monague and Ivan both stood up, and started for the door.

"Let me wish you the best of luck, Dr. Berkowitz."

They shook hands for the final time, although Ivan hated to do it. But, by the time he walked past the spouting fountain in the center of the quadrangle, Ivan had never felt better. With elation, he muttered to himself those remembered words that Martin Luther King, Jr. made famous in a speech many years ago,"I'm 'free at last...free at last.' "

CHAPTER 21

The Coincidence

When Ivan announced his resignation from Jesuit University, the only sincere regrets at the university came from a number of students who felt that Dr. Berkowitz had been the best teacher they had ever known. Betsy also regretted his decision, but she told him that she understood. He promised that he would not abandon her, a promise she knew he would keep. When Ivan left, he tearfully hugged and kissed her good-bye, knowing they would always be related by tragedy, a bond that could not be broken.

The press release in *The Houston Chronicle* showed a picture of Dr. Ivan Berkowitz shaking hands with the newly-elected President of the United States, Mr. James Harrison Woodrow. Standing in the background was an approving Lt. General Oliver Wakeman. The brief article said,

"President Woodrow has appointed Dr. Ivan Berkowitz to the position of Executive Director of the Environmental Division of NASA. Berkowitz, a 47 year old Nobel Prize winner from Jesuit University, will bring a new level of knowledge and experience to the agency...an agency that has been obsessed with improving its public image ever since the Challenger accident in the mid-80s."

Ivan loved his new job. He began each day adrenalized with enthusiasm for his work. Some mistook Ivan's zeal as an imitation of Wakeman's, but there was a huge difference between the two. Wakeman's enthusiasm exuded from his hyper-activity, mixed with his blind, militaristic devotion to duty; while Ivan's surge was strictly related to the rush of a new encounter. Ivan recognized the excitement and wondered if these were the same juices that sponsored romantic love. Regardless, the feeling was rejuvenating.

Ivan enjoyed the opportunity to apply his scientific knowledge to practical rather than academic situations. He also enjoyed interacting with adults for a change. These were professionals who could be told what was expected of them, not students who had to be taught how everything should be done. But what he loved most was his involvement with the United Nations, plugging into a new, global network of fellow researchers who shared his love for science.

Typically, the Environmental Council met once a month at the United Nations building in New York City. There would be a breakfast meeting, an outside presentation, reports from various sub-committee chairmen, old business matters to be voted on and finally, new business to be proposed. Whatever got out of the Council intact was presented to the General Assembly by the Chairman of the Council. The Council had been chaired by the U.S. Ambassador to the U.N. ever since its inception.

In addition to monitoring and reporting on the condition of the planet, the Environmental Council was also responsible for proposing legislation to the General Assembly, and recommending warnings and penalties for violators of U.N. laws, codes, resolutions and ordinances. The cast of participants included many lawyers, industrialists, economists and professional politicians, but fewer scientists than Ivan expected.

━━━

Like most romantic interludes, the excitement wore off as Ivan became familiar with the defects of this political body. At first, all he seized upon was the idealism of the Council's mission statement,

"Our purpose is to monitor and protect the well-being of the planet Earth..."

He was thrilled about being involved with such a prestigious group. It's lofty goals inspired him like Liberty's torch. But eventually, Ivan's naiveté was cast aside. Like peeling the veneer off a pressed-board door, Ivan, once again, recognized the ugliness of politics.

Most of the information disseminated to the Council members was greatly diluted and politicized by the editors and handlers back home...even his own. What had not been explained to Ivan during his recruitment was that all outside communiqués had to be submitted to and approved by Lt. General Wakeman and his committee of outside directors. This unwelcomed committee routinely applied a political spin to Ivan's research in order to reflect the official party line. The outside directors were professional political consultants appointed by President Woodrow's Chief of Staff. Their shallow purpose was merely to protect and promote the President's image.

After observing the performance of the Council for almost a year, Ivan became increasingly cynical. He decided that at best, the Council was ineffective, and at worst, misleading. Not only was the information circulated by the Council contaminated, the Council proved to be completely impotent when it came to assessing penalties against environmental violators. A warning was the harshest action ever levied by the Council. The Council was a joke, Ivan concluded. And so was the United Nations.

He learned to internalize the disappointment, rationalizing that his job was like all jobs: none perfect. Once again, he just had to roll with economic reality and play the game. He was getting too old to do much else.

ɯɯ

When in New York, Ivan usually stayed at the Waldorf-Astoria, although occasionally he liked to stay on Central Park at the Plaza. He decided early on that if he had to go to New York at least once a month, he might as well enjoy it.

On this occasion, two years after accepting his position at NASA, he had chosen the Plaza, specifically requesting a room high up in the building, facing Central Park. It was spring once again. The view from his room allowed him to see that the grass was still dormant, but the trees in the park were showing tiny lime-green leaf buds.

It was a crisp morning...blue skies, but chilly enough to see your breath. Ivan expected it to warm up quickly, so he didn't wear an overcoat, just his usual dark suit and loud tie. Like Mac, Ivan loved flamboyant neckwear. It had become his trademark. Betsy had given Ivan all of Mac's ties when he died, a gift that really didn't match Ivan's personality. But the ties constantly reminded him of Mac's flamboyant way of life, and each tie Ivan added to Mac's collection made the same statement.

The taxi dropped Ivan off in front of the United Nations building where he and dozens of others plodded across the concrete plaza toward the entrance, like drones returning to the hive. He attended his breakfast and acquainted himself with the day's agenda. The presentation part of the agenda, which was coming up next, was broken into three parts.

The first was an historical account given by the Russian Ambassador to the U.N. He covered the destruction of the Baku oil fields in 1905, when revolutionaries started the blaze that drove the Rothchilds and the Nobels out of Russia.

The second segment was given by the Oil Minister of Sumatra.

158

He gave a fifty year chronological account, from the late 1890s to the end of World War II, detailing horrendous exploitations of natural resources in Borneo and Sumatra. The violators had been the English, the Dutch, the Americans, and the Japanese. They had acted irresponsibly for motives of profit or war.

The third segment was the most dramatic of all. It was an account told by the U.S. Ambassador to Kuwait of Saddam Hussein's destruction of the Kuwaiti oil fields in 1991, a crime against humanity, a crime against nature, and a crime against Mother Earth. He went on to mention Saddam Hussein's use of chemical agents against the Kurds in the north, and the destruction of his own country's vast marshlands in the south. The destruction of the marshlands not only ruined the environment, but virtually exterminated the Marsh Arabs who lived there, and untold numbers of plant and animal species who depended on the wetlands.

Following the Gulf War, the U.N. imposed economic sanctions against Iraq, but these sanctions, for the most part, were circumvented. The speaker argued that in this case, economic sanctions failed to punish those responsible for committing the crimes. It was Saddam and his military who deserved the punishment, not the general population of Iraq. Yet the international community allowed Saddam to continue to rule, and they allowed him to rebuild his military.

The speaker was calling for justice. It was a bold speech, saying exactly what everyone had privately thought for years, but had been afraid to say publicly. According to the speaker, Saddam Hussein, and others like him, should be held accountable for their crimes. The speaker proposed that the United Nations should play the role of enforcer, and that the Environmental Council and the Human Rights Council should increase their efforts to bring violators to justice. The speaker was U.S. Ambassador Julio Masito.

Ivan couldn't believe his eyes and ears when he realized that Julio was the man. His previous perceptions of Julio as a young assistant to Mac, a Hopi Indian who left his reservation and went to college, a desk officer in Washington with the State Department, a newlywed husband and father, expecting his first child. . . all of these images were cast aside by this young man who was so bold, who was so charismatic, who was so magnetic that he had captured the attention of the entire room.

All but a few Arabs applauded loudly when he finished. Julio had stepped into the spotlight in a big way, and almost everyone who witnessed his debut loved it.

At age 40, Julio was certainly young to have such responsibility. Someone in the State Department must have taken an interest in Julio's career, Ivan thought. That was typically how young overachievers broke out of the pack. And those who tried to break out of the pack without that sponsorship were usually crushed by the political machine at the first opportunity. Someone important had endorsed Julio, and Ivan couldn't wait to find out who it was.

The last time the two had seen each other had been at Mac's funeral, about eight years ago. And while Julio had matured noticeably over those years, he wasn't the only one. Ivan had gained a few pounds, his sideburns had turned gray, and he had acquired a few extra lines in his face. They had both changed jobs. It was obvious that they would have some catching up to do.

When Ivan approached Julio, there were five or six Council members surrounding him shoulder to shoulder. Ivan was getting frustrated standing in the second row, and was about to lose patience, when the guy in front of him finally turned his shoulders to leave, allowing Ivan just enough room to slip into the inner circle.

"Dr. Berkowitz!" Julio said, stopping his conversation in mid-sentence as soon as Ivan stepped into the ring.

"Ambassador Masito," Ivan said, embracing him with both arms, patting him solidly on the back. "What a coincidence! I can't believe it's you stirring up the hornet's nest, making such a fuss."

"Well, Dr. Berkowitz, I just thought this would be a good forum to vent the feelings of the people from my host country without jeopardizing their safety. You see, they have to live next door to their enemies, and I don't, at least not forever, anyway."

Ivan responded, "Be careful, my friend. You're not out of harm's way yet. That was a mighty bold talk you gave us." Then Ivan leaned close to Julio's ear to ask, "Is there any way we can have dinner tonight, on me?"

"That would be perfect, Dr. Berkowitz, perfect. Where do you want to meet?" Julio asked.

Rather than blurt out the name of some restaurant, Ivan asked Julio how he could get in touch. Julio wrote a number on the back of his card and said,

"Leave a message if I'm not there. I look forward to visiting with you. We have a lot of ground to cover."

"Yes, you might say we do," said Ivan, the master of understatement.

ᵀᵀᵀ

They met at 8 p.m. at Tavern On The Green, a well-known restaurant located within the borders of Central Park. Julio had never been there before, and his first comment was, "I can't believe we're in the middle of New York City, surrounded by all these beautiful trees. Central Park reminds me of the Havasupi Reservation in the bottom of the Grand Canyon—almost a Garden of Eden."

"It's a little touristy, but I'm glad you like it. Now, first things first. Nobody's near us, it's just you and me. So let's get back to basics: I'm IVAN, and you're JULIO, remember?"

"I apologize for being more formal. And while I'm apologizing, let me apologize for not congratulating you long ago on the Nobel Prize. I was in Egypt at the time, but that's no excuse. Anyway, please let me make retribution by treating you to dinner."

"No, no, no. Not this time young fella. I invited you out to dinner," Ivan reminded him.

"Well, then it's just my lucky night. In fact, maybe we should go to the nearest Indian casino, I'm feeling so lucky."

Ivan laughed before getting serious, "Right, Julio, maybe we

161
ᵀᵀᵀ

should go tonight before you make too many speeches like the one you made today. If you keep that up, your good luck might not hold up very long. You're flirting with some dangerous stuff there, some very dangerous stuff. To some, the most dangerous threat of all can be the truth, and that's what you told us today."

"Maybe so, but somebody needs to say it," Julio countered.

Changing the subject, Ivan asked Julio about his family and what all had happened to them over the years. Speaking first about his pride and joy, Julio told Ivan about his two children, a daughter named Amelia who was seven years old, and a son named Julian who was five. They were keeping his wife, Mary, very busy these days. Julio then backed up several years and talked about their many moves, from Washington to Mexico City, then back to Washington, then to Cairo and finally to Kuwait City.

When Ivan asked who in the State Department had taken an interest in his career, Julio smiled before answering, "The Secretary of State."

That explained a lot to Ivan. Before being appointed to the President's Cabinet, the Secretary had been the Under-Secretary, nurturing Julio's development and steering opportunities Julio's way. But Julio had done a terrific job all along, and so his accelerated climb up the ladder came as no surprise to anyone.

When it was Ivan's turn to share, he began by refreshing Julio's memory of the diskettes that Mac had left behind, and then proceeded to tell of his research, the publishing of his book, the debate he had with Willis Barker, his demotion, Barker's threat, Liebermann, the Nobel Prize and finally his resignation and move to NASA. He told Julio about the U.N., the Environmental Council, and why it was so lame.

Julio figured as much, but nevertheless, he was astounded by all of the ups and downs that Ivan had faced. Here they were, brought together by chance, both ambitious, both successful, both with powerful friends, and both with powerful adversaries.

When Julio returned to Kuwait City, a car bomb at the airport exploded right in front of his limousine. Two U.S. Marines in the car ahead of Julio's died in the explosion. There was no phone call; there was no letter. Nothing but the remnants of the burning car that served as the terrorist's calling card.

CHAPTER 22

The Appointment

Late one night, Ivan was home watching TV with Katrina, and saw the CNN coverage of the car bombing in Kuwait City. The news story included excerpts from CSPAN's coverage of Julio's speech to the United Nations' Environmental Council. The report speculated that perhaps there was some linkage between the two events.

Ivan was shocked at first, because Julio was the target of the bombing, but then Ivan adopted an I told you so attitude. His protective instincts took over, and he checked his watch to see what time it was. It was just past mid-night in Northshore, but 9:10 the next morning in Kuwait City. He decided to try to give Julio a call at the embassy.

After speaking with three international operators and two receptionists, Ivan finally got Julio's secretary. She had been trained to screen the Ambassador's calls carefully, and only after Ivan said that the call was of a personal nature, and that the Ambassador knew him well, did she ask him to hold for a moment to see if the

Ambassador was available to take his call.

"Ivan! How are you?"

"I'm fantastic, but the real question is how are you?"

"I'm fine, really, I am. I knew the two servicemen who died, and I think it is so sad, especially for their families."

"It is terribly sad. I just saw the news report, and goddamn, that was a serious blast. What do you think can be done about it?"

"The Secretary of State is working on it right now. He called me last night to say that my security detail would be doubled, but I'll have to stay put for a while to avoid any appearance of running from terrorism. It doesn't bother me that much, but it gives Mary and the kids a case of nerves."

"I'll bet."

"Apparently the Secretary met with the Director of the C.I.A. late yesterday, but all the Director promised was a complete investigation and a full report, whatever that means. I don't think anyone has ever really gotten a full report out of the C.I.A."

"Well, you better hold your tongue, at least until you get reassigned. Please don't get yourself killed over there. I just called to say that Katrina and I are worried for you."

"I'll be more careful. Don't you guys worry."

At the end of the conversation, Julio asked Ivan to call Betsy and tell her hello for him. Ivan promised he would, but added, "My life would be in danger if I called her right now. It's almost 1:00 in the morning here."

After hanging up, Ivan helped Katrina up from the sofa, turned out the lights and led her to the bedroom. They were both exhausted.

彡

Two years later, Ivan was again watching the news at home when CNN announced that the U.S. Ambassador to the United Nations had resigned. President Woodrow called a press conference to announce that he had appointed 42 year old Julio Masito to fill the position, subject to confirmation by the Senate. The President, now in his third year in office, stood tall at the podium. His long mop of gray hair was swept to one side, so that it did not flop down in front of his gold-rimmed eyeglasses. He appeared to be an interesting mix between a disheveled rounder, and a sophisticated intellectual...the classic look of a progressive Democrat. Regardless of party politics, Woodrow made a distinguished impression, and appeared presidential in every sense of the word.

Following the press conference, television political consultants argued back and forth about the merits of the selection. The Republicans pointed out Ambassador Masito's youth, inexperience and inflammatory diplomacy. The Democrats aired interviews with Mexican, Egyptian and Kuwaiti diplomats who all supported Julio's nomination.

The Republicans countered by saying that President Woodrow, who was soon to be up for re-election, had simply made a populist choice for political reasons. The Democrats touted Julio's resume, a Native American born on the Hopi Reservation in Arizona, a college graduate with honors, a scholarship recipient, a distinguished alumni of Georgetown's Graduate School of Foreign Service, and a career diplomat who had rocketed through the ranks of the diplomatic corps.

At the end of the news story, President Woodrow's closing statement during the press conference was shown again. Woodrow repeated,

> "It is about time that we honored all Native Americans with this appointment. Who might represent our nation better in the international arena than this young man from Arizona, Ambassador Julio Masito."

The Republican response included a clip of the CSPAN coverage of Julio's speech at the U.N., and the subsequent car bombing in Kuwait City. They tried to make Julio appear irresponsible in his actions, almost deserving of the attack, but their argument backfired.

At the end of the broadcast, the results of a CNN political poll indicated that the American people loved this man named Julio, although they did not know him well. The polls were sympathetic with the President. Julio was a perfect choice.

Very few were more thrilled by the appointment than Ivan and Katrina. The two of them immediately called Betsy to tell her the news.

ᵀᵀᵀ

Ivan's first occasion to see Julio following his return to the United States was in New York City. Following the assignments of previous U.S. Ambassadors to the U.N., Julio had been asked to chair the Environmental Council. It was a great day for Ivan. His excitement was apparent to all who sat near him at Julio's inaugural breakfast meeting. After calling the meeting to order, Ambassador Masito began by telling everyone how glad he was to be a part of this very distinguished group, and he promised to devote a very high level of energy to his new responsibility.

Secondly, he told the Council to expect some change. His first order of business would be an attempt to de-politicize the process, and to access raw data as opposed to accepting at face value various party line statements from political consultants. He intended to do this by having third parties confirm the data they reviewed.

The last point Julio tried to make was that he would work very hard to strengthen the compliance and enforcement responsibilities of the Council, and he expected full co-operation in this effort from each of its members.

Again, he told everyone how glad he was to join them, and how he looked forward to working closely with each and every one in the room. His opening remarks were very well received. Julio was their new commander.

CHAPTER 23

The Cover-up

On most occasions, when Ivan made his monthly trip to New York, Julio and he would go out on the town at least for a beer. Every now and then they would include their wives, so the four of them became very good friends. They would attend plays or concerts or ballets or sporting events together or maybe just relax at a favorite New York restaurant. Whatever they did, it was always a good time. Conversations about business would be left behind intentionally, so they could relax and be entertained.

Recently, however, Ivan seemed to be having trouble leaving his work at the office. Something very serious was disturbing him, and Julio was the only person Ivan could relate to who might understand or care. And more importantly, Julio was the only guy Ivan trusted.

His problems began when he first learned about Lt. General Wakeman's approval policy regarding external communiqués. The editorial authority that Wakeman exercised was bad from the start, but lately it had been getting worse. Julio's call for the Council to de-politicize the information flow had been completely ignored by the political advisors who nearly controlled the actions of the Council members. Third party data that contradicted the official statements was vigorously refuted, causing excessive debate on the floor of the Council, which typically degenerated into useless conflagration. Julio didn't know quite what to do about it, but he did realize that his idealism had been undermined. And Ivan was getting tired of fighting with Wakeman.

Finally, Ivan told Julio that the censorship was becoming very consequential. His research was revealing some very serious problems, problems that ultimately could threaten the very survival of the planet. He told Julio that the editors at NASA were silencing his alarm because in the eyes of the handlers, the news was politically untenable.

Julio seemed very disturbed and asked Ivan to begin meeting with him privately each month to review Ivan's personal findings. Julio said he wanted to monitor the level of editing in the official NASA position. The two of them stopped going out on the town altogether. They had too much work to do.

Ivan had mathematically determined a progression of circumstances that could cause the planet's atmosphere to reach a point of destabilization. Beyond that point, he predicted, the Earth's ordered system that has sustained life, as we have known it, could accelerate toward collapse. Once that point was reached, efforts to reverse the condition would be futile. The condition would continue to worsen without remedy. And not only had Ivan calculated the point at which that would occur, but he had plotted past and present conditions of the atmosphere and concluded the very worst. Unless humanity reversed its behavior quickly, the state of the environment could reach the point of no return. The news was catastrophic, but no one wanted to hear it.

ᛟ

Back in Houston, Ivan thumbed through his messages, and noted that some staff member from Senator Cheney's office had called. Cheney was the Chairman of the Senate Intelligence Com-

169

mittee, and was a very high profile Republican. For sometime, he had been identified by the media as a man with presidential ambition. It was no secret that he and President Woodrow weren't the best of friends. Most would say their relationship embodied that dynamic tension that was important to a healthy political system. But the dynamic tension between a Republican-controlled Senate and a Democratic President sometimes tested the definition. Ivan responded to politicians on both sides of the aisle pretty much the same, with distrust and contempt.

Even though President Woodrow had appointed Ivan to his position with NASA, his enthusiasm for Woodrow had been lost after seeing the President's minions eviscerate his research. For the most part, Ivan had learned to hate politics, conceding that he simply wasn't politically inclined, that he was basically ineffective in a political setting. He sorrowed for himself as a victim of politics, suffering through political currents each day, wondering if a political riptide would one day take him out altogether.

Ivan returned the call to the Senator's office, and learned that Senator Cheney wanted to meet for lunch later in the week. Ivan had no idea why, but he agreed, asking if he should invite Lt. General Wakeman to come along, also. The answer was an emphatic no. The Senator wanted to meet with Ivan alone, and he would be contacted later in the week to learn exactly when and where. That was it. Ivan was told not to mention the meeting to anyone. The Senator's trip to Houston was highly confidential.

On Thursday at mid-morning, Ivan got the call. He was given a street address in a residential neighborhood as the place where they would have lunch. It was all quite strange, but clearly Senator Cheney didn't want to be seen in public. Again, Ivan was reminded not to mention the meeting or the address to anyone...just show up at noon.

The house was in University Park near Rice University. It was small, but well kept. There were two cars already in the driveway. He went to the front door, and was let in before he knocked. A fairly young guy was standing there, looking over Ivan's shoulder as he came inside. He smelled Cajun cooking, but as much as he loved Cajun food, it wasn't enough to give him an appetite. Seated in the dining room was Senator Cheney. He stood to shake hands with Ivan when he entered the room, gesturing to him to please sit at the other end of the table. It was set for only two.

The Senator had brought his own cook with him, and the young fellow who had met Ivan at the door. Ivan couldn't tell if the young one was a staff lackey or a security guy. When the food was served, the cook closed the door between the dining room and the kitchen, and the young man closed off the dining room from the living room, giving the two complete privacy. Only then did Senator Cheney get to the point of his trip, and the reason for their meeting.

"Dr. Berkowitz, I realize you haven't been told much about why I wanted to see you. Let me begin my story with some history, and then you'll understand more clearly."

"Years ago, a one-billion-dollar unmanned NASA space probe, called the Mars Observer, was launched from Cape Canaveral. The probe traveled over 450 million miles to Mars. It was supposed to map the surface of the red planet, a project that would last almost two years. But it never happened. Instead, the Mars Observer mysteriously disappeared on arrival. Do you remember any press about it?" asked Senator Cheney.

"Vaguely, sir. I do." Ivan answered.

"Well, the press did not rant and rave too much, but the White House went crazy. The President wanted some answers. Anyway, the Air Force branch of the military was asked to investigate the matter, just to see what the hell was going on at NASA. At the time, Major Oliver Wakeman was placed in charge of the investigation. Before Wakeman could make heads or tails of the matter, Congress came along and terminated funding for all planned and future exploratory projects.

"In fact, the entire focus of NASA was changed. The only problem was that Wakeman was too far into his investigation financially and otherwise to just back out, making the President's request look like just another stupid waste of taxpayers' money. The compromise reached was that one of the new divisions of NASA would be responsible for military projects that involved national security matters, so Wakeman was made Executive Director of the Military Division. It was the same ranking position you have now over the Environmental Division."

Senator Cheney paused to take a sip of water before going on with his story. "Well, Wakeman continued his investigation of the missing Mars probe under the guise of military projects undertaken in the interest of national security. Nobody said a word about it. Several years went by and everything seemed to be fairly normal. A few Presidents came and went, but NASA kept on, with Wakeman running the Military Division."

Cheney again reached for his water, realizing that he was doing all of the talking. "When I became Chairman of the Senate Intelligence Committee, I learned through one of our contacts at NASA that the Military Division had continued over the years to conduct unmanned exploratory missions disguised as military research projects, all in contempt of Congress. Wakeman knew a leak of such news was unbearable for any President, so the exploration program was run by a very select few who understood the secretive nature of their responsibility. They also understood the consequences of a leak. If this cover-up was blown, it would make the Iran-Contra Scam of the 1980s look like pocket change, because of the enormous costs involved. If any President got caught, whether he knew about it or not, that President would be crucified by the American people. When I first learned of it, a Republican was in the White House, so I decided that I couldn't blow the whistle."

Cheney looked down at his empty water glass, and asked the cook to come in and fill it. Not until they were alone again did Cheney start again, but before he did, he covered his face with his hands and rubbed his eye sockets and forehead to relieve his tension.

"When Woodrow was elected, my knowledge about the NASA problem was tempting to disclose, but it was also very risky to me, since I had failed to disclose the same information earlier during the Republican administration. My decision to not blow the whistle worked fine until recently. My contact at NASA has told me some news that will leak into the press, no matter what I decide to do.

"Rumor has it that an unmanned probe to Jupiter returned an ice sample from one of Jupiter's moons...Europa, I believe. The sample contained evidence of protozoan life presumed to have existed before the surface of Europa got so cold that it froze over. My source speculated that the core of Europa might have contained sufficient ambient heat to support life at one time, but once the core cooled, it was too far removed from the Sun's warmth to be sustained."

Ivan was stunned. He could not speak, although he was amazed and intrigued.

Cheney went on. "Shortly after the ice samples of Europa were analyzed, the members of the probe project team began to get sick, and mysteriously died of their illnesses. There weren't any hospital records to review. I have been afraid to go public with any of this for my own safety, but last week even my contact at NASA disappeared. Now I have to do something about it, but I'm not sure what."

Ivan interrupted the Senator with a question, "Senator Cheney, with all due respect, sir, what exactly does all of this have to do with me?"

"Dr. Berkowitz, let me try to answer. If Wakeman has anything to do with this, and I'm sure he does, its not likely that he's acting alone. Wakeman is not a rogue shark. He's no lone wolf. He is a man who carries out orders. I need to know for sure if Wakeman's orders have been coming from the White House or from the military. No doubt, these deaths and disappearances lead to one or the other. We either have a President giving out execution orders, or a military that has gone far astray. Either way, we are in dire straits, Dr. Berkowitz. I need your help."

This time, it was Ivan who covered his face in his hands and rubbed his forehead to relieve the stress. He backed away from asking more questions and simply said, "Senator, you've given me a lot to think about. I can't answer today, but I will give you an answer, soon."

"Dr. Berkowitz, I don't need to caution you about how

dangerous this can be. This must not be discussed with anyone, no matter what your answer is. Please don't be long in getting back to me. I'm afraid we don't have much time before the other side concludes whatever strategy they have put into play," Cheney pleaded.

"I'll talk to you soon, Senator. Very soon," Ivan said.

With that, Ivan excused himself, shook Cheney's hand, and opened the door leading to the living room. The young man got up from his chair, and peered out the cut glass windows at the front door. Once he felt secure, he opened it for Ivan, who left without saying another word. Ivan couldn't wait to get out of there. He had recorded the entire conversation.

ᵛᵛᵛ

Even though Cheney had issued a warning not to say a word to anyone, Ivan felt that a phone call to Liebermann was in order. Ivan wouldn't breech Cheney's confidence or divulge any details, but he wanted to make some inquiries, particularly about Oliver Wakeman.

"Liebermann," was all that he said when he answered.

"Howard, this is your favorite Russian-American astrophysicist calling. How are you?"

"Ivan, I'm fine, couldn't be better. How's everything with you?"

"Well, you oughta know by now. Every time I call you, my life is topsy-turvy. I'm sorry to say that its sorta screwed up again. Did I call you at a bad time?"

"Oh no, now's as good a time as any. But I thought you were taken care of forever, Ivan. What's wrong? What is it this time?"

"Maybe all I need is a little help understanding Oliver Wakeman. You've known him for quite a while. Tell me about Wakeman."

"What's the matter, Ivan? Are you and Oliver not getting along?"

"It's more than that, Howard. I just want to learn what makes him tick. Didn't you know him when he first came to NASA?"

"Yes, yes I knew him. He was recruited right out of the Air Force. If I recall, he was assigned some special project when he came. He's done pretty well for himself since those days, hasn't he?"

"Yeah. I suppose so. Howard, do you remember that NASA probe that disappeared around Mars a while back? Did Wakeman's special project have anything to do with that?"

"Ivan, where are you going with these questions? I can't really help you with Wakeman unless I know where you're going with all of this."

"Howard, have you kept up with Wakeman over the years? Is Wakeman today a White House guy or still a military guy?"

"Ivan, hold it. Hold it. What's going on here?"

"I'm sorry, Howard. It's just that I seem to have gotten myself into trouble again, and I'm trying to understand what I'm up against...who I'm up against."

"Ivan, you're talking nonsense. What is it?"

"Howard, let's back up. When did you first meet Wakeman?"

"Ivan, you're backing me into a corner. The truth is I met him only four years ago through a guy at Jesuit University who was trying to help you out behind the scenes, back when you needed some help."

"Who was that, Howard?"

"It was your Chancellor, Ivan...Chancellor Monague. He told me that he didn't want to see you get hurt in all that mess back at Jesuit U. He asked me to try to work things out for you. He figured that sooner or later you'd come to me if you ever thought about leaving J.U. I was just playing facilitator. I really don't know Wakeman personally at all."

"So how did you know Chancellor Monague?"

"Ivan, I've known Chancellor Monague since the day you were employed at Jesuit University. I placed you there, remember?"

"Howard, are you telling me that all that stuff about you and Wakeman being old friends was a hoax?"

"Ivan, I lied so that you wouldn't feel so manipulated. You have to remember, you're a very valuable American asset. You always have been, and you always will be. It has always been my job to protect you. That is all that I was doing."

Ivan was speechless. He felt like a puppet.

"Howard, I just don't know what to say. I need to think about all of this. I've gotta go. Thanks for all that you have done for me."

With that, Ivan hung up the phone, realizing that Howard was working both sides of the fence.

CHAPTER 24

The Speaker

When Ivan hung up, he suddenly became extremely nervous, almost panic-stricken. He agonized over why he always stumbled into trouble. He had only intended to find out more about Wakeman, but more likely he had only tipped his hand to Liebermann.

"Damn!" he muttered under his breath. "If Liebermann tells Wakeman about that call, I'm in some deep shit. God, I wish I hadn't done that. Now I don't know what I'm gonna do."

Feeling caught in a speed trap, he decided that he had to call Julio. While Julio didn't know anything really about Wakeman, or NASA for that matter, his advice was always worth hearing. But unfortunately when Ivan called, all he got was a voice recorder. He hung up in frustration, unwilling to leave a message.

The next day, Ivan had better luck. In a very brief call, he simply told Julio that they needed to meet soon, privately. Ivan asked if they could meet tomorrow, if he could arrange to fly up to New York that evening. Since the monthly Environmental Council meeting was the day after anyway, it worked out conveniently for both of them.

ᛇᛇᛇ

As agreed, Julio met Ivan at noon the next day in the lobby of the Plaza. Like the rest of New York City, they decided to take a walk in Central Park. It was a pretty day. By the time Ivan finished telling his story about meeting Cheney in Houston, Julio was just shaking his head in disbelief over Ivan's misfortune.

The two of them talked about options. Ivan's first option was to say yes to Senator Cheney, placing him in the cross-hairs of Wakeman. The second option to say no to Cheney, placing him in the cross-hairs of Cheney. Julio decided that the best thing for Ivan was an exit strategy. It was time for Ivan to get out of the crossfire, before he was caught dead in the middle.

Julio told Ivan that he needed a new forum to trumpet his message anyway, one that was not so politically sensitive, one where he could say whatever he wanted without wearing the muzzle of political advisors. His message was too important not to be heard. Julio advised his friend to take up public speaking on the college campus circuit, at least for a while anyway. There, Ivan could say whatever he wanted, so long as he didn't directly implicate his adversaries.

The next day, Ivan failed to show up for his monthly meeting at the United Nations. He had taken the Amtrak Northeast Corridor Commuter Train out of Penn Station to Washington, D.C. He owed Senator Cheney a visit. Ivan didn't want to call him ahead of time, because the Senator would only insist on some secretive meeting place. Ivan wanted to walk into the Senator's office unannounced, take a seat, and wait to see him. It was important that everything be out in the wide open. Ivan was quitting NASA.

As soon as he returned to Houston, he did the same thing with Wakeman. Wakeman seemed to be as surprised as Cheney about Ivan's decision. Neither anticipated the move. Cheney appeared frustrated, as though he was back at square one, and Wakeman seemed relieved, making Ivan feel like he had made a wise decision. When asked what was he going to do with himself, he just

178
ᛇᛇᛇ

said he was going to take some time off, relax, enjoy life a little, and maybe travel some with Katrina. The exit strategy seemed to have worked well. The only string attached when he left NASA was Cheney's warning to keep what he knew to himself, forever.

Ivan didn't waste any time meeting with a booking agent to launch his new career. Given his resume, the only question in the agent's mind was, "How much money will this guy bring?" There was no doubt that every college in America would want to book him. Ivan replied that he wanted to maximize his exposure, rather than the money. With that instruction, the agent booked him solid for an entire school year, beginning in the fall.

Ivan's earliest presentations focused on the general state of the Earth's environmental condition. It was a fabulous talk that received widespread attention in each community where he spoke. By the end of the fall, Ivan had turned up the volume a notch by emphasizing the magnitude of our environmental problems, giving his listeners a glimpse of the trend lines, and where these trends could lead us.

By mid-winter, Ivan's reputation as a doomsayer had taken his publicity far beyond the boundaries of campus newspapers. He was getting offers to appear on all of the TV talk shows. His popularity was exploding.

By spring, he unleashed a new book called *The Point of No Return*. The critic's reviews said it was astonishingly frightening, though too technical to interest the average reader of paperback novels. But once the book hit the shelves, Ivan's followers bought every copy until it became a best seller. Those who could understand the mathematic equations in the book confirmed the significance of Ivan's discovery. The scientific community was rumbling that Dr. Berkowitz could possibly win another Nobel Prize. His mercurial notoriety had reached a new high.

It was late April when the booking agent called to tell Ivan of a schedule change. Ivan's tour was taking him through the Midwest, and he was supposed to speak at Northwestern University in Chicago the following week. The agent said, "Dr. Berkowitz, next week has been changed to Northshore. Jesuit University must have wanted you real bad, because they agreed to pay your cancellation penalty, and double your fee. The arrangements have already been made. I didn't think you would mind, so I've already given notice to Northwestern University."

"But I wanted to go to Chicago. It's not the money, dammit. Jesuit University is the last place I want to speak," Ivan protested.

"Dr. Berkowitz, I apologize for not consulting with you first. The change has already been made. The new contract is signed. I'm really sorry. I thought the change would make you happy."

"Well, it doesn't. Let's get one thing straight. I don't want to have this mix-up again. I've got to approve everything, do you understand? This is my life you know."

"Yes, sir. I understand and apologize. It won't happen again."

Ivan was mad, but there was nothing he could do about it. Trying to make the best of the situation, he called Betsy to tell her he would be coming to town and, of course, she was thrilled. In her voice, he knew that she had missed him. She said that she had been keeping up with his whereabouts through the media. Only two weeks before, he had been featured on the cover of *Time Magazine*. She had shown it to all of the girls at her office, bragging that the famed Dr. Berkowitz had been her husband's best friend. Betsy asked if she could invite these girls over to a small reception or a tea to meet Ivan while he was in town, but he declined.

"Betsy, if you don't mind I'd like to keep a low profile, if that's possible. I feel like I stirred up enough controversy last time I passed through town. How about we just go get a bite to eat? You and Mexican food are the two things I miss most around Northshore."

"No problem, Ivan. Call me as soon as you get here. I can't wait to see you."

It had been three years since Ivan had set foot on the campus at Jesuit University. Nothing had really changed. The fountain in the middle of the quadrangle had been turned off, and the trees had been recently trimmed. Those were the only differences he could see. It was beautiful, actually. Ivan caught himself reminiscing about the first time he had driven onto the campus. Quickly his nostalgia was dominated by the negative experiences that had haunted his tenure at J.U.

He was scheduled to speak that afternoon in the large auditorium on the edge of the quadrangle. The place was filled with students who wanted to hear the man who, by reputation, overshadowed all others on the subject of the future. They were hoping Dr. Berkowitz would tell them how to fix the world. They were young and energetic enough to do it in their own minds, if only the older generations would get out of their way and let them. It reminded Ivan of his own youthful feelings when he had been a college student.

The President of the Student Government Association was having trouble getting the crowd quiet so that an introduction could be made. Finally, the S.G.A. President plowed ahead uncomfortably, telling of Dr. Berkowitz's credentials. When he mentioned Ivan's former teaching experience at Jesuit U, a section of students stood up and booed, taunting Dr. Berkowitz. They jeered when the S.G.A. President compared Berkowitz to visionaries like Arthur Clarke, Carl Sagan and Stephen Hawking. The hecklers were on a mission of their own. Ivan knew it was going to be one of the longest afternoons of his life.

The group of hooligans was fairly well-organized, with banners that said "HOAX," "BINDING FARCE," "NEVER RETURN," and "TRUST JESUS." Ivan did the best he could, trying to give his normal presentation to the remaining ninety-five percent of the students. But is wasn't any fun. The hecklers made sure they were so disruptive that the campus security had to throw them out.

When they refused to leave, the security officers were forced to place them under arrest, totally upstaging Ivan's presentation. The real story of the day became the student unrest, and the violence. Sadly, a couple of football players who wanted to hear Dr. Berkowitz speak, went over to the hecklers, and started fighting with them. It was near bedlam. The show was over.

As sick as Ivan was about the way things went that afternoon, he didn't break his date with Betsy to go to their favorite Mexican restaurant. In spite of the dismal day, it was great to see her. When Ivan told her what had happened, she was horrified. Somebody set that whole thing up she concluded. It didn't sound like there was anything spontaneous about it. But like the prophets of old, Ivan said he would just knock the dust off his sandals and get out of town. The only problem was that his flight didn't leave until the next day.

The next morning, Ivan was brushing his teeth while listening to one of the morning talk shows on TV. He had already showered and shaved, and was almost ready to go down to the lobby for a free continental breakfast and a cup of coffee, when his phone rang. It was Betsy.

"Ivan," she was crying. "Ivan..." she couldn't talk.

Ivan told her to relax, to sit down and catch her breath. Everything would be fine, he said.

"The newspaper, Ivan. Have you seen the local newspaper?" Betsy asked him.

"No, Betsy. I'm just getting up, but I'm sure there is one outside my door. Let me go take a look."

Outside Ivan's door was a *U.S.A. Today*, but no local paper at all. He came back to the phone and told her that all he had was a national paper.

She said, "Ivan, you've got to see the campus paper, and the city paper. You won't believe it. Call me back as soon as you've read them. I'm so sorry, Ivan. Please call me."

Ivan finished dressing and headed out the door. He knew that he could find both papers just outside the Student Union Building, so there he went.

The headlines of the campus paper read,

"FORMER PROF CAUSES RIOT"

The article blamed Ivan for the entire episode, showing pictures of students being handcuffed and others fighting, while those in the background held up their "TRUST JESUS" banners. The article said that Dr. Ivan Berkowitz had always been a controversial figure at Jesuit U. His employment was eventually terminated for insubordination. According to Dean O'Leary, who was quoted several times in the article, Berkowitz had, furthermore, engaged in conduct unsuitable for a tenured professor at Jesuit University, as depicted by photos taken of Berkowitz leaving a hotel room with the wife of another former J.U. professor, who was also terminated for conduct unbecoming to faculty members. The pictures appeared in the article. The innuendos were devastating.

"Oh my God!" Ivan exclaimed silently. "This is pure libel and slander. This is character assassination. Those pictures were taken at the Mayfair Hotel in Miami. It must have been Liebermann. I can't believe it. I trusted that bastard!"

Ivan didn't even bother looking at the local paper. He had seen enough. He called Betsy and told her he had seen the news.

His next call was to Katrina.

CHAPTER 25

The Messenger

Ivan never wanted to return to Northshore...never, ever again. He called his agent to remind him to stick to his schedule. No more changes...not for love, or money or anything. The agent made his apologies all over again. After calming down, Ivan spent the rest of the week working on his coming presentation. It was time to make a few changes.

The day he was to give his next speech could not have been more beautiful. His spirits were lifted because Katrina had joined him. She was going to record his presentation, something Ivan liked for her to do each time he made major revisions. She truly supported him all the way. Her trust had not even been rattled. She strengthened him in his resolve to fight back. Before he left the hotel room that morning, Katrina said to him, "Your enemies have no idea what they're up against. Now they're gonna meet Ivan the Terrible. Woe unto them. God pity their souls."

It was a perfect day to launch a counter assault. Ivan's adrenaline was pumping, his motives were right, and his heart was pure. Because the weather was so beautiful, the program was moved outdoors in the sunshine, among the blooming flowers and budding trees. He knew it would be well-attended, and he was prepared to give them their money's worth.

Ivan had never felt better. He hadn't realized what a burden it had been to bottle up suppressed information for so many years...but he was ready to put this burden down and speak freely. After his introduction was made, Ivan stepped forward to the podium and gripped the sides firmly. He was relaxed...unconcerned with the consequences of whatever it was he was about to say. All he was concerned with was the truth. Nothing else mattered. He was confident that the truth would set him free. He looked out over the crowd and began to speak.

"Years ago, I spearheaded some research that led me to write *The Binding Force*. It's true that there was some controversy that followed the publishing of the book. At Jesuit University, the controversy was defined in a debate that I had with the head of the Religion Department at that time, a debate which continues even today. I left my teaching profession at Jesuit University because those in power within the administration were intolerant of the views that my research embodied.

"After winning the Nobel Prize, I accepted a position with NASA, hoping to be free of political impediments, hoping I could continue my research in a way that would maximize my personal development, and my contribution to society at-large. But I was mistaken. My research at NASA revealed problems that no one wanted to face, and so again, those in power ignored the warning, killing the messenger in effect with their editorial policies.

"The final straw during my relatively brief tenure at NASA came when I was asked by the Chairman of the Senate Intelligence Committee to be a "mole" within NASA for the purpose of reporting on a longstanding fraud against the American people, a conspiracy that had turned deadly, and one that brought fear to those who knew of it."

The crowd of students started rumbling loudly among them-selves and then fell silent, hanging on Ivan's every word.

"Under the guise of 'military research', NASA has for years conducted unmanned exploratory probes against the direct in-structions of Congress. Only a very tight circle even knew about it until one of the missions discovered something too big to keep quiet. And like the barking dog that catches up to the car, those responsible for the stealth operation didn't know what to do about the discovery. They decided that nobody could talk, so people started dying. Somebody ordered the research team to be mur-dered."

The students who had been sitting on the lawn now stood up, realizing that this news was too important to hear sitting down. They got loud again for a moment, but quickly hushed so they could hear more.

"Controversy has always been hard to take but hardest of all for those who like the status quo. And who would be threatened by news that evidence of life had been found in ice samples taken from the frozen surface of Europa? Not only those who shouldn't have been looking in the first place, but each of us, each human being who has forever believed that we are at the center of God's universe.

"You see, we have become blinded by politics that serve to protect the status quo, and also by our religious institutions, that have perpetuated a doctrine of separation between God, man and the rest of creation. This legacy of western civilization is what I call 'the dividing force', the antithesis of all that I have learned in my research. It is 'the binding force' that refutes this belief that mankind stands at the center of creation, as though God created us for his own entertainment. And what is so tragically ironic is that humanity, with its narcissistic views, is heading down the path of self-destruction, jeopardizing all of life as we know it. It is a controversy that confronts us all. We cannot escape it. And we're not going to take it anymore. It's time to start the revolu-tion. It's time for our salvation to begin."

The college kids loved the fiery words. The message was

getting through. They screamed out their support for Ivan and what he stood for. He was working them into a frenzy.

"I left NASA so that I could be heard. Many of you know that I have written a new book, entitled *The Point of No Return*, which spells out my message. But listen, young people, I am here to tell you that my message is urgent. We, as a planet, are going to destroy ourselves if we do not change. And we must change soon."

On the third floor of the Science Building, a high-powered scope was focused on the gray hair in Ivan's sideburn. When the assassin gently squeezed the trigger, a muffled pop was heard by only a few on the edges of the crowd. Ivan's head exploded like a watermelon that had bounced off a truck, leaving no doubt in anyone's mind that he was dead before he hit the platform. No one even tried to save him. They just stood there in shock, mortified by the sight. Ivan was gone. Someone had, indeed, killed the messenger.

BOOK THREE

Julio's Legacy:

The New Creed

CHAPTER 26

The Pilgrimage

That same afternoon in New York City, Julio was sitting at his desk, alone in his office at the U.N. His thoughts were interrupted by a vision, and he slipped into a semi-conscious dream-state.

Again, he was an eagle in the Fourth World, flying low, sharing his message with all who would listen. He passed over a nest of snakes and circled. One of the snakes struck down another eagle with his deadly fangs. He circled closer, and saw that the eagle that had fallen was Evava, his older brother. It was too late to prevent the confrontation. The venom had been injected. His brother was dead. All he could do was mourn.

When he awoke, Julio felt sick to his stomach, weakened by the loss that he had experienced in the dream. He stopped his work, cancelled his afternoon schedule, and went home early, wanting to be with his family. That evening, Julio was watching the network national news when he heard the anchor reporter say,

"History, once again, has repeated itself. A fifty-two year old Nobel Prize winner, Dr. Ivan Berkowitz, was slain today on the campus of Kent State University, while giving an outdoor public address. Those students who witnessed the shooting were horrified. The news sadly reminds us all of days past, when four protesters of the Vietnam War were killed on the campus of Kent State by the National Guard."

Almost before the words were spoken, Julio knew why he had gotten sick that afternoon. It had been the same when Mac had died. His vision had only cushioned the shock, but it did not stem his pain or his anger. He counted Ivan's enemies, wondering who among them was so threatened that they would kill, or have him killed. There had been no mention in the reporting of anything Ivan had said in his speech, but it was announced that his funeral would be in Northshore, Indiana.

ᵥᵥᵥ

Julio shared the tragic news with Mary and his children before scheduling a morning flight from New York to Chicago. He wanted to visit with Betsy and Katrina before attending Ivan's funeral. After a sleepless night at home, he got up early and packed for his trip. As he was leaving, he kissed Mary good-bye in the bedroom and walked out his front door. At his feet, Julio noticed at least a dozen small, yellow lumps scattered across the sidewalk. He stooped down to take a closer look, picking up in his hands a lifeless little bird. It was a dead canary.

Julio immediately went back inside and called his security team, asking that they keep an eye on his house while he was away. He cleaned up the mess on the sidewalk, and then went back into the bedroom to tell Mary that there had been a change of plans.

"Mary, I've changed my mind about all of this. I want you and the children to go with me to Chicago."

"You what?"

"I know its late notice, but I really think its the right thing for us to do."

"Julio, we're not even packed."

"I know that. We'll take a later flight. I think its important that you go."

"The kids are going to have a fit."

"That's O.K. They've never been to Chicago. Maybe they'll enjoy getting out of town."

"That's wishful thinking. This is a funeral, darling, not a field trip."

"No doubt. But they need to go with us. See what you can do."

"All right. Just tell me when the flight leaves."

"I don't know yet. Let me call the airlines."

Julio didn't want to alarm Mary, so he didn't mention anything to her about the canaries. And he definitely wasn't going to say anything to the cab driver, who had been silently waiting out front to take him to LaGuardia. He just gave the guy a twenty dollar tip, and told him that there had been a change of plans.

Mary seemed perplexed about the change, but she didn't argue. Julio got on the phone and booked seats for everyone on a later departure. He also called Betsy McFarland to see if she could pick them up at O'Hare, and drive them to Northshore. Betsy said she would meet them at the terminal building, just outside the baggage claim.

After retrieving their luggage, Julio led his family outside, where Betsy was waiting for them. He spotted her immediately, and walked around to the driver's side to give her a hug. He introduced his family, and they all piled into her car.

As they drove back to Northshore, Betsy announced that Ivan would be buried right next to Mac. She had given up her own plot, and ordered a headstone just like Mac's. Both men had been born in the same year, but Mac died at the age of 41, while Ivan lived eleven years longer until the age of 52. Betsy and Katrina thought they belonged next to one another. They were both martyrs in the eyes of those who knew and loved them.

The Jewish burial service was very emotional, and before it was over, Katrina's composure simply collapsed. Julio, Mary and Betsy were there to comfort her, but the effect on all of them was compounded by the prior loss of Mac. When the Rabbi finished reading from the Old Testament and reciting traditional Jewish prayers, everyone present at the service walked past Katrina and threw a handful of dirt onto the casket that had been lowered into the grave. Each person said a few words of mourning as they passed by for the last time.

Once the crowd began to disperse, Julio sent his family to the car, so that he could spend a few minutes alone with Betsy and Katrina. The three of them embraced each other in a huddle of despair. In addition to grieving for Ivan and Mac, Julio felt a certain pressure, whether real or imagined, to keep up the good fight that his friends had fought to their end. It had been a struggle against those in power, who had institutionalized their hierarchies and their agendas. It was a fight against institutions that wanted to preserve the status quo in a world that had to change in order to survive. The call to fight came not from these widows, but from Mother Earth herself, who spoke to Julio through these weeping voices.

Before leaving the burial site, he spent a few moments by himself, in prayer. He prayed for Ivan just as he had for Mac years ago. Julio asked Taiowa, the Great Spirit and Supreme Creator, to unite the Sun Father, Tawa, and the Earth Mother, Tuwa Katsi, in a Song of Creation, and to guide Ivan's spirit during his journey back to the womb of Mother Earth.

Katrina and Betsy stood behind Julio as he prayed, and when he finished, they asked him if they could visit for just a moment longer, before he returned with his family to New York. Betsy reached into her purse and gave Julio the diskettes that Mac had left in the book locker at Jesuit University, the diskettes containing the Constantine Papers. She told him that as far as she knew, the only other copies in existence were in the hands of Howard Liebermann. Julio winced when Betsy said his name.

Then Katrina asked Julio and Betsy to please walk her back to her limo. When Julio opened the door for her, she reached inside the car to grab something off the back seat. She handed Julio two cassette recordings: the first one wrapped in a note-sized piece of paper, secured by a rubber band, and the second labeled Ivan's Last Speech. Julio took the rubber band off the first, and opened the note that had been wrapped around it. The note said,

"Katrina,
      Give this to Julio, if anything unfortunate should ever happen to me. He will know what it is. I love you so much.
                                                    Ivan"

Julio was befuddled when he read it because he didn't have a clue, and wouldn't until he was able to go home and listen to it. The same would be true of Ivan's Last Speech, since the media hadn't mentioned a word about the contents of what had been said that day.

Katrina reached inside the limo once again and emerged with copies of Ivan's two books, each with a hand-written inscription signed by Ivan. In the first, Ivan said he hoped the world might one day recognize the common threads of *The Binding Force* that connect us all. In the second, Ivan begged the world to change before reaching *The Point of No Return*. Both messages conveyed a sense of urgency.

Julio knew that Katrina and Betsy had armed him to continue the fight. The surge of emotions that came with their final embrace said to each that this embrace might be their last.

When Julio returned home, he took both cassettes into his study and closed the door. He first took the unlabeled cassette from its paper wrapper and inserted it into a player. He put on a set of headphones so that only he could hear, not knowing what might be on it. Initially, he recognized Ivan's voice and then heard the voice of a stranger. But within moments another voice was heard, that of Senator Cheney. It was the meeting Ivan had taped in Houston, a tape that could potentially topple a Senator, a Lt. General, or even a President.

The second cassette was more chilling. He listened to his friend send out his warning before the muffled pop of the gun silenced him. Julio was crying when he turned off the recorder. He felt too weak to shoulder the burden that only he could bear. He decided in that moment that he must make a pilgrimage home to recover his strength. He needed to return to the Hopi Way. The Hopi Reservation seemed farther away than a plane ride, farther than any journey. Julio had almost forgotten his past, his culture, his religion, his traditions, his Hopi family and friends. He had to re-learn that which he had forgotten. He needed to be born again. It was time to go home.

ᵀᵀᵀ

He had never taken his wife and children to visit the Hopi Reservation. Being afraid of interracial and intercultural rejection on both sides, he avoided even the possibility. But now was the time to have them with him. He needed them. He needed every ounce of strength he could muster. He could not separate from them.

During the cross-country drive, Julio tried to tell his family what to expect. The children were excited, expecting an adventure, while Mary was anxious, expecting to be judged unfavorably for being a pahana. Julio knew both were wrong, but as hard as he tried, he couldn't amend their preconceptions or their premonitions.

When he stepped out of the jeep that he had rented in Phoenix, the Hopi Indians in the plaza of New Oraibi didn't even look his way, as they continued on with their lives. They likely presumed that the driver of the jeep was a pahana from the government or possibly even a tourist who didn't belong there. Julio's ego had grown accustomed to so much fanfare in the western world that he suddenly felt alone, unrecognized, disappointed, and then humbled. Julio decided in that moment that he would not cut his hair again to conform to western standards. He seized on the humiliation of not being received, and he began his rehabilitation, knowing that before he left, he would be a Hopi, once again.

196

He walked into the offices in the Tribal Council Building and met briefly with the Chairman, who was the only one who expected his arrival. In less than five minutes, he returned to the car smelling like pipe smoke. Julio assured Mary and the children that the Chairman had welcomed them all.

The next order of business was to visit his mother and sister, and introduce them to his family. They walked to the house that Julio grew up in and knocked on the door. A short, round woman opened the door, and saw her son standing before her for the first time in many years. Her smile revealed a missing tooth, but told a story about how much she had missed Julio. She opened her arms and threw herself around him, and he did the same. Within moments, Julio's sister joined in the embrace, and the three hugged each other without speaking a word.

"Nampeyo, this is my wife, Mary. And Mary, this is my mother, Nampeyo."

"It is an honor to meet you, Nampeyo," Mary said.

Then Julio introduced his sister, "And this is my sister, Mina. Mina, please meet Mary."

Mina spoke first, saying she was happy to know the woman who had captured Julio's heart.

Next, the children were introduced, first, Amelia, and then, Julian. Nampeyo leaned down to give each of them a hug, and so did Mina. Julio and Mary were excited to finally have the family together, after so many years of separation. Their reception had been warm, and their fears of rejection were unfounded.

Nampeyo stood back and looked closely at the children. Then she said, "Amelia resembles Mina, don't you think, Julio?"

"Yes, I've often said so to Mary. She has Mina's pretty hair and dark eyes, and her pretty smile. But she has Mary's features, don't you think?"

"Yes, the best of two worlds," Mina laughed. They all laughed together.

Then Nampeyo spoke, "And Julian, what a beautiful name. You look just like your father, but you will be even taller. Your grandfather was tall, and strong. He would have loved to have known his grandchildren, and he would have been proud of both of you. I am so glad you have come to visit us. Mina and I adore you all, and we are honored to meet you at last."

Julio told his mother that they had met with the Chairman, and they would be staying in the same mesa-top cliff dwellings that Julio and Dr. Mac had used 15 years ago. He told her they were going to get settled-in and would see her later. His family loaded up in the jeep and headed out of town, ascending the winding road that would take them to the top of Third Mesa.

When they arrived, Julio felt that he had entered a dominion where time stood still. Once Julio showed his family the room where they would be living, he then went to the room next door where he planned to stay, alone. There were some practices that he had to follow that he didn't want to impose on his family. He asked Mary to take charge of the children, while he went out to gather wood for cooking food during the days, and to keep the rooms warm during the chilly nights.

After gathering an ample supply, Julio trekked down the mesa to the nearest spring-fed creek where he bathed himself in mud, smearing it all over his body, marking the beginning of his fast. He returned to his family's pueblo room with a jar full of water and then disappeared again to the confines of his own room, where he baked like a potato in the afternoon heat, meditating on the Hopi word "koyaanisqatsi", a word that meant "a world out of balance". He completely let go of logic and reason, letting emotion and intuition guide him through his prayer. By mid-afternoon, he had reached a hypnotic state, void of all distraction, sensing only the sounds of silence.

The next morning, Julio asked Mary and the children to go with him to visit what used to be his father's kiva, a very sacred underground ceremonial chamber with a symbolic sipapu or hole of emergence cut into its top. They removed their shoes before entering the kiva through the small door of an antechamber positioned on the side. Following Julio's instructions, the children were given beans to plant in the kiva floor, beans that would quickly germinate under the oven-like conditions caused by the hot afternoon sun. Julio asked Mary and the children to care for them each day until harvest, always on the eighth day after planting.

Julio continued his fasting for the next several days, trekking each morning to a different monument of nature before returning to his hut to meditate and pray. He took his wife and children with him on these hikes so they could appreciate the beauty of their surroundings, and see the sights where their father grew up. Julio was in a prayerful state of mind all day long. The children were awed by their father's spirituality , a side of him they had not experienced before. Mary, on the other hand, was concerned, unable to even approach her husband while he was soul-searching with such intensity. She chose to keep her distance, until he invited her to be close. Like the children, she had not witnessed this side of him before either.

On the seventh day, Julio got up at dawn and left his family sleeping, while he trekked to Old Oraibi. He wanted to visit Prophecy Rock, an ancient petroglyph that charted the two paths that the world could follow. The first path led to liberation through purification rites practiced in Hopi ceremonies. The second path led to destruction through pleasure, greed, convenience, profit and personal gratification, symbolized by a single petroglyph called the Gourd Full Of Ashes. The inscribed stone was as sacred to the Hopi as the Ten Commandments were to the Jews, but not even Hopi tradition knew how it got there. It simply had always been there.

Julio spent the balance of the day in total solitude, perched 600 feet above the desert valley on the edge of a mesa cliff. Just as the sun was setting, he experienced a vision, or perhaps it was a visitation, he wasn't sure.

It was Kwahu, the divine messenger, the eagle dancer. The eagle dancer told Julio not to be afraid before saying, "It is time for me to tell you just who you are, so that you can fulfill your purpose...so that you can honor your responsibility. While the Hopi have never strayed from the path of responsibility, so many others have. You must try to lead them away from the abyss. This is your purpose. But like the Phoenix, you will have to rise from the ashes before they will listen."

Julio awoke from his trance with his feet dangling over the edge of the cliff. The panoramic view stole his breath, and caused his heart to stop beating, while he scrambled away from the edge as fast as he could. He dared not even look back, afraid that he might slip or be dragged over by some unseen enemy. He went straight home, anxious to be with his family. He had found what his soul had been searching for, a message from Kwahu. He was almost ready to assume his responsibility. But there was one more Hopi tradition that he had to follow before his return to the Hopi Way would be complete.

It had been eight days since the beans had been planted in the kiva floor by his children. Julio invited Nampeyo, Mina, Mary and the children to join him in the kiva, for on this eighth day, Julio would need his family more than they would know. Mina helped Julian and Amelia cut the sacred bean sprouts and tie them into bundles, so they could be used in a stew that Nampeyo helped Mary prepare. Mina dug out an earth pit and began baking pikami, a ceremonial pudding that would be the main course of this holy meal. She had already prepared piki, the ceremonial wafer bread that would be served.

The aroma of food was almost enough to make Julio faint, since he hadn't eaten a bite in over eight days. He appeared drawn in the face but happy, no longer tormented as he seemed to be when he first started his fasting. His anguished soul-searching seemed to be near an end, and Mary could tell that his search had not been in vain. She was sure that he would be stronger than ever before, after he left the kiva.

When the meal was ready, the family gathered close together to share in their love and thoughts for each other. As they broke bread together, they pulled each other closer and closer to the center, making their circle tighter and tighter as the meal was consumed. When they had finished, Julio said a blessing and then served each of them a cup of the sacred bean stew, which they drank together as a sacrament of communion. They tightened the circle again, touching one another shoulder to shoulder in prayer, joined in the Hopi Way, sharing the warmth of the common womb, the kiva.

Suddenly the silence was broken. Into the kiva sprang several kachinas, members of Hopi society, dressed in full costume, personifying the spirits of animals, plants and persons. They danced about the family, at first frightening Julian and Amelia with their ghoulish appearance. But before long, the children remembered what their father had taught them on the ride out to Arizona. They quickly lost their fear and began dancing themselves with these larger than life spirit-creatures.

After watching the children dance, Julio went to each family member and kissed them good-bye. The kachinas lifted him onto their shoulders and helped him crawl out of the sipapu, symbolizing his emergence into the world.

As soon as Julio emerged from the kiva and stood tall, he found himself looking into the eyes of another kachina. His appearance was frightening, although Julio had seen the kachina many times before. He reached out and gave Julio a young eagle whose feet were bound by a rope, holding him captive to a wooden perch. The kachina told Julio that it was time to make a sacrifice of the eagle, the most mysterious and controversial of all Hopi traditions. Julio took the young eagle with him, not saying a word to the kachina.

Nourished from the meal back in the kiva, Julio began his final journey. He was to sacrifice the young eagle at an altar built on the most sacred of all Hopi grounds, at the top of the 12,600 foot high San Francisco Peaks. When he finally reached the altar, Julio looked at the horizon in all directions before looking down upon the high plains city of Flagstaff. He and the young eagle were on top of the world.

He knelt at the altar with his sacrifice. The young eagle was clutching his perch nervously, and looking deeply into Julio's soul. Julio said a Hopi prayer, and then let the eagle go, refusing to complete the sacrificial deed. He defied the tradition of even his own people.

When he let the young eagle go, it circled above his head before spiraling higher and higher, until eventually the eagle disappeared into the heavens. But even though he could not be seen, Julio could hear the eagle's unique cry, a message that only Julio could understand. The eagle said to him, *"My brother, now you stand alone in my place at the altar."*

CHAPTER 27

The Initiative

During the next few weeks, Julio found himself compulsively jotting down his thoughts on a legal pad, ideas that he knew would stir the political pot. He had challenged himself to come up with a list that had no boundaries, no conventions, no limitations, no rules, no preconceptions. It was a wish list that required a changed world. It would take a changed world to convince Julio that his friends had not died in vain.

At the next breakfast meeting of the Environmental Council, Julio announced the news of Ivan's death, even though he presumed they all knew. While Ivan had not attended a Council meeting since his resignation from NASA, most members of the Council remembered the contribution of Dr. Berkowitz with a great deal of respect. Ambassador Masito, as Chairman of the Council, took the opportunity to publicly eulogize his friend's life, and lament his tragic and untimely death. Dr. Ivan Berkowitz would not be forgotten.

Following the breakfast meeting, the Council was scheduled

to hear the outside presentation segment of their meeting agenda. Julio canceled the scheduled speaker, and took the podium over himself. With the assistance of a finely choreographed slide show, Julio presented in detail the findings that Ivan had published in *The Point of No Return*. He concluded the presentation by playing the tape entitled Ivan's Last Speech. It was a dramatic presentation that spawned the most spirited floor debate that Julio had ever witnessed.

After lunch, the Council re-convened, not knowing exactly what might lie ahead. Julio returned to the podium, with his legal pad in hand.

"Ladies and gentlemen of the Council, please allow me to push the new business segment of today's agenda forward. Thank you for your indulgence on this point of order.

"Today, as Chairman of this Council, I would like to introduce to you a new initiative that is intended to alter the course of history, but more importantly, an initiative that will alter our prospects for the future. I believe that we, as representatives of humanity from all over the world, stand at a crossroads, and we must choose today the path that future generations will travel, just as our predecessors chose the path that has brought us to this point. The choice we face is either the path of responsibility or the path of self-destruction. Many will scoff at this new initiative, especially those who want to stay the course that we are on. But as the late Dr. Berkowitz has shown, we cannot continue to travel this road. At all costs, we must avoid the point of no return.

"Today, I will ask that a special committee be formed that will become responsible for drafting new legislation which, if approved by this Council, will be submitted to the General Assembly. This legislation will seek to empower the United Nations with jurisdictional authority over sovereign governments on matters that concern the planet as a whole. This legislation will address the following: environmental and natural resource protection; nuclear, biological and chemical risk supervision; disease and pestilence control; food, famine and disaster relief; human and animal rights supervision; and international law enforcement.

"These issues have not been adequately addressed within sovereign borders. The consequences of irresponsible actions can effect us all. We are responsible for the well-being of the planet. Therefore, I am proposing that the U.N. increase its direct involvement in each of these areas of common concern."

The Council applauded loudly, rising from their seats to give Julio a standing ovation. None of them really knew where this would lead, but it was very well-received.

"I will also ask that a second committee be formed to study, draft and submit their recommendations to this Council on how to best enforce an enhanced U.N. role, should it come to pass. This committee shall give consideration to all forms of enforcement, ranging from economic, to judicial, to police, to military.

"The focus of this legislation should be on two specific levels of enforcement: the first level would pertain to violations by sovereign governments, and the second level would pertain to violations by individuals who have responsibility for the conduct of those sovereign governments."

"With respect to such cases where charges against an individual have been made and substantiated, I would suggest that the U.N. consider prosecuting that individual through the World Court. The Court should rule on the case, whether the individual chooses to defend himself or not.

"If in fact, it is determined that the crimes of the accused are so heinous that the death penalty is warranted, then so be it. Such a sentence should be carried out under the supervision of the United Nations, giving secondary regard to method.

"To serve as an example, such a court system should be able to sentence characters like Adolph Hitler, Idi Amin, or Saddam Hussein, for their crimes against humanity, in particular, and against the world, at large. And the U.N. should be willing to execute whatever sentence the World Court renders. Perhaps this would curb the maniacal behavior of certain politicians who have grossly abused their power, and neglected their responsibilities. Anyone who seeks to harm the world will have to answer for their actions.

"I would further suggest that if the World Court proves to be an ineffective alternative, then the U.N. should set up its own Judicial Council. Perhaps it is time for a Global Constitution that would provide the basis for resolving international disputes. The world is in need of a progressive judicial system.

"But before the U.N. expands its role, the U.N. should examine itself carefully. This expanded responsibility must be assumed only by individuals who want to serve others, not themselves. In order to assure that the U.N. continues to be a representative rather than a self-serving body, term limitations must govern our members, so that our respective constituents are truly represented. The responsibility is too great to be shared by only a few.

"Before our next meeting, I will appoint two individuals to head up these new committees. Their first order of business shall be to select members of this Council to serve on their respective committees. If you are asked to serve, please commit yourself to the task of carrying out this new initiative. I certainly hope that the remainder of this Council will be supportive in every way, although my experience causes me to expect some opposition. Pro or con, let me say that all input is invited, and I will serve as a conduit to assure that it is channeled into the process.

"The importance of this measure cannot be over-emphasized. Without knowing how long it will take to reverse our deteriorating environmental trends, I cannot give assurance that these changes will be enough. But, if the research of Dr. Berkowitz has merit, reversing these trends is critical to our very survival. That is why I bring this new initiative to you with a sense of urgency. The message is that we, as responsible human beings, must make a fundamental change."

Again, the Council members stood to applaud, but Julio wondered how they would respond after reporting home to their superiors. Julio knew he had a long way to go before his initiative received a mandate. As he put his legal pad back into his briefcase, he reminded himself that it was only a wish list.

CHAPTER 28

The Testimony

As soon as Julio returned to his office, he tried to call the Secretary of State. He thought that he had better warn the secretary of any fallout that might result from his address to the Environmental Council at the U.N. Julio expected to be chastised for not gaining approval for his comments before delivering his speech, but he knew that such approval would never have been obtained. His only option was to go it alone, outside of policy, and hope that the world didn't cave in around his ears.

The Secretary was on the phone when Julio called, but once the Secretary knew who was holding, he terminated his other call and answered abruptly.

"So now you call me, after the cat is out of the bag. Goddammit, Julio, the whole world is calling me. What the hell did you say up there?"

"I just suggested that the U.N. step up its role, mainly with respect to environmental matters, but I went a little beyond that, I suppose."

"A LITTLE BEYOND THAT? Everyone I've talked to said you called for the establishment of a fucking world government! You've strayed a little far this time, haven't you?"

"Let me send you a recording of the entire meeting. Then you can judge for yourself."

"Don't bother. My staff is setting up a video of the whole thing right now. Why don't you remain where you are for the next few hours, so I can get you if I need you."

"Yes, sir."

"Julio, hold on a minute. I'll be right back to you."

Julio could hear the Secretary yelling, even though he had obviously muffled the phone receiver. Then he came back on the line.

"Shit, Julio! The President wants to see me in the Oval Office right now. This is gonna be the last fall I'm going to take for you. Do you understand?"

"Yes, sir. Thank you, sir."

Julio hung up the phone and sat back in his chair. He decided to turn on the T.V. and watch the news channel, while he read his mail and returned a few calls. He wasn't going anywhere until he heard back from the Secretary, or the President, or both.

It had been less than two hours since the U.N. meeting had adjourned, but already the news channels were covering the story. Julio put down the mail and turned up the volume with his remote control. The TV journalist reported that Ambassador Masito's new initiative encompassed far more than merely environmental issues. The reporter criticized Julio for overstepping his bounds, but praised him at the same time for his bold attempt to strengthen the resolve and the effectiveness of the U.N.

The media spokesman was very articulate, and seemed to endorse the scope of the initiative. All things considered, Julio thought it was the best coverage he could have possibly expected.

ꝿꝿꝿ

Julio waited there in his office all afternoon, but never received a phone call from the Secretary of State. Right or wrong, Julio

208

assumed that no news was good news, and thought that he would try to touch base with the Secretary later, just to smooth things over.

The next morning, when Julio's driver arrived to take him into the city, the news papers were laying on the back seat, as they were every day. Julio picked up *The New York Times*, and to his astonishment read the headlines:

"SECRETARY OF STATE RESIGNS OFFICE

President James Harrison Woodrow, now in the first year of his second term of office, announced the surprise resignation of the Secretary of State late last night, citing 'personal reasons' for the unexpected departure. The Under-Secretary will act as the Interim Secretary and is expected to fill the vacancy in Woodrow's Cabinet as soon as his appointment can be confirmed by Congress."

Julio was deeply disturbed by the news. He regretted the President's decision, but couldn't do anything about it. Julio felt partly responsible for the President's action, but it was too late to change directions. And even if he could, he would not.

When Julio arrived at his office, a stranger was waiting for him in the reception area. Julio's administrative assistant followed the Ambassador into his office and closed the door. Julio asked, "So, who's the guy in the reception area?"

"He says he's from Washington. He didn't say much, only that it was imperative that he talk to you alone. He wouldn't let anybody else help him."

"O.K., O.K. I'll handle him. Thanks for warning me."

Julio walked back out into the reception area. The stranger stood and asked, "Are you Ambassador Julio Masito?"

"Yes, what can I do for you?"

The young man didn't introduce himself or anything. He simply said, "This is for you."

After handing the envelope to Julio, the stranger turned around and left, not saying another word. Julio looked down to see who the envelope was from, and realized that he had just been served his first subpoena to appear before the Senate Foreign Relations Committee in Washington D.C. It was Julio's turn in the barrel.

꙰꙰꙰

Normally, a Senate hearing on foreign policy would be a closed door session. The U.S. didn't typically discuss its foreign policy positions before the public; but on this day everything was different. When Julio walked into the room where the hearing was being held, TV lights and cameras were turned on and rolling. And CSPAN wasn't the only camera in the room either. It was obvious to Julio that this coverage had been set-up with a purpose, but he wasn't sure why. All he had been told was that the President was furious about all that had transpired at the U.N.

After the meeting was called to order, the Republican Chairman of the Senate Foreign Relations Committee made an opening statement to the public, and to those in attendance at the hearing. He said that following the resignation of the Secretary of State, it was appropriate to review all U.S. foreign policy, from top to bottom.

The Chairman announced that the proceedings would begin by examining the United Nations, citing alleged irregularities in the implementation of U.S. policy, and citing examples of misconduct by Ambassador Masito. Based upon the Committee's findings, the Chairman said that appropriate steps would be taken to remedy all such irregularities, and to strictly implement and enforce foreign policy goals that were shared by the legislative and executive branches of government.

Following his introductory remarks, the Chairman set forth a schedule for testimony, asking that testimony begin in three days. The first witness to be called would be Ambassador Julio Masito.

꙰꙰꙰

Three days later, at the appointed time, Julio was sworn-in to testify. He submitted for the record a copy of the minutes from the last meeting of the U.N. Environmental Council. Individual copies were handed to each Committee member, although none of them even bothered to glance at the document. Obviously, they had already done their homework.

Next, the Chairman of the Committee invited Julio to give his opening statement. These remarks had also been prepared in writing for distribution and for the record. His opening statement was very straight forward and plainly spoken, giving the necessary background leading up to the U.N. meeting, including the circumstances that surrounded the death of former U.N. Environmental Council member, Dr. Ivan Berkowitz. Following the death of his friend, Julio thought it would be appropriate to pay tribute to Dr. Berkowitz, and the contribution he had made to the Council.

Julio took full responsibility for the new initiative that followed. The initiative, he said, was basically a wish list of changes he believed would make the United Nations more effective.

The TV cameras were rolling, capturing every word spoken.

When he had finished giving his opening statement, the Chairman of the Committee called for a brief recess, asking all of the Committee members to meet jointly with him behind closed doors before re-convening the hearing.

ᛉ

One of the members on the Foreign Relations Committee was the Republican Senator from Arizona, Senator Robert Chisem. Senator Chisem had been a long-standing ally of Julio's, and Julio had gone out of his way to help Chisem on several occasions in the past. Now, Julio thought, would be a good time for the Senator from Arizona to repay those favors. Julio wanted to know what was going on behind the scenes.

During the recess, one of Chisem's staff members discreetly passed Julio a note that said, "Meet me." It gave an address and a time. That was all.

When the hearing re-convened, each Senator was given a certain amount of time to ask questions of the witness. Each took his turn, beginning with flattering, complimentary remarks, and ending with a rash of questions meant to discredit Julio. The only exception was Senator Chisem, who yielded his time to the next

Senator. The interrogators asked about Julio's background, his education, and his former work experience. They talked about his association with Dr. Ivan Berkowitz, who they characterized as a lunatic, mad professor and womanizer, distributing black and white pictures of Ivan Berkowitz leaving a hotel room with Betsy McFarland. They also distributed pictures of angry students pointing fingers at Ivan Berkowitz at a campus speaking engagement. The attack wore on.

Next, the questions turned specifically to the Environmental Council meeting at the United Nations. The Senators challenged Julio's authority to put forward such an initiative. They suggested that Julio's directive usurped the sovereign power of the government of the United States of America, the country he was supposed to be serving. They concluded their smear campaign by painting Julio as an inexperienced, token appointment by a progressive Democratic President. Without saying it, the impression the Senators tried to make was that Ambassador Masito was an unqualified choice for the job.

The Chairman of the Foreign Relations Committee summarized that Ambassador Masito had not acted in the best interests of the United States Government. The Chairman accused Julio of exercising poor judgement, that was negligent at best and seditious at worst. Julio was cautioned to remember those he was serving, and he was warned not to indulge in any further personal crusades, at the expense of the American people.

Having issued those staggering judgments, the Chairman then adjourned the hearing until the next day, when Ambassador Masito would give a response in his closing statements. At the conclusion of the interrogation, the Chairman asked each member of the Committee to please meet with him once again in his chambers.

It was only 1:30 in the afternoon. Julio pulled the note out of his pocket that had been handed to him by Senator Chisem's aid. Knowing that his career was in serious jeopardy, he saw no reason why he shouldn't see what this crumpled note was all about.

The note gave an address that appeared to be near Georgetown, but Julio didn't immediately recognize the place. Scribbled at the bottom was "3:30." That was all.

Julio's driver took one look at the address and said he knew where it was. It was the launch for the Georgetown rowing team, an interesting spot, right on the Potomac. Jogging trails along the water's edge were all that stood between the crews and the viewing stands. The scenery was spectacular...shells full of college oarsmen, straining their muscles in rhythm to the call of their coxswains, rowing up the river with graceful but powerful strokes, competing to be the fastest boat in the water.

Julio took a seat on the bleachers and watched the boats for a while. He had arrived a little bit ahead of 3:30, so that he could get acclimated. Julio wasn't sure who he'd be meeting, and he was slightly apprehensive. While there were occasional walkers and joggers heading up and down the trail, he was the only one sitting in the viewing stand. He checked his watch. It was 3:34, and he wondered if anyone would show at all. The only soul in sight was a lone jogger, dressed in a warm-up suit, and wearing a baseball cap. He emerged from the shadows underneath Key Bridge, and slowed his gait to a walk. As the runner caught his breath, he looked out into the water, before turning to face Julio. With a great sense of relief, he recognized Robert Chisem, the only friend Julio had that day in all of Washington.

The Senator from Arizona climbed the rows and took a seat. He started by saying how sorry he was to see Julio tangled up in all this mess, but he added, "You have to admit, Julio, you sorta asked for it this time."

Julio was glad to see him, and had to agree, "Yep. I've got nobody to blame, Robert...just me."

"Well, I can't exactly get you off the hot seat, but I can try to tell you what's going on behind closed doors."

"You know you don't have to do this for me."

"Hey, how many times have you bailed me out of a mess? This is the least I can do."

"Well, thanks."

"All right, here's the deal. Every time the Chairman recesses and calls the Committee members into chambers, he is taking the pulse of the American public. The chairmen of the Senate committees have always hired political consulting firms, who poll the public on an array of issues. But now the Senate has access to real-time polling. With the TV coverage this hearing is receiving, the viewing public can answer pollsters' questions with their remote control channel changers. There are several Washington-based consulting firms equipped to tabulate the responses, and transmit a summary report to their clients within minutes of the actual event. The report is faxed into the Chairman's office, and then projected onto a holographic screen."

"You're kidding?"

"Nope, I'm not kidding. And let me tell you, it changes the way we do things in government. Today the Chairman called for a recess right after you gave your opening statement, remember?"

"I remember."

"Well, the public was fairly fond of you, but your identification rating was low, so the Senators felt free to go after you without the public responding negatively. It gave the Senators a chance to play big shots on national TV. Get it?"

"Yeah."

"So guess what they did? They came back in there after the recess, and really tore into you."

"O.K. Robert. Now, what can I do to prevent it from happening tomorrow?"

"Just keep in mind that if you can drum up public sympathy for your actions, the Senators will be informed of that, and they will back off. If the public doesn't side with you, then the Committee will develop a wolf pack mentality, and devour you."

"All right, so where do I stand right now?"

"After the interrogation today, we were all called back into chambers to see how the public reacted. Interestingly enough, the statistics showed that the Senator's efforts to belittle you created a backlash of sympathy. The public said that while you are young and idealistic, you are thought to be terribly honest, a quality non-existent among politicians. The statistics indicated that nothing more than a reprimand is justified under the circumstances. But before you go celebrating, my friend, let me remind you that we have another day to go, and these polls can be very fickle. They aren't too different from the live or die wishes of the crowds at the Roman Coliseum during the gladiator days. So far, this crowd wants you to live, but be careful, my friend. Be careful."

With that, Senator Robert Chisem patted Julio on the knee and stepped down the rows of bleachers to the jogging trail. Julio thanked him for the advice just before the Senator started his run again heading up the river and disappearing around the bend. Julio sat there in the bleachers for at least another thirty minutes thinking of how he could put that information to good use.

ᛉ

The next morning when the hearing re-convened, Julio re-positioned the microphone on the table in front of him and said, "Mr. Chairman and distinguished members of this Senate Committee, I understand your concern as you expressed it to me yesterday afternoon, and I will not waste time defending myself in the face of your honored judgement. However, there are a few points I would like to make today, especially on behalf of my deceased friend, Dr. Ivan Berkowitz, who for obvious reasons cannot defend himself.

"First of all, I would like to refute all allegations intended to disparage the character of Dr. Berkowitz. Ms Betsy McFarland, shown yesterday in the pictures with Dr. Berkowitz, was the wife of Dr. Berkowitz's best friend, Dr. Nigel McFarland, whose life was also ended unexpectedly. For the record, let it be known that the relationship between Dr. Berkowitz and Ms McFarland can only be accurately described as a longstanding friendship. The pictures you have shown today depict the twosome traveling to Miami together to investigate the death of Betsy's husband. Let the record be clear on this for the sake of Ms Katrina Berkowitz and for the sake of Ms Betsy McFarland, two wonderful and dear women who have suffered enough by the murders of their husbands.

"The second point of defense I would like to make on behalf of Dr. Berkowitz regards this Committee's depiction of him as a mad, rebellious professor. Let me remind the Committee that Dr. Ivan Berkowitz was a well-respected, Nobel Prize-winning physicist...a brilliant scientist of the highest order. You have discredited him only because Dr. Berkowitz had repudiated the government's official positions on matters that involved his NASA responsibilities. I would like to make clear to this distinguished Committee why Dr. Berkowitz resigned his position from NASA and the Environmental Council.

"The conclusions that Dr. Berkowitz drew from his research led him to believe that the planet's upper atmosphere is becoming unstable, information that was edited from his reports to the Environmental Council by Lt. General Oliver Wakeman, and his political advisors. Dr. Berkowitz was, of course, frustrated and offended by the omissions, but privately he was able to communicate his concerns to me, off the record. These concerns were clearly stated in his book, *The Point of No Return*, published after he left NASA more than a year ago.

"Secondly, I submit this tape for the record." Julio reached inside his coat and pulled out a tape, which he handed over to the Committee. "Shortly before Dr. Berkowitz's resignation from NASA, he was approached by Senator Cheney, Chairman of the Senate Intelligence Committee, to discuss a matter which I believe is connected to the death of my friend."

The Chairman of the Foreign Relations Committee placed his hand over his microphone and began whispering to the Senator sitting next to him. He then quickly cut-off Ambassador Masito and called for an adjournment, so that the Committee members could review the tape privately before proceeding any further. The hearing abruptly ended, and was scheduled to re-convene the next day.

That evening in a Georgetown restaurant, Julio was eating alone. He was approached at his table by a young man in his mid-twenties. It was the same aid of Senator Chisem's that had given Julio the note that led to Julio's meeting with the Senator.

The young man spoke some kind words of introduction before leaving a folder on the table that he said was from the Senator. Julio thanked him for his trouble, and offered to buy the young man's dinner. The staff worker declined the invitation, saying he had to get back up on Capitol Hill. Senator Chisem was still at his office.

When the young man was gone, Julio opened the folder to read its contents. The folder contained real-time polling feedback from Julio's testimony earlier that morning. The information indicated two new trends: one, that the viewership was expanding rapidly, increasing the ratings of the channels that were broadcasting the hearing; and two, that Ambassador Julio Masito had dangled a teaser in front of the public that a major political scandal was on its way, and the public couldn't wait to find out more. The media would be in a frenzy by the time the hearing resumed.

The pages in the folder said one more thing. Senator Chisem had four security guards assigned to protect Julio as long as he remained in Washington. Julio's friend was concerned.

᙮᙮

The next morning, Ambassador Masito could hardly get through the crowd that blocked the way to the Senate room, where the hearing was being conducted. Every local network, five cable news companies, and numerous newspaper journalists were crammed into the under-sized room with their lights, cameras and microphones focused on Julio.

A message for Julio was presented on his arrival by the young staff worker for Senator Chisem. The message indicated that Julio's identification with the viewing public had soared, along with his popularity. Loyalty from the public was now a problem for any Senator intending to discredit or smear the Ambassador. The real-time polls had come to Julio's rescue.

᙮᙮

When the hearing resumed, Julio was allowed to continue reading his closing statement in accordance with procedural rules, uninterrupted by questions from the panel. He said a few kind words of greeting to the Chairman of the Committee, and to its distinguished members, before resuming his testimony.

"Senator Cheney tried to recruit Dr. Berkowitz, but he declined. Those of you who have heard the tape of that conversation realize that Senator Cheney was very alarmed about his situation — perhaps even concerned about his personal safety. He needed someone on the inside of NASA to keep him informed. Dr. Berkowitz decided that he would not be the Senator's informant, and so he resigned.

"At this time, Mr. Chairman, I would like to submit to the Committee one additional tape for the record. This tape is that of the last public speech that Dr. Berkowitz ever made. His speech ends at the moment of his death, but I think you will find that the motive behind the killing can be discovered somewhere between the Cheney tape and the Berkowitz tape. Dr. Berkowitz knew enough to be dangerous to the people who ordered his assassination.

"In closing, I would like to call for a special investigation into the death of my friend, Dr. Ivan Berkowitz. Furthermore, I would ask that the investigation include within its scope a complete review of NASA's activities, going back to those days when NASA first employed Lt. General Oliver Wakeman. The scope of the investigation should encompass NASA's finances, and the deaths of those persons referred to in the Cheney tape as the 'probe project team'. As Senator Cheney himself said, it is important that the American people learn who is behind this entire story."

CHAPTER 29

The Probe

Julio knew that the fallout caused by the tapes would be enormous. Once the special investigation had been completed, the venue of the hearing shifted to the Senate Judicial Committee. The Judicial Committee was mostly comprised of trial lawyers and judges, who were better qualified than the panel of Senators on the Foreign Relations Committee to conduct the high-stakes proceedings.

Julio's testimony before the Judicial Committee was the first in a series of testimonies that eventually led to Senator Cheney, and to Lt. General Oliver Wakeman. Nothing before had captured the attention of the American public like the NASA Probe, the media's new generic name given to the investigation of NASA and the related proceedings. According to the TV ratings, not even the daily soap operas could compete.

Several high profile officials had their careers on the line, if not their very lives. It became apparent over the many weeks that followed that many would go to jail for charges that ranged from perjury, to fraud, to murder. Following Senator Cheney's testimony, he resigned his position as Chairman of the Senate Intelligence Committee. But, testimony had largely pinned the responsibility for the NASA Probe on Wakeman, and now it was Wakeman's turn to speak.

Most people who knew Oliver Wakeman knew that his political skills and instincts were quite savvy. But during the hearing, Julio observed that Wakeman made the impression of a very stoic military officer. For days he appeared in full dress, giving the most minimal of responses to the Senators' questions. He made the impression that he was merely a good soldier, serving his country, and his Commander-In-Chief.

But, the TV news anchors who were following the proceedings commented that the scope of Wakeman's interrogation and testimony had advanced far beyond what they expected. The Republican Senators were now trying to probe into President Woodrow's knowledge of the scandal. Wakeman resisted their questions to the bitter end, but when confronted with murder and conspiracy charges, not even Wakeman could stand the heat.

ᚲᚲᚲ

For several weeks, Julio followed the NASA Probe on Court TV. He watched the monitor every day while he worked in his office at the United Nations. During the course of the proceedings, the special investigator confirmed that NASA had for years conducted unauthorized, unmanned exploratory missions. He confirmed the discovery of protozoan life preserved in the frozen ice samples taken from Europa. He confirmed the extermination of the probe project team; and most importantly in Julio's mind, the special investigator had successfully prosecuted the man responsible for their deaths. Oliver Wakeman was behind bars, awaiting criminal prosecution in the federal court system.

ᚲᚲᚲ

The next phase of the investigation focused upon the involvement of the White House in the cover-up. As testimony from White House staff members was taken, President Woodrow called

Ambassador Masito to the Oval Office for a private meeting. When Julio arrived in Washington, he was picked up at Langley Air Force Base by the Secret Service and taken to the White House. Before clearing security, Julio was scanned for weapons and recording devices, and then ushered in to meet with the President.

They talked for a while about foreign policy before the President got down to the real subject at hand. Woodrow began by saying that he had looked the other way when he learned that NASA was operating outside the boundaries Congress had approved. He looked the other way because it was the path of least resistance. He didn't want to stir up a hornet's nest that would damage himself and a few former Democratic Presidents who had helped Woodrow's career.

"I thought, at the time, that I couldn't afford a political scandal early in the life of my new administration," he said. The President stood and looked out the window. He was very subdued, to the point of being despondent. "Wakeman swore to me that he could keep a lid on all of this, so it seemed like I didn't have a choice but to go along. I didn't give a rat's ass about NASA or any of that bullshit, until this report appeared on my desk that said we had discovered some goddamn prehistoric ice fossils or some shit on one of Jupiter's moons. Then I knew that the lid was coming off, no matter what Wakeman said.

"Wakeman and I had a chat about the problem, and we decided that the exploration program had to be dismantled. That was it. Looking back, it was a poor choice of words on my part. We didn't discuss how the probe project team would be dismantled, only that it had to be done. Wakeman decided for himself that the best way to dismantle the team was to terminate its members. That was a unilateral action on his part. I had nothing to do with those deaths."

Julio interrupted the President to ask, "And what about Dr. Berkowitz? Did you decide that he had to be dismantled, as well?"

"Wakeman never discussed the Berkowitz problem with me. But by that time, Wakeman was totally out of control. To this day, Wakeman swears he had nothing to do with Berkowitz. And even if he did it, I couldn't have stopped him."

There was silence between the two that continued for some time. Then the President asked Julio a question, "Why, Ambassador Masito, have you come after me with this scandal? Just tell me why?"

The President was looking out the window again, with his back turned to Julio. Before he could answer, the Chief of Staff barged into the room. He announced to the President that Vice President Borland had been served with a subpoena.

The President sat down behind his desk and spun his chair around, so that once again, his back was turned to Julio and the Chief of Staff. As the two of them quietly exited the Oval Office, President Woodrow continued to stare out the window, his thoughts lost somewhere beyond the Rose Garden.

ᴡᴡᴡ

Julio returned to New York, wondering why President Woodrow had wanted to meet with him. It was an awkward meeting. It was almost like Goliath knew he would be slain by David, and he wanted to meet his nemesis before the show down on the battlefield.

Back in his office, Julio tuned in to Court TV to continue following the drama that was unfolding in front of the Senate Judicial Committee. Court TV's Nielsen ratings were sky high. Viewers had not been exposed to this level of political scandal since Watergate.

The anchor broadcaster for the network was interviewing a Republican advisor who was offering his opinion of the Democratic Vice President. Kendall Stewart Borland was described as a Texas Democrat whose family had made millions in the real estate market. They had acquired mortgages on commercial and multi-family properties at huge discounts from the Resolution Trust Corporation in the early 90s. The family's wealth enabled Borland to quit his job and run for office. His flamboyant campaign style suited Texans to a "T", and like so many wealthy Democrats, he stumped around the congressional district making

222

promises to the underclass that big government would level the economic playing field.

Borland's promises were enough to get him elected to Congress. After serving two terms as a Congressman, Borland ran successfully for U.S. Senator. President Woodrow took notice of him when he was campaigning for the presidency. Political polls indicated that American females were attracted to Borland's flamboyant style. The polls also indicated that Woodrow needed to strengthen his popularity with the female sector of the electorate. Nothing else mattered. Borland was chosen as Woodrow's running mate.

Julio looked up from his desk and saw Borland take the oath and sit in the witness chair, surrounded by a host of attorneys. The Vice President spent the next hour reading excerpts from his written opening statement, proclaiming that he had not done a thing wrong, nor did he have knowledge of anyone who had.

When testimony resumed the next day, Borland was asked to give quite a bit of detail about his past, questions that led to his relationships with his largest campaign contributors. According to testimony, Vice President Borland had a vast war chest of political action committee money. He also had served on the Board of Directors of a major Texas-based aerospace/defense contracting company, prior to his election to Congress. After assuming public office, Borland's father took over the seat on the aerospace/defense contractor's Board. It was disclosed that over half of the company's revenues came from unspecified sales to NASA, and the balance was made up of rocket component and testing equipment sales to the Air Force, for their fleet of intercontinental ballistic missiles.

The Vice President's testimony was interrupted by a request to call Oliver Wakeman, once again, to the witness chair. He was ushered into the room by guards, since he was in the custody of prison officials.

Wakeman wasted little time in naming an executive officer of the Texas aerospace/defense company who had been his supplier over the years. He testified that all of the component parts for the exploratory probes had been made by this Texas company. Viewers had little difficulty associating the Vice President with the problem.

Wakeman's testimony was then followed by that of the executive, who specifically confirmed that Kendall Borland had knowledge that the component parts were being used in an unauthorized, unmanned exploratory probe project that had continued at NASA for years.

🟆🟆🟆

It was highly unusual for a President of the United States to give testimony. Executive privilege was their escape. But with the Vice President in jeopardy, Woodrow thought that he was left with little chance of survival unless he pleaded his own case. With Woodrow preparing to testify, the public was held hostage to their televisions. The NASA Probe had become the talk of every household in America, and throughout much of the world.

Julio had learned to get his work done, even though the television stayed on in his office almost all day long. Now it was Woodrow's turn in the barrel, and Julio wanted to watch it all.

After receiving the oath, President Woodrow delivered his opening statement: "Mr. Chairman and distinguished members of this Senate Judicial Committee, today I appear before you to testify on my own behalf, and on behalf of the American people. I want this Committee and the American people to know that I have always tried to serve the best interests of the American people, though some of you might accuse me of particularly serving the interests of those who voted me into office.

"In my judgement, every conscious action or omission that has fallen to my charge of responsibility has been decided upon in the favor of the American public taken as a whole. As your President and Commander-in-Chief, such decisions have not always been easy decisions, and in hindsight, I certainly would decide differently today if faced with the same information that this distinguished body now possesses. But often, we are not given the opportunity to change directions. And let me be perfectly

224

clear...saying that I would do things differently is not an admission of guilt. It is only a re-evaluation of circumstances and outcomes.

"Today, I will give an account of my decisions which relate to this particular hearing. I am prepared to lay out the circumstances which surrounded those decisions, in so far as those circumstances directly affected my decision. I am not prepared to delve into such circumstances for the purpose of drawing any other persons into this judicial arena. I am the President of the United States. I am ultimately responsible for actions taken by the Executive Branch of our government. When this hearing is over, I hope you and the American people will know that I have served and will continue to serve this country with all of my heart, with all my soul, and to the very best of my ability. At all times I have acted in accordance with both the spirit and the letter of the oath of my office."

Following the President's opening comments, the brief recess that normally followed was waived. The Chairman of the Judicial Committee went straight forward with the interrogation, calling on the distinguished Republican Senator from Virginia to lead the questioning.

"Mr. President, thank you for being here with us on Capitol Hill this morning, and let me be the first to say that we all regret the circumstances which require your testimony.

"Mr. President, as you know, we have heard from a multitude of witnesses, which all started with the testimony of Ambassador Julio Masito. Hopefully, we are near the conclusion of these proceedings, and soon, we will all put these trying times behind us.

"Perhaps an appropriate starting place today would be to pick up the testimony of Senator Cheney, the former Chairman of the Senate Intelligence Committee, who testified that he had knowledge of the NASA military probes prior to your election as President. Let me refer you, Mr. President, to page 363 of Senator Cheney's written testimony, and then, if you would, Mr. President, please tell this Committee of the first occasion when you personally learned that NASA was operating beyond the legislative and budgetary constraints imposed upon NASA by Congress."

Before Woodrow could speak, his attorney reached across the President to cover the microphone with his hand. The counselor whispered some words of advice to the President, as he thumbed through the lengthy text of Cheney's testimony that was before him. The attorney then slid the document in front of the President, and opened it to the page referred to by the Senator from Virginia. It appeared that the President cut his own lawyer off in mid-sentence, when Woodrow finally cleared his throat, and spoke into the microphone. He seemed impatient to get on with this dreadful and unavoidable day. The President was ready to testify.

After the first day of Woodrow's testimony, the public perceived Woodrow as just another fallible politician. But a majority of viewers felt that he should have exposed the entire illegal operation immediately upon learning of its existence. That had been the President's flaw in the public's mind, at least through the first day of testimony. So far, it all seemed to be forgivable, and that was exactly the perception that Woodrow's attorney wanted the public to have at this stage of the game.

On the second day, the panel of interrogators took a step further, asking Woodrow about his relationship with Oliver Wakeman. The testimony of several White House aids had confirmed that Wakeman had met several times with the President, and the first of the meetings had occurred at or about the same time as the Europa discovery. According to previous testimony, meetings between Wakeman and Woodrow continued over the following months as the covert probe project team began to disappear.

At the end of the second day, the public's judgement was more harsh. They strongly suspected Woodrow's direct involvement in the cover-up. The second day was not a good one for Woodrow.

On the third day the President's testimony continued: "Senator, at that point in time, and to the best of my knowledge, I do not recall learning of any Europa discovery. My meetings with Lt. General Oliver Wakeman were for informational purposes only, and he typically would inform me about issues that related to NASA's realm of responsibility. I only assumed that NASA was operating within the boundaries of its charter."

"Mr. President," interrupted the Republican Senator from the State of Missouri. "I believe that your previous testimony, and the testimony from Senator Cheney, has already established that you had been informed long before these meetings with Wakeman that NASA was operating outside of its charter. I believe that you said earlier that you looked the other way so as not to involve your predecessors. Let me remind you, Mr. President, that you are under oath, and if you would like to amend your testimony in any way, please do so at this time."

The President was flustered. He seemed to have lost his composure, at least momentarily, and he adjusted his posture in his chair before whispering something to his attorney. Then he continued, "Yes, Senator, thank you for pointing out what might appear to be a discrepancy in my testimony. But let me be very clear about this whole matter that you have raised. Wakeman and I never discussed any unofficial business. While Cheney had disclosed to me the NASA problem, I certainly didn't want to know any more about it, feeling that it could only be a can of worms. In hindsight, I should not have stuck my head in the sand on this matter, but that is exactly what I did. My meetings with Wakeman had nothing to do with Europa."

The Chairman of the Committee then interrupted the President and called for a recess. He said that when testimony resumed, the Senate Judicial Committee would hear the testimony of a special witness, Ms Shirley Hawkins, the President's own secretary. After making the unexpected announcement, Woodrow's attorney pulled the microphone in front of himself so that he could speak on behalf of his client.

"Mr. Chairman, I object to this inclusion of testimony from a witness that has not been identified to us or and has not been deposed by the special investigator. If this testimony is allowed, then I request a lengthy recess following the testimony of my client, so that we might have ample time to review it before continuing."

"Yes, Counselor, I understand. We will hear the testimony of Ms Hawkins, and your request for a break afterward is granted."

With that, the Chairman pounded his gavel and the hearing recessed.

When the hearing resumed, Ms Shirley Hawkins stood to be sworn-in, and then she took her seat, facing the panel of Senators with a great deal of poise. She knew them all, and they all knew her as the Chief Executive's gatekeeper. Knowing that she could make or break their access to the President, every one of the panelists had paid homage to her at one time or another. On this day, it would be no different. Once again, she was their access to the President.

The Senator from Texas was the first to address her, "If you don't mind, Ms Hawkins, please tell us a little bit about yourself: where you are from, where you went to school, how you came to Washington, who you have worked for...that sort of thing, Ms Hawkins."

Shirley gave an account of herself as though she were interviewing for a new position. She was very professional in her delivery, and by the time she finished, everyone in the country wanted to offer her a job. The Senator from Texas continued,

"Now Ms Hawkins, you mentioned that your family had moved around quite a bit when you were growing up, like most military families. But you did say that you spent most of your high school years in Huntsville, Alabama, where your father worked at Redstone Arsenal. Is that right Ms Hawkins?"

"Not exactly, Senator. My real father died in Vietnam, when I was an infant. I was raised by my step-father."

"So, your step-father then took responsibility for you when you were quite young, and for all intents and purposes, would you say your step-father provided for you well, and took care of your family when you were growing up?"

"Yes, Senator. He was a wonderful man, and I thought of him

always as my daddy, even though we didn't share last names."

"And where is your step-father based today, Ms Hawkins? Is he still at Redstone Arsenal in Huntsville, Alabama?"

Shirley Hawkins lowered her head when she answered, "No, sir, Senator. My step-father is dead."

"Ms Hawkins, I know this is terribly painful for you, but please tell the Judicial Committee what happened to your step-father.

"Many years ago, my step-father moved from Huntsville to Houston, Texas. I didn't go with them, because I was already living in D.C. at the time. Dad told me he had been transferred to Houston to work on a NASA-related military project, but he never discussed the details with me. It was top secret. He called it a 'black project', which meant nobody could know about it. Anyway, I never discussed it with anyone, not even the President. We never discussed personal matters anyway.

"My step-father has been dead now for just over a year. He died of some very rare viral disease that killed him in less than five days. They cremated his body before an autopsy could be performed, saying that it had to be done for the sake of public safety, and to minimize the risk of the virus spreading. His death caught me totally by surprise.

"Just before he died, Lt. General Oliver Wakeman from NASA had been meeting with the President. I noticed each time he came in that he was extremely reserved in his conversation, and he rarely spoke to me other than to give his name and the time of his appointment. After Dad died, I finally decided to ask the Lt. General if he knew my step-father, although I did not tell him that we were related in any way. Wakeman said he was sorry, but he had never met or heard of such a person. That is when I knew that something was wrong, and I began listening to his conversations with the President."

Following the completion of Shirley Hawkins' testimony, the President's counsel asked for a recess. They argued behind closed doors for an hour and a half whether they should call Oliver

Wakeman back to the stand. Woodrow emphatically denied, even to his own counsel, that the conversations referred to in Shirley Hawkins' testimony ever took place between Wakeman and him. The problem was that Wakeman was the only witness who could repudiate the testimony of Shirley Hawkins.

The President's counsel knew Wakeman was being held on murder charges, and they didn't want to risk the President being implicated by Wakeman in those crimes. It was a no win situation for Woodrow, so counsel decided to let Ms Hawkins testimony stand without opposition. It would simply have to be the President's word against hers.

When President Woodrow's testimony resumed, he maintained his innocence with regard to every point raised by Shirley Hawkins' testimony. It appeared to Julio, who had been watching most of the proceedings on television, that the President and the Vice President were not going to surrender to the Republicans, no matter what. This would be a fight to the bitter end.

CHAPTER 30

The Election

When the dust settled, history had been made. Never before had both the President and Vice President of the United States of America been jointly impeached. According to the Constitution, the Speaker of the House was the next in line to take over the Executive Branch of government, and so the White House was turned over to the Republicans.

The Speaker of the House was Congressman Rus Hamilton from a small town in South Carolina. According to the polls, he was considered to be one of the most staunchly conservative members of the Republican Party. His career had been built on muckraking the Democrats, and there was no one in Congress whom the Democrats despised more. Partisan politics had never been uglier. When Speaker Rus Hamilton was sworn into office as the President of the United States, the entire city of Washington was in turmoil. As a peacekeeping gesture, his first executive order was to grant a full pardon to both James Harrison Woodrow and Kendall Stewart Borland.

☛☛☛

As quickly as ex-President Woodrow had fallen from grace, Ambassador Julio Masito began his rise to stardom. The media loved him, and so did the public, but none loved him more than his peers at the United Nations. Diplomats from all around the world were awed by the mystique of this young Indian, who, at least in their minds, had single-handedly deposed an American President. They almost worshipped him.

Julio was besieged by calls from publicists trying to schedule him on TV talk shows. All the attention he was getting made it difficult for him to return to his professional routine, and impossible to have a normal personal life. Nothing was the same.

Back in New York at the United Nations, Julio was being watched very carefully by the newly-appointed Secretary of State, and his administrative assistants or 'watch-dogs'. They were keeping Julio on a very short leash, making him submit written reports to D.C. on every action taken. He was buried by the bureaucracy, who wanted to make sure that he didn't have enough time to think for himself. They took away any chance at creativity, forcing him to follow policy and procedure every step of the way.

But the State Department could not control everything. Sadly, the Secretary-General of the U.N. had a debilitating cerebral hemorrhage. The stroke was not fatal, but it forced his sudden retirement. The General Assembly had to replace him. When the votes were counted, the overwhelming majority had cast their vote for Julio Masito, chosen to lead the United Nations as its new Secretary-General.

☛☛☛

The inauguration of Secretary-General Julio Masito was elaborate by any measure, and well-attended by heads of state from all over the world. He relinquished his job as the U.S. Ambassador, and no longer reported to the State Department. Now Julio could cast-off the yoke of his former bosses. He was free to speak his

☛

mind. He was free to lead. It was his turn at last.

The media followed Julio everywhere he went, elevating his stature with sensational stories. They portrayed him as a miracle worker. People began to believe that this man could actually lead humanity in a new direction. Soon after taking office, Julio once again pulled out his wish list, and called a meeting with the chairmen of the various U.N. committees. He outlined his agenda for them all, building a consensus among the leadership that he hoped would eventually translate into grassroots support for change.

When the time was right, Julio addressed the General Assembly in a televised broadcast that was seen by the whole world. Most viewers who watched the new Secretary-General became excited by his call for change, although many were unnerved. When he concluded his address, Julio announced that he would embark on a world-wide goodwill tour to spread his message of peace, hope, understanding and harmony. He came across as more of a spiritual leader than a politician, and the world celebrated his arrival.

ⵣⵣ

Invitations from nations all over the world poured into Julio's office, each hoping that the Secretary-General would visit them on his tour. He had to plan his itinerary very carefully to maximize the impact and effectiveness of his mission. Among his many invitations was a letter from the Pope, inviting Julio to visit the Vatican. It was an elegant invitation, handwritten by the Pope himself. Julio rubbed the thickness of the elaborately embossed stationary, weighing the pros and cons of accepting the invitation. Julio knew that he had more than politics to discuss with the Pope.

For centuries, the office of the Pope had been the most powerful on the planet; but now, Julio was beginning to run a close second, and was closing the gap. The trend analysis of most media companies indicated that Julio's star was still rising, while the Pope's stature was embattled by all the controversy that came with being in charge of an inflexible institution in a changing world. In fact, the Church seemed to have fallen into a state of turmoil, divided over various social, theological and political issues. And to those on the inside of the Church, the trouble was much deeper.

For years, Vatican insiders had heard rumors of evidence which could potentially undermine the Church's authority. The rumors had been suppressed, but yet they persisted, causing doubt and disillusionment to spread among certain members of the Church's clergy. Debates on the subject were disallowed. Dissenting clergy were ex-communicated. Sympathetic resignations were prolific. The Church seemed to be on the brink of breaking apart.

The Pope couldn't afford to be overtaken in popularity by the newly elected Secretary-General of the United Nations. The Pope was attempting a show of solidarity, but Julio wasn't quite ready. An agenda needed to be negotiated. Maybe then a meeting with the Pope could be arranged.

CHAPTER 31

The Emissary

Julio decided to write the Pope a polite letter of regret, suggesting that a preliminary business meeting be arranged with an emissary. The letter explained that a highly publicized meeting between the Pope and himself would be premature, if certain matters of mutual importance were not reviewed beforehand. Julio imagined that his letter would not be well-received. He wondered if the Pope would respond to his letter at all.

At the Pope's instruction, a meeting between Secretary-General Masito and the Pope's emissary was scheduled at the offices of St. Patrick's Cathedral in New York City. On the day of the meeting, Julio was met at the front door by a priest who ushered the Secretary-General to the rear of the sanctuary. They turned through some doors that separated the Church's offices from the public areas of the Cathedral. The priest asked the Secretary-General to please have a seat, and to make himself comfortable. The

Cardinal would be with him shortly. Almost as soon as Julio sat down, a very formally dressed clergyman appeared, introducing himself as Cardinal Marciano Angelico, the Pope's appointed emissary. Julio had never seen or heard of Cardinal Angelico before. All Julio knew was that Angelico was the Pope's man.

The two went into a private conference room and closed the door. While they were getting acquainted, the Cardinal seemed interested to learn all that he could about Julio. He wanted to know what it had been like to grow up on the Hopi Indian Reservation. The Cardinal contrasted the experience with his own upbringing in the Catholic Church. Eventually they compared liturgy as it related to Hopi religious ceremony versus that of the Roman Catholic Church. It was a non-confrontational, pleasant beginning that Julio found quite interesting. Both men discovered more similarities than either originally presumed. But, of course, there were some very distinct differences as well.

When it was time to move on to other topics of conversation, the emissary asked Julio one final question to conclude their ecumenical discussion. "So, Mr. Secretary-General, given your cultural, social and religious background, please tell me what you think of Christ?"

Julio answered the question without hesitation, "I believe that Jesus of Nazareth understood exactly who he was, a human who recognized that his humanity was divine. But I also believe that the Church, long ago, put an exclusive spin on the written account of the life of Jesus, leaving the Church's followers dependent upon the Church to interpret the written words."

The Cardinal gave Julio a hostile look, but he did not interrupt the Secretary-General. Julio continued, "This dependency has blocked, in my opinion, the Church's followers from making the same discovery that Jesus made. By offering its followers life after death, the Church shifted the focus of its followers to a future promise, and away from our present responsibilities. The Church has not helped us define who we are, and what our purpose might be. I believe that Jesus understood his identity and purpose very clearly. Jesus, in my view, recognized that he was connected to

All. I believe that Jesus of Nazareth rebelled against institutions that blocked the Way, and for that he was killed."

Cardinal Angelico gave an apologetic response in defense of the Church's theological views concerning the Christ. Then the Cardinal asked Julio another question, "What do you mean when you use the phrase, 'the Way'?"

"According to the Church and its scripture, Jesus used the phrase himself when he said, 'I am the Way...'. Hopi Indians also use the expression to describe their religious journey. They call this the Hopi Way. But when I personally refer to the Way, it means to me the Way for all people...the path of responsibility. I think this is the same meaning that Jesus implied. I believe that Christian literature best describes the Way in *The Sermon On The Mount*."

Cardinal Angelico was impressed with Julio's familiarity with the subjects that they had been discussing, but both of these men knew that they were not meeting for the purpose of discussing theology.

Julio steered the conversation back toward his youth, back to his college years. He told the Cardinal about meeting a Jesuit University professor named Dr. Nigel McFarland, an archeologist who spearheaded a dig on the Hopi Reservation. The Cardinal listened. Julio continued the saga, telling of his trip to Istanbul with Dr. McFarland the following summer.

The story went on. Julio mentioned the discovery that had been made, and brought back to their sponsor, Mr. Joseph Baldone, a prominent businessman from Chicago. Julio then told the Cardinal that later on, he learned that Dr. McFarland had discovered more than what was returned to Mr. Baldone.

"Dr. McFarland also discovered a set of manuscripts that he brought back for himself. These papyrus scrolls turned out to be a collection of early Christian gospels, along with a couple of other documents written during the early Christian period."

The Cardinal was sitting on the edge of his chair.

"Dr. McFarland worked on translating these manuscripts for years, but unfortunately his life ended before he could publicize his findings. His findings differed considerably from the gospel texts that were canonized by the Church. He knew his discovery would cause quite a stir among the establishment. In fact, I remember him saying 'controversial' would be a gross understatement.

"But before there was any controversy at all, Dr. McFarland supposedly committed suicide. In fact, soon after Dr. McFarland's death, his wife received a million dollar life-time annuity from the Church, if only she would not contest a mysteriously amended will that named the Church as the beneficial recipient of the Constantine Papers.

"For twelve years, the Church has found a way to keep the Constantine Papers buried. I imagine that they are too great a threat to the Church's authority to be released to the public."

Cardinal Angelico's mouth seemed to have gotten very dry, and so had Julio's. They paused for a moment, while the Cardinal stepped out of the conference room, and asked the priest if he would please bring them both something to drink. When he returned to the conference room and got settled once again, Julio went on.

"This whole story probably makes no sense to you. Over the years, have you ever heard of the Constantine Papers?" Julio asked.

"No, no, never," the emissary responded.

"Well, perhaps you should tell this story to the Pope and ask him this question. Ask him if he has ever heard of the Constantine Papers. I would like to hear his answer. If the answer remains a mystery, then I suggest you begin your inquiry starting with Monsignor Thomas Bates in Northshore, Indiana, or perhaps he is now Bishop Bates. It's been several years since I have seen him. Anyway, I would like to hear back from you on this if you don't mind. You see, Dr. Nigel McFarland was a very dear friend of mine."

The emissary made a note of the Secretary-General's request.

Then Julio continued. "There are other issues we need to discuss. If I may change the subject, the first order of business that I want to pose to the Church regards the state of our environment. You are probably wondering what in the world does the environment have to do with the Church."

Cardinal Angelico looked perplexed.

"Well, I'll try to explain," Julio continued. "As I understand it, the Church has always held that God created man and that man was given dominion over all other creatures. This, in fact, is stated in the book of *Genesis*, the first chapter, verses twenty-six through twenty-eight. Now, please let me get to the point of all this. Our environment is in serious jeopardy, and so are we. I firmly believe that we have made a mess of our responsibility regarding the environment, whether one believes in the *Genesis* version of creation or not.

"The Church must do more to move us away from the brink of self-destruction. The Church should begin to emphasize this question of responsibility. The Pope can help with this.

"The second order of business that we should discuss is the Church's resistance to change. New information forces us to periodically re-examine our world views. The Church must do more to help its followers understand these changes. For the most part, it would seem that the Church has chosen to simply ignore these changes. But these changes cannot be ignored. The Europa discovery is only an example of what will follow. Eventually, humanity might become even further removed from center stage in the theater of the universe. The Church must help its followers understand. The Pope can help them make the transition."

The Cardinal was only listening, playing his role as messenger to the Pope.

"Tell the Pope that I need his help. Tell him that perhaps the two of us can make a difference.

"And tell the Pope one more thing. Please tell him that if he chooses not to budge...if he refuses to help me...then tell him I am prepared to lead the world alone. If he stands in my way, then I am prepared to release a copy of the Constantine Papers into the global PC network. Pandora's Box will be opened."

Cardinal Angelico was speechless. Julio was the first to stand, extending his hand to the Cardinal, thanking him for coming to visit, and thanking him for serving as emissary to the Pope. Before letting go of the Cardinal's hand, Julio looked him in the eye and said, "Tell the Pope that I would love to meet with him, but let me hear back from you first."

Angelico only said, "I will tell him," and then he turned to leave.

CHAPTER 32

The Frame

Julio never heard back from Cardinal Angelico or the Pope. Julio felt certain that the Pope knew about the Constantine Papers, and he assumed that no news from the Pope meant that the Church was coming after him next. He made arrangements for the diskettes of the Constantine Papers, and Mac's diary, entitled the Istanbul Project, to be released to the public through the Internet. Julio's standing instructions said the diskettes would be released only if he was harmed in any way.

He penned his second letter to the Pope, stating the terms of this arrangement, hoping that it would discourage the Church from interfering in the work that Julio had to tackle alone. He was afraid that if he released the Constantine Papers now, he wouldn't have a means to hold the Church in check.

When the Pope received the letter, he was incensed. He called for the head of Vatican Intelligence, Cardinal Marciano Angelico.

The Pope told Cardinal Angelico that the Secretary-General was blackmailing the Church with this empty threat. "Unless he can produce more than a copy of some diskette that contains translation work of documents that do not exist, he has nothing. The public will not respond unless he can produce the originals...and that he cannot do.

"We must find a way to discredit the Secretary-General before he tries to discredit us. I want you to find a way, Cardinal Angelico. Tell me when you have an answer. We must defend the Church's honor, in the name of God."

"Yes, your Holiness."

꒰꒰꒰

Cardinal Angelico instructed his staff to ascertain what they could about the Secretary-General, but nothing new was discovered that might achieve the desired results. After working on the assignment for weeks to no avail, the Pope called a frustrated Angelico back to his quarters and said to him, "Our prayers have been answered. We have found a way."

"Please tell me, your Holiness. I have not been able to find a weakness."

"The Lord tramples His enemies, Cardinal. That is what we must do to Julio Masito. I have asked Cardinal Ruffino, our Vatican banker, to join this meeting so that he can explain what must be done."

Cardinal Angelico heard footsteps in the vestibule. He stood to greet the banker, wondering what scheme had been plotted against the Hopi Indian. After speaking to Cardinal Angelico, Cardinal Ruffino kneeled to kiss the hand of the Pope, before taking his seat.

The Pope began the meeting by saying, "The Lord has called the three of us to fight a holy war. What is said here today must remain in sworn secrecy in the name of Christ. Is this understood by each of you?"

In unison they replied, "Yes, your Holiness."

Then, at the Pope's direction, Cardinal Ruffino took charge of the discussion. He told Cardinal Angelico that recently, he had been approached by a high ranking Swiss bank officer responsible for managing the Vatican's huge deposits and investments at the bank. For years, the Swiss banker had shared privileged information with the Vatican, in exchange for the generous deposits. Upon request, the Vatican had access to a listing of all numbered bank accounts, and their related authorized signature cards. Information for money was their quid pro quo.

Cardinal Ruffino opened a folder that contained several documents, including photocopies of a numbered account set-up form, the authorized signature card, and a copy of recent bank account statements. The Cardinal leaned forward toward the Pope's chair with a magnifying glass in hand, and asked him to look at the signature on the card. It was the signature of Shirley Hawkins, the former secretary of ex-President James Harrison Woodrow.

The Pope gleamed a smile, and passed the folder and magnifying glass to Cardinal Angelico. Then Cardinal Ruffino went on. "We have traced the flow of funds to an account of the Republican Party, and have reason to believe that Senator Cheney, the former Republican head of the Senate Intelligence Committee, was the mastermind behind the impeachment of President Woodrow. He lost his job in the aftermath, but my guess is that he got well-paid for his troubles, if the balance in Ms Hawkins' account is any indication. Anyway, now that we have evidence that the American government has been defrauded, we must decide how to use this information to our best interest, so to speak."

The Vatican banker gloated over his cloak and dagger discovery. He paused to allow the Pope to respond.

"You are saying that the trail leads to Senator Cheney?"

"Yes, your Holiness."

"Might the trail lead to our adversary, the Secretary-General?"

"It might, your Holiness. Let me work on it a little longer."

"Yes, take your time if you must, but please, see what you can come up with."

Cardinal Angelico couldn't believe what he had just heard. The Pope had just asked Cardinal Ruffino to falsify the evidence so that it led to his enemy. He wondered what the difference was between a holy war and any other.

Cardinal Angelico cringed the next time he was called into conference with the Pope and Cardinal Ruffino. He knew that he would be asked to play a role in all of this. The banker had already played his. This time, Ruffino brought a new folder to the meeting that he pushed across the table to Cardinal Angelico. The folder contained a road map to the demise of Julio Masito. While thumbing through it, Cardinal Angelico became frightened, but he couldn't show it. The folder said that the Church could get to anybody, if only they wanted to.

When Angelico closed the folder and placed it back on the table, the Pope said to him, "Now, Cardinal Angelico, it is your turn. I want you to arrange a meeting with James Woodrow. You tell him the good news. Tell him that he will be President, again."

CHAPTER 33

The Arrest

In Washington, the Republicans launched a legislative assault on the Democrats, from the moment Woodrow left office. President Rus Hamilton would propose a new bill with his congressional cronies standing by his side on national TV, and the Republican-led Congress would rubber stamp it.

There wasn't much the Democrats could do to prevent it other than filibuster, but that wasn't very effective. The Democrats were being strong-armed. The only meaningful check and balance that had existed between the Executive Branch and the Legislative Branch of government had been Woodrow's ability to line-item veto the bills that were sent to the White House to be signed into law. But ever since his departure, it appeared that the White House had simply become the new residence of the Speaker of the House, not the residence of the President of the United States.

The public sensed this deterioration in the separation of power, and responded in short order. At first, the poor and the young were the only visible dissenters. On TV talk shows across America, the Republicans simply dismissed these voices of protest as non-productive elements of society, and therefore, unworthy of a voice in government. But the reaction to that attitude was swift and strong. Riots began in the urban areas, particularly in those where major colleges or universities were located. The Republicans got the message loud and clear, and they made efforts to pacify those who had been offended. But the college students were the only ones who accepted their apology. The poor had nothing to lose, so they kept on burning and looting.

James Harrison Woodrow had almost slipped into obscurity, returning to his hometown of Jefferson City, Missouri. He announced to the public that he was planning to write his memoirs. His press agent continued to maintain his client's innocence in the media, but Woodrow absolutely refused to make public appearances.

Occasionally, he had to get out of the house, and one day when he was returning to his car with a sack of groceries, a young man dressed in a black suit and a white collar approached Woodrow in the parking lot. Secret Service agents jumped out of a parked car to stand between the man and Woodrow. The clergyman introduced himself as Father Frank Seeley, the most senior representative of the Roman Catholic Church in Jefferson City.

He had a letter to give to the ex-President, which was intercepted by the Secret Service agents, briefly examined, and then handed to Woodrow. The Father gave the agents a business card to hand to Woodrow as well, and then he turned to leave. Woodrow thanked him, and then ducked into his car and headed home.

The envelope from the Vatican was very formal in design and printed on very high quality, richly textured paper. Curiosity made him want to tear the letter open and read it, but he thought that perhaps he should wait until he was alone, given the peculiar method of delivery. He stuck the letter in his jacket pocket.

Once he was inside his office at home, he opened the letter and read its contents. It was a letter from Cardinal Marciano Angelico, the emissary of the Pope, asking for a meeting with the ex-President. The letter suggested that they meet at St. Patrick's Cathedral in New York City, and several potential dates were suggested that might be convenient to Mr. Woodrow. The letter ended by saying,

"Information vital to your political future has come to the attention of the Vatican. This information could reverse the events that resulted in your ouster from office. Please agree to meet at your earliest possible convenience. Confirmation of an appointment date should be communicated through Father Franklin Seeley, in Jefferson City, Missouri. I look forward to meeting you.
Cardinal Marciano Angelico,
Emissary to Pope Pius XIII"

Woodrow was confounded by the inferences in the letter. He thought that the intrigue warranted checking out, so he selected a date to meet with the Cardinal. What the hell, he thought to himself, I've got nothing to lose.

At the appointed hour, Woodrow and his Secret Service agents walked in the front door of St. Patrick's on Fifth Avenue, just like the twenty-five tourists that stood in front of him. A few of them recognized Woodrow, and one guy spun around and took a flash picture, temporarily blinding the ex-President. The Secret Service agents were beside themselves, totally uncomfortable that very few security arrangements had been made beforehand with the Church. Woodrow told them to relax. Nobody, he said, was interested in killing an impeached President.

Once the crowd in front of Woodrow cleared out of his way, a priest came forward and introduced himself. He led Woodrow and his entourage to the same offices that Cardinal Angelico had used when he first met with Secretary-General Masito. The ex-President was ushered into a conference room and the doors were closed behind him, leaving the Secret Service agents in the reception area.

Inside the conference room, Woodrow marveled at the appointments. The old wood molding and the paintings were very beautiful. In fact, the wealth of treasures that existed throughout Catholic churches all over the world was awesome, he thought to himself.

In that instant, his thoughts were interrupted by the opening of the door, and the entrance of Cardinal Angelico. Woodrow stood to introduce himself, amazed by the clerical garb that adorned the Cardinal. Although more sanctimonious than valiant, his appearance wasn't unlike that of a highly-decorated, five-star general in full dress, exuding power and authority. Woodrow became confident that the Church was not fooling around, that this meeting would be of a very serious nature. He decided to remain passive, content to let the Cardinal tell him what this was all about.

"Thank you, Mr. President, for troubling yourself to meet with me. As I mentioned in my letter, there are some very important matters that we must discuss that concern you. If you don't mind, I would like get right down to business by taking the next few minutes to tell you why you have been contacted."

"Please, go right ahead. I have become very curious."

"What I am going to share with you is extremely confidential. The information that we have will eventually find its way to the public, all in due course. But you must not reveal to anyone that the Catholic Church was a source of this information. It would be very dangerous."

"That goes without saying," Woodrow replied, although he felt a little uncomfortable with the Cardinal's mention of danger.

"Not long ago, Vatican Intelligence became aware that a numbered bank account was opened for the benefit of Ms Shirley Hawkins."

Woodrow's mouth fell open.

"The flow of funds to the account has been very difficult to trace, but it appears that an international political organization that supports a world government is behind the bribe that was paid to Ms Hawkins. We believe that the villain that stands behind your impeachment is the Secretary-General of the United Nations, Julio Masito."

Woodrow was momentarily speechless. He tried to maintain his poise. Then, with as much composure as he could muster, he asked, "What was his motive? Why would he be better served by Rus Hamilton?"

"If you had been successful in removing him from office, his plans couldn't be executed."

"Does the Church have any proof of this?"

"We think so. But, remember, the Church cannot involve itself in these matters, at least not openly. The burden of discovery and proof will be yours. But I can help you find what you will need."

Woodrow was astounded. He didn't know where to begin. The Cardinal volunteered to get him started.

"Here is a file that contains all of the bank information confirming what I have told you. Questions will come up along the way. If you need me, then tell Father Seeley and a meeting will be arranged. When you are ready, we will help you launch your counterattack in the media. Just say when."

In less than a month, James Harrison Woodrow was ready to begin the fight for the White House. His return to power would be unprecedented. Just before initiating a media blitz, he called Father Seeley to set up a meeting with Angelico.

Woodrow's second meeting with Cardinal Angelico was brief. They discussed timing, resources, contacts, and witnesses. When the meeting adjourned, Woodrow was confident that his office would be restored. Everything had fallen into place. As he shook Cardinal Angelico's hand in gratitude, the Cardinal said, "Tomorrow, your adversary will make headlines in the American newspapers. It will be a minor incident, but a good place to start your campaign. Good luck, Mr. President."

The next day, photographs were taken of a bunch of jailed young hoodlums who firebombed a Federal building in downtown Washington. They told reporters that they wanted to overthrow the U.S. Government. None of them were citizens of the

U.S., they were all under eighteen years of age, and none of them were carrying green cards. They claimed that their leader was Julio Masito. In jail, they chanted his name over and over again...Julio MASITO! Julio MASITO! The press had a field day.

Julio was very upset by the coverage, and he vehemently denied any association with the group. He characterized them as misdirected, uninformed and criminal. But as the weeks wore on, similar disturbances continued to occur across the country, and there was nothing Julio could do to stop it.

In the meantime, Julio noticed through the media that James Harrison Woodrow was beginning to make public appearances all over America. He was delivering the same populist speeches that had gotten him elected twice before, except this time he wasn't running for office. Julio decided to follow Woodrow in the polls, to try to determine what his true political motive was. The polls, as he expected, continued to indicate that the American public would never truly forgive an impeached President, but the polls did show signs that Woodrow was making a faint comeback. Still, it didn't make any sense. Julio wondered to himself what had prompted Woodrow to come out of his shell.

ㅠㅠ

Ever since the impeachment, Shirley Hawkins had become somewhat of a media celebrity. She had been invited to appear on all of the TV talk shows, and had even been offered a huge sum of money to make a centerfold appearance in one of the "magazines for gentlemen". She publicly declined the offer, issuing a statement that bashed the very thought of a magazine company exploiting her rise to popularity for merely serving her country. The statement made her even more adored and credible in the eyes of the public. Shirley Hawkins seemed to be the only living symbol of honesty and integrity in Washington, D.C.

That is why it came as such a huge shock to America when Shirley Hawkins was arrested. Headlines around the world carried the story:

"SHIRLEY HAWKINS ARRESTED!
Testimony Tainted By Payoff"

She was shown on CNN in handcuffs, surrounded by police who were protecting her from an angry mob. She was charged with conspiracy, bribery and treason.

Only then did it dawn on Julio why Woodrow had elevated his profile.

━━━

Just like the rest of America, Julio was stunned by the turn of events. The level of turmoil in American politics, and in American cities, was cause for concern to everybody, but Julio was much more than concerned...he was alarmed. His name had been tossed around in the media, indirectly associating him with seditious activities. Many of the illegal aliens who had been arrested were deported after telling the police and the media that Julio Masito was their leader. They all claimed to stand in favor of world government. Their slogan was "America Must Die, So The World Can Live." The image painted in the minds of Americans was threatening. Julio's popularity in the polls started to tumble.

To counter this disinformation, Julio decided to address the subject in a speech to the General Assembly of the United Nations. He stood tall at the podium in front of a full house with a worldwide television audience listening to his every word.

"Ladies and gentlemen, delegates to this Assembly, citizens of the world. Unfortunately today, I must tell you that everything that I stand for is being undermined by those who do not want to see the world take steps in a new direction. My detractors would have you believe that I stand for a world government that would supersede all of the governments represented by this esteemed body. That is simply not true. As you know, there are certain issues that undoubtedly concern us all, issues that I have previously outlined before this Assembly. I firmly believe that as we go forward, these issues must be addressed jointly, in partnership.

"But do not be misled. This is not a question of power and

authority, as many would have you believe. It is a question of survival and responsibility. You have all witnessed the unrest and turmoil in the streets of America. You have probably heard my name associated with much of this violence. Let me tell you all that I have nothing to do with these hooligans. I am a Hopi Indian, through and through. The very word 'Hopi' means 'peaceful people'. These groups represent those who want to undermine everything that I stand for. Do not let these manipulators destroy our true purpose. Do not let them interfere with the important decisions that we all face. Please, we must choose the path of responsibility in these matters of mutual concern. We must follow the Way."

In that instant, live on television, F. B. I. agents stormed down every aisle of the Assembly, surrounding the Secretary-General at the podium. They handcuffed him on the spot, charged him with conspiracy, bribery and treason, the same charges that had been brought against Shirley Hawkins. The arresting officer read the Secretary-General his rights. His voice was picked up by the microphone at the podium, and carried around the entire world.

Julio Masito, the Secretary-General of the United Nations, had been arrested.

CHAPTER 34

The Cemetery

Back in Jefferson City, Missouri, Father Franklin Seeley waited patiently in the reception area to see James Woodrow. He had been waiting for an excessive amount of time, but he would wait however long it took. The message he had been asked to deliver was urgent. It had to be communicated immediately. Finally, the door to the office opened and Woodrow stepped out to greet the Father. No time was wasted before the ex-President asked what it was that they needed to talk about. They walked back into Woodrow's office and closed the door.

"Sir, Cardinal Angelico has sent me to tell you that there is one final step that must be taken before the White House is once again yours."

"Yeah? What's that, Father? Ask and you shall receive," Woodrow laughed.

"It's Senator Cheney, sir."

"What about Senator Cheney?"

"I'm afraid he must be done away with, sir."

"What?"

"You must get rid of him, Mr. President."

"Why?"

"He knows too much, sir. He knows everything. In truth, Senator Cheney knew about Shirley Hawkins long before we did."

"Father Seeley, you're not from around here, are you?"

"No, sir. I was just sent here from Rome when you moved back to town, sir. I am originally from California."

"You're not really a parish clergyman, are you?"

"Vatican Intelligence, sir."

"Now, Father Seeley, are you telling me that Cheney was behind the Shirley Hawkins payoff?"

"Yes, sir."

"You mean Secretary-General Masito had nothing to do with it? He's just a fall guy?"

"That's correct, sir. Masito was our problem. We had to find a way to discredit him. Now that we have done that, it is your turn, Mr. President. Senator Cheney is your problem. I'm afraid you have no choice in the matter. He must go."

"But I don't do that sort of thing."

"Here's a phone number," Seeley said, sliding a piece of paper across Woodrow's desk. "Set up a meeting with Howard Liebermann. He can help you get the job done. He does this 'sort of thing'."

"Why don't you arrange it? Why do I have to do it?"

"Come on now, Mr. President. Mr. Liebermann is Jewish. He is not one of our own. Besides, this business is more suited for politicians than clergymen, don't you agree?"

"And what if I don't?"

"I suppose it'll be Rus Hamilton for the duration. And watch out for Senator Cheney. I hear he can be quite nasty himself. I imagine he will try to keep Hamilton in office, one way or another. He probably figures that an impeached President won't be missed too badly."

Woodrow realized for the first time that he was under the

Church's thumb. He picked up the phone and dialed Liebermann's number.

⟨⟨⟨

"Liebermann," was his answer.

"Mr. Liebermann, this is James Woodrow."

"Yes, Mr. President. I've been expecting your call."

"Would it be possible for you to fly to St. Louis tomorrow? We need to meet privately."

"Yes. That can be arranged."

"Good. Please call my secretary with your flight information and my driver will pick you up at the airport. Let's shoot for sometime around noon. Our meeting shouldn't last more than an hour, so you can catch a mid-afternoon flight back to Miami."

"Yes, sir, Mr. President. I'll shoot for noon tomorrow."

⟨⟨⟨

Woodrow sat in the back seat of the limo behind the driver, looking out bullet-proof windows that were tinted so darkly that no one on the outside could see in. In route to the airport, photographs of Mr. Liebermann had been shown to the Secret Service agents assigned to protect Woodrow. The agents recognized Liebermann the instant he walked out of the terminal. They escorted him to the limo and opened the door to let him in. One of the agents climbed in behind Liebermann. Once the door was closed, the driver pulled away from the airport, while the agent checked Liebermann for weapons and recording devices. After he checked out clean, the limo stopped to let the agent return to the car that followed. Then Woodrow pushed the control button that raised the partition that separated the driver from the passengers, so they could have some privacy.

Woodrow dispelled the small talk and got right to the point of the meeting.

"Mr. Liebermann, what is your relationship with Senator Cheney?"

"I've worked for him in the past. I am not working for him now."

"What would it take for you to work for me?"

"That depends. What would you have me do?"

"Senator Cheney has become quite a nuisance."

"A Senator?"

"That's right."

"That'll be expensive. Five hundred thousand dollars, cash. Small denominations. Half up front, half when the job is done."

"Cancel your return flight and check into one of the airport hotels. My driver will deliver half the money to you tomorrow. When can I expect the job to be completed?"

"Oh, it won't take long, Mr. President. Only a week or two."

"O.K., my driver will deliver the other half to Miami when I read about this in the newspaper. Don't ever contact me again. Is that understood, Mr. Liebermann?"

"Yes, sir. You'll never hear from me again."

"One last question, Mr. Liebermann. What's the going price for an impeached President?" There was a pause, "On second thought, don't answer that question. Just look for the delivery tomorrow."

"Mr. President, don't worry about a thing. You won't be an impeached President long enough for me to consider your question. You'll be right back in the White House before you know it. It was a pleasure meeting you, sir."

Woodrow wondered how much Liebermann knew after making that remark about his return to office. Woodrow could only hope that the job got done and he never heard from the murdering bastard again. With the push of a button, he lowered the privacy window, and asked the driver to drop Mr. Liebermann off at the Marriott Hotel. Their business meeting had concluded.

Cheney wasn't difficult to find. Liebermann just dropped by his office in Washington and insisted upon waiting to be seen. He used an alias, claiming to be the government affairs officer of a newly formed political action committee from Cheney's home state. When Cheney walked past the waiting area on his way to the men's room, he recognized Liebermann immediately, but chose not to speak to him. On his return from the rest room, Cheney told his secretary to cancel his afternoon schedule. He grabbed his coat and brief case and motioned to Liebermann to follow him out of the office, telling his staff that he would be out for the remainder of the day.

Cheney didn't speak a word to Liebermann until the two were out of the building. Only after they were completely alone did their conversation begin.

"For God's sake, Howard! What the hell do you mean just walking into my office like that?"

"Calm down, Senator. Just calm down. I didn't use my name back there. Nobody in your office has a clue who I am. We need to talk. That's all."

"Well, why can't you call me like everybody else?"

"Phone records, Senator. Phone records. Besides, last time we talked, I recall you emphatically told me to never call your office."

"I believe it was 'never contact me', period!"

"Well, we need to talk."

"What is it, Howard?"

"I'm parked right here, Senator. We can't have this conversation on Capitol Hill."

Liebermann drove Senator Cheney due west down Constitution Avenue, and then crossed the Potomac on the Fourteenth Street Bridge. They turned northwest up the George Washington Memorial Parkway, and took the exit into Arlington National Cemetery. Howard found a secluded spot and parked the car, asking the Senator if he objected to taking a walk. It was a cold day in Washington, so both men wore their gloves and coats to stay warm. They walked alone among the countless white gravestones that marked the resting places of so many who had died serving their country.

"The Democrats are making their move. They want the White

House back," Liebermann began.

"I know."

"So far, the blame for Shirley Hawkins has gone to the Secretary-General, not the Republicans."

"Yeah. Let's leave it that way, Howard."

"I found out that it's the Roman Catholic Church who wants to get him. They're scared to death of the guy."

"Where'd you hear that?"

"Woodrow. Woodrow told me."

"Why are you talking to Woodrow?"

"It's a job, Senator. Woodrow wants me to do a job."

"I thought you only worked for me, Liebermann. Now you're working for both sides of the aisle?"

"Not necessarily, Senator. What's it worth to hit an impeached President?"

"Goddammit, Howard. I don't know. What are you talking about?"

"I'm talking about money, Senator. How much money is it worth to keep Hamilton in the White House?"

"Howard, I'm just worried about damage control at this point. Given the circumstances, the Republicans are lucky the curtain hasn't fallen. We'll take whatever allies we have, including the Roman Catholic Church, if that's what it takes to preserve the party. With a Republican-controlled Congress, Woodrow's a lame duck President anyhow. He's not worth killing."

"Thank you, Senator. It's been a pleasure working for you."

In that instant, a silenced .22 caliber bullet from a hand gun that had been cloaked beneath Liebermann's coat tore through Cheney's rib cage. He fell straight to his knees, and then took a second low caliber bullet to the head. Liebermann dragged the corpse over to the nearest gravestone, and propped the body up in a sitting position.

Then he took a switch blade knife from his pocket, opened the blade with the press of a button, and stuck a note to the chest of the dead man. He had not seen a soul in the cemetery on this cold day, so he walked back to the car, casually put his gloves and coat in the trunk, and drove away, humming a song like he had just taken another stroll in the park.

The next day, the headlines of *The Washington Post* said,

"SENATOR FOUND MURDERED IN ARLINGTON CEMETERY
Note Says, 'America Must Die, So The World Might Live...
Free Julio Masito'"

Howard Liebermann picked up his copy of *The Miami Herald* and saw the headlines. His wife wouldn't stop talking about what a terrible state the world was in, with people being murdered and all. Howard ignored her, but she kept on going until he finally told her to please shut up. The phone rung and he answered to avoid her wrath.

"Liebermann."

"Mr. Liebermann, can you meet downstairs to pick up your delivery?"

Liebermann recognized the voice immediately. It was that of Woodrow's driver. Apparently he had the second instalment for the job. "Yes, I'll be right down."

Howard told his wife he would be right back. He was going to run a quick errand. When he walked out of the building, he noticed a black limousine with tinted glass windows parked under the porte-cochere to the tower. Liebermann couldn't see in, but the rear door opened and a voice invited him to get in. It was the voice of Woodrow, who patted the leather upholstered seat, inviting Liebermann to go for a drive.

Once the limo pulled away, a second car followed. Woodrow started the conversation. "The polls say that the public believes Julio Masito doesn't have a thing to do with all of this, even though we've built an air tight case against him. It looks like attacking Julio isn't going to be very popular. That means I've got one more job for you to do."

Just as he finished speaking, Woodrow slid a case across the seat to Liebermann. It was his second instalment of $250,000 for the Cheney job. Liebermann opened the case and saw the cash, but he didn't bother to count it. He closed the case back up and listened.

"I need for you to arrange a meeting with Julio Masito. I'll set it up if you tell me when you can do it. You need to make a deal with him. If you succeed, there's another $250,000 in it for you."

"And if I don't?"

"Then half."

"O.K. What's the deal?"

Woodrow and Liebermann talked for another forty-five minutes before the limo dropped him back at his tower. He carried the case upstairs and stored the cash in a safe that he kept in his office. Before Howard closed the door and spun the tumblers, he pulled the diskettes of the Constantine Papers and Nigel's diary, the Istanbul Project, out of the safe. The diskettes were those that Ivan and Betsy had brought to Miami eight years before. They hadn't realized at the time that they had been in concert with the devil.

Liebermann looked down at the diskettes he was holding in his hands and smiled confidently. "I'm gonna be a rich son-of-a-bitch before this is all over," he muttered to himself, as he replaced the diskettes into the safe and closed the door.

CHAPTER 35

The Deal

The U.S. Attorney-General's office controlled all access to prisoner Julio Masito. Private visitations were highly restricted. Even so, Woodrow was confident that a meeting could be arranged, since he had appointed the Attorney-General to office. After deliberating with the Justice Department, a deal was going to be offered. Howard Liebermann would actually make the offer. Woodrow wanted no part of the negotiations.

A meeting date was chosen that allowed Liebermann enough time to complete his homework. First, he had to fly to Chicago, to meet with Baldone. Then, he needed to go to Istanbul, to meet with the Turkish government. Julio Masito was going to be offered a deal that he couldn't refuse.

"Secretary-General Masito, my name is Howard Liebermann."

"Yes. I know who you are," Julio replied.

"Have you been told why this meeting has been arranged?"

"Yes. They told me you had some kind of proposal to make."

"That's correct. If you co-operate, we believe that a settlement can be reached."

"Why should I believe you?"

"You don't have to believe me. If you agree to the terms of the settlement, I'll have James Harrison Woodrow himself give you written assurance that the deal sticks. We'll make it legal."

"You are a killer, aren't you?"

"What makes you say that?"

"I had a vision about you."

"And is that why you mistrust me?"

"Yes."

"Why else?"

"For money, you would kill your own mother."

"Yeah, well...apparently you're worth more alive than dead at this point. At least to somebody. That's why we're having this meeting. But you're right about one thing. I don't really care one way or the other. In fact, if I had it my way, you'd be dead just like the rest of your buddies."

"You killed them, didn't you? You killed Nigel McFarland and Ivan Berkowitz, didn't you?"

"Didn't you read the newspapers? McFarland killed himself. I just happened to be there to watch. And Ivan just couldn't keep his big Russian mouth shut."

"And Senator Cheney?" Julio asked.

"Live by the sword, die by the sword."

Julio was silent. He didn't speak another word to Liebermann the entire meeting. Liebermann was left with no option other than to deliver the deal. He knew there would be no more conversation.

"Woodrow will arrange for the Attorney-General to offer you a light sentence, just a couple of years at a minimum security prison, if you plead guilty to one of the lesser charges that you face. You can plead guilty to sedition. Remember that the other charges you face include treason and conspiracy to murder Senator Cheney. They both carry the death penalty."

"If you choose to plead not-guilty to sedition, then you will be extradited to Turkey where charges have been filed against you for pilfering their national treasures. Already, Mr. Joseph Baldone and Dr. Myers Watson stand ready to testify against you in the U.S., and Mr. Mustafa Alomar is prepared to testify against you in Turkey. You see, Mr. Masito, you were an accomplice whether you knew what was going on or not, and it doesn't matter in their eyes. In Turkey, the penalty is the guillotine."

Julio did not flinch.

"So, tell me Mr. Masito, what do you want to do? Like I said before, it doesn't really matter to me, one way or another. I'm getting paid just to deliver the deal."

Julio did not respond.

"Then so be it. Your extradition proceeding will get under way tomorrow. If you defend against extradition, then you'll be made to look like a common thief, and then a murdering traitor. If you remain silent, you will likely be in route to Istanbul by the end of this week. Your blood shall be on the hands of the Turks, not the Woodrow administration. Actually, if I were you, I'd take Woodrow's offer. Mr. Masito, are you even listening to me?"

Julio did not answer.

CHAPTER 36

The Litany

When Howard Liebermann and Mustafa Alomar first met with the Turkish government officials at the U.S. Embassy in Istanbul, the Turks did not like the sound of playing a part in the execution of a Secretary-General of the United Nations. It was true that fifteen years ago, Turkish laws had been broken. Everyone agreed that early Christian sculptures, icons and manuscripts had been smuggled out of the country, but it was also true that Turkish government officials, in office at the time, had been paid handsomely to look the other way. In the final analysis, the Turks knew they were being asked to do the dirty work of the U.S. Government. They wanted to know what was in it for them.

It didn't take long for the U.S. Ambassador to produce Turkey's multi-billion dollar shopping list for restricted U.S. manufactured military hardware, and place it on the table. The Ambassador offered them the entire list, and a 100 percent U.S. Government loan, to facilitate the purchase. It was a hard deal for the Turks to turn down.

ᛏᛏᛏ

When the news was announced that Julio Masito, the Secretary-General of the United Nations, would be extradited to Turkey, people from all over the world were shaken. On the day that he actually boarded a jet bound for Istanbul, there were uniform reactions around the globe. In smaller communities, people gravitated toward their town centers and held vigils on Julio's behalf, praying for his release. In the larger urban areas, mass demonstrations occurred, accompanied by civil disobedience.

As his flight was in route over the Atlantic, hundreds of thousands of Turkish men, women and children filled the streets of Istanbul. They congregated in the plaza in front of the prison where Julio was to be held and shouted out their feelings. Eventually, the crowd grew tired of the hysteria and began to organize.

It started as a murmur and graduated to a chant. The mob repeated their mantra over and over again, saying only the name, "JULIO." A summoner broke into the gaps between repetitions, saying the name singularly, only to be echoed by thousands of voices. It built to a battle-cry, making those inside the prison feel like Joshua was leading the litany. Some feared that the prison wall might come tumbling down if the crowd's fervor increased by even a decibel. Others inside the prison hoped that it would. But everybody on both sides seemed to agree, they wanted Julio to be free.

Live televised reports from Istanbul delivered the mantra to communities scattered across the entire planet. Those who had been demonstrating or holding vigils were caught up in the same chanting, echoing the name, "JULIO." Nothing like it had ever happened before on the planet Earth. Nothing even close.

One of those watching the CNN broadcast was the Pope. Within minutes of witnessing the phenomenon that was unfolding in Istanbul, he placed a call to Turkey's head of state, asking him to have mercy on the Secretary-General. Because of the fury of the Turkish people, the Pope wanted a change of venue. He was worried that the Turkish connection would be investigated too thoroughly if Julio was executed. And, he feared that the Constantine Papers would be disclosed in some way. Then, the whole world would be looking for a smoking gun.

He made his request in the name of mercy, as though it was Julio's soul he was worried about.

The Turkish government officials were also watching the reactions of the people. They had not been comfortable in the first place, but now it was getting out of control. The Turks decided that the deal that had been agreed to regarding the purchase of military equipment, and the loan that went with it, were not enough to justify taking on Julio Masito. They did not want to sully their hands.

When Julio boarded the flight back to the U.S., cameras representing news agencies from all over the world were focused on him. His calm demeanor in the midst of the storm elevated his mystique in the eyes of many to a level reserved only for deities. When the door to the plane was closed in preparation for take-off, the Turkish people started their litany again, shouting out his name, "Julio... JULIO...Julio...JULIO...Julio...JULIO...!"

CHAPTER 37

The Trial

In the United States, Woodrow was busy trying to resurrect his strategy. In his mind, Julio Masito would become politically unstoppable, if he wasn't silenced altogether. Woodrow pressured the Attorney-General to go for the throat, bringing a full-blown treason charge, including sedition and conspiracy to commit murder. The prosecutors used the note found with Senator Cheney's body as circumstantial evidence that the Secretary-General was an accomplice in the murder, and the leader of a political group responsible for the death. The treason charge included references to Julio's initiative at the United Nations, which the prosecutor said was a blatant attempt to usurp the power and sovereign authority of the United States of America. The Attorney-General was seeking the death penalty.

The charges were filed in the federal court system, moving the trial off Capitol Hill. In preparation, Julio's accusers rehearsed their script over and over again, knowing that the last successfully prosecuted treason case involving the death sentence in the

United States had been in 1951, when Julius and Ethel Rosenberg had been executed for passing atomic secrets to a Russian spy.

ᵀᵀᵀ

The toughest obstacle that the prosecution faced was Julio's popularity. The polls continued to reflect global support for the jailed Secretary-General, even though the government thought its case would be convincing to a jury. Regardless of the evidence against him, people in the streets seemed to be determined to stand behind Julio until he was vindicated. They continued to show their support through acts of civil disobedience in the cities, even though Julio made a plea to his supporters to please remain non-violent in their protests.

But the advisors of ex-President James Harrison Woodrow figured out a way to counter Julio's popularity. They hired the services of one of Hollywood's leading production companies, known for its advertising capability, and its successful track record in changing public opinion.

The strategic plan was to conduct a heavy media blitz on TV that would lessen the tensions in the cities, and build grassroots support for Woodrow's staged comeback. The campaign was structured to drum up a strong sense of nationalism, while at the same time portraying Julio and his ideas as threatening to all patriots.

The final impression made upon the viewers was that Woodrow should rightfully be restored to the White House. His return would signal the preservation of the American way, and bring to an end the conspiracy against the American people...a dangerous conspiracy that had resulted in Woodrow's wrongful impeachment. The advertising suggested that justice would prevail and America would be saved.

ᵀᵀᵀ

In addition to buying the services of Hollywood's finest talent, Woodrow's political advisors also hired a Madison Avenue firm to further improve the public's perception of the ex-President. The Madison Avenue firm was responsible for conducting the campaign in the print media and on talk radio programs. Woodrow was going to have the best image money could buy.

ππ

When the trial began, neither Hollywood nor Madison Avenue had done much good. The real-time polls still indicated that world-wide, Julio Masito was not going to be abandoned. In Washington D.C. and in the Vatican, there were many closed-door meetings taking place.

Ironically, it was the Pope who dealt the death blow. He appeared in a globally-televised CNN broadcast. It was a special news report that interrupted their normally scheduled programming. The Pope delivered his message in seven different languages, and those watching in the United States had to wait patiently until he spoke in English. The pronouncement was brief, but it was shattering. The Pope played his trump card. It was the ultimate slander. He simply said, "The world should be aware that Julio Masito might well be the anti-Christ."

ππ

The trial concluded fairly quickly, with Julio never speaking a word in his own defense. On the last day of the trial, you could have heard a pin drop when the foreman of the jury stood in the jury box and read aloud to the judge each charge against the defendant and each verdict by counts. The jury had unanimously found Julio Masito to be guilty of each charge brought against him.

The courtroom broke out in pandemonium, silenced only by the pounding of the judge's gavel and the bailiff's commands that there be order in the court. The judge then asked the defendant to rise as he read the verdicts. Immediately after the reading, the judge pounded his gavel to restore order in the court. There was a haunting silence. The judge peered over the top of his reading glasses at the defendant, radiating the full power of his authority as he spoke.

Julio chose not to look darkly into the eyes of his accusers or his judge. He only wanted to remain calm. He was searching for peace within himself, and so he didn't let his focus turn outward. The only words that he heard the judge say were, "...death by lethal injection."

That was all he heard.

CHAPTER 38

The Execution

As soon as Julio was found guilty of treason, the General Assembly of the United Nations voted to strip him of his office as their Secretary-General. During the same day, on a different stage, Congress voted to fully re-instate James Harrison Woodrow to the office of the President of the United States of America.

In all the commotion, Julio paused to speak to the press as he was being escorted out of the courtroom. He said that he remembered learning the Pledge of Allegiance when he was a young boy. He remembered placing his hand across his chest and saying the pledge proudly, even though his forefathers forbid the practice.

There must have been a dozen microphones thrust into his face when he said,

"America has always struggled to be one nation, under God, indivisible, with liberty and justice for all. The struggle itself has made the United States of America such a strong nation. Now more than ever, we, the people, must endeavor to abide by these words...before it is too late."

During his last days, Julio was visited by his mother, Nampeyo, and his sister, Mina. They brought with them some bean stew, which the three shared together in communion, before saying their good-byes, tearfully.

Julio was also allowed to see Katrina Berkowitz and Betsy McFarland, the widows of his two best friends in life. He reminded the two women that the diskettes would be released to the public following his execution. He warned them to be prepared for the aftermath. They hugged and kissed him good-bye, and thanked him for everything he had done on behalf of their husbands. They promised to keep the torch of truth burning, and to pass on the legacy of three great men.

On the day of his execution, Julio was allowed, for the last time, to see his wife, Mary, and his two children, Amelia and Julian. He was affectionate with each of them, and told them over and over how much he loved them. They were so brave, but in their eyes, Julio could see their pain. For the past few weeks, Mary and the children had cried themselves to sleep every night. Their grieving had already begun. After so many tears, Mary was learning to cope with her emotions. But the children could contain themselves no more, and their emotions welled up and spilled over, once again.

They wept for their father, and for each other. Julio threw his arms around them both, and tried to make them smile by telling them that he would wait for them in the clouds. But they could not be comforted. Finally, Julio smiled at them and with great courage, his children wiped their tears away and tried to smile back...for their father's sake. They knew their dad wanted them to be happy in life, and to celebrate their time together, rather than mourn their time apart.

When Julio was led into the room where he was to be executed, the bright lights and cameras came on once again. He was strapped to a gurney and hooked up to a machine. As his executioners were adjusting the fittings, Julio lifted his head and looked directly into a CNN camera. Then he spoke his last words.

"Do not despair. Be assured that you are connected to All. It is this holy communion that transcends all circumstances.

"Now, in these final moments, I profess to you my faith in God, the individual and collective All. I have come to recognize that our individual and collective actions define the human features of God's nature, and so we have true responsibility. The recognition of true responsibility gives us purpose. The exercise of responsibility gives us fulfillment. The path of responsibility is the Way. It is the path which I continue to travel, as I cross over the threshold into a new realm. The Way leads to holy communion with All. Our salvation resides in this symbiotic and holy communion.

"I leave you now, asking that you grasp your purpose and fulfill your responsibility. Be creative if you are able. Give back what you have taken when you can. Keep your sense of balance in all things.

"Peace, love, hope, and understanding will help you follow the Way. So will honesty, trust, courage and commitment. Try to maintain a spirit of prayer and meditation. This will amplify the power of communion.

"Even so, you will not always be able to follow the Way. There will be times when you will stray from the path. Your mistakes will hurt others, and on occasion, you will need to be forgiven. But do not let the concept of forgiveness lessen your sense of duty. Make retribution for your mistakes. Do not lay your responsibilities at the feet of others, taking comfort that you will be forgiven for your apathy or rebellion. This is a false hope.

"True hope is centered in your divinity. It anticipates a sacred experience. Let true hope, rather than dogma or delusion, be your compass in life...and in death. We should live in the cradle of hope, for there we also die.

"Now close your eyes as I close mine. When hope seems to retreat, you must learn to embrace your imagination. There will be times during your journey when your imagination is all that will sustain your hope. But it is enough.

"To my dearest wife, Mary, and my beloved children, Amelia and Julian...not even death can separate us. We shall be connected...forever. Remember my love always."

Julio then took a few deep breaths and exhaled, appearing very relaxed. He slipped into a state of meditation, just before the machine injected the poison. For a moment he saw his vision of the eagle and the snakes, but he forced the vision from his thoughts. He did not want to dwell on things past. It was time to look forward, to prepare for the journey he was about to take. With eyes still closed, he began to chant a Hopi supplication, a prayer of true hope, and then came the sound of silence. Julio was gone.

EPILOGUE

The day that Julio died, Betsy McFarland went through a drawer full of old photographs that Mac had taken on his many trips over the years. She retrieved one taken of Julio that first evening when she and Mac had arrived on the Hopi Reservation. It was taken during the summer solstice celebration. The Hopi called it the Niman Ceremony or the Going Home Ceremony. It marked the end of their perennial ceremonial cycle. Following the dance at sunset, the mythological kachinas that inhabited the village returned to their spiritual home in the San Francisco Peaks, just outside of Flagstaff.

The photo showed Julio in full costume, dressed as the eagle dancer. It was a sensational picture, backlighted by a raging bonfire that cast a glow about Julio's figure. His eyes seemed full of magic, sparkling like diamonds, radiating the spirit that his costume portrayed. That night, in a vision, Julio realized that one day he would become Kwahu, the divine messenger.

Betsy took the photograph with her to Flagstaff, Arizona, where she met up with Katrina Berkowitz at the airport. The two of them drove out to The Landslide, and watched the sunset while they reminisced. They wrote down what they could remember of the last words that Julio had spoken. When they returned to town and checked into their hotel, Betsy and Katrina called the local newspaper to tell them that they wanted to run an anonymous, full-page ad in several national papers. The gentleman who took the call was glad to help them.

ᵾᵾᵾ

The funeral service was held on the Hopi Reservation and was closed to the public. Mary, Amelia and Julian stayed on the reservation with Nampeyo and Mina. The five of them prepared Julio's body for the funeral. They began by washing his hair in yucca suds, and rubbing his body with sacred corn meal, before dressing him in his favorite clothes. The children put a special Hopi necklace around his neck, and placed photographs taken of themselves in their daddy's pockets. Nampeyo kissed her son and placed a white cloud mask over his face...a ceremonial mask that prepared Julio to join the cloud people. Last of all, Mary draped a blanket over his shoulders to keep him warm, and placed some piki bread and strips of meat near his body so that he would not hunger during his final journey.

Typically, the Hopi buried their dead sitting upright in their grave, in a fetal position. A planting stick would be placed in the grave to help the deceased climb to the land of the cloud people. But the Tribal Chairman thought Julio's spirit was so powerful, he should journey to the realm of the Spirit Father. The Chairman decided Julio's body would be set ablaze atop the San Francisco Peaks. There, in the presence of Taiowa, Julio, the eagle dancer, would be transformed into Kwahu, the divine messenger. His destiny would be fulfilled.

When the funeral service began, a small procession drove out of New Oraibi to the base of the sacred mountain. From there, six Hopi men, dressed in ceremonial garb, carried Julio's body up the mountain. The family and guests followed, grieving with each

276
ᵾᵾᵾ

step taken. Once they reached the summit, the men lifted Julio
onto a wooden platform. Everyone stayed until the funeral pyre
completely burned out. When it was over, there was nothing left
but smoke and ashes. Julio's body was gone; but his spirit remained. The Tribal Chairman told those who were present that if
they listened very carefully, the voice of Kwahu could be heard
forever.

A week later, Mac's diskettes appeared on the Internet and the
Church couldn't do a thing to prevent it. Soon thereafter, *Time
Magazine* carried a story entitled *The Istanbul Project*. The writer
interviewed Mr. Joseph Baldone, Dean Willis Barker, Monsignor
Thomas Bates, and Chancellor Preston Monague. They all denied
having any knowledge of the Constantine Papers, saying that any
such claim was purely a hoax. The authenticity of such a story,
they said, could never be confirmed without producing the original manuscripts.

The only person inte.viewed who supported the story was
Betsy McFarland, who provided bank statements and a copy of
Mac's amended will to the author. She claimed that the Church
had paid her hush money over the years. She took it because she
didn't understand the significance of the Constantine Papers, and
she needed the financial assistance. The Church countered that
the payments were unrelated to the will, and were made to support a suffering widow, who hadn't the financial means to support herself. Besides, they added, the Church's inheritance under
the will was meaningless.

There remained a lot of unanswered questions, but most people
just let the whole story fade away without the original documents
to validate the claims made by the diskettes.

Then, almost five years after Julio had been executed, another
amazing story was featured in *Time Magazine*. This one made the
cover, and was entitled *The Constantine Papers*. The article

proclaimed the existence of the original documents.

The documents were made public by Cardinal Marciano Angelico, who was defrocked and ex-communicated by the Church. The former Cardinal told the whole story to the press, including his participation in the framing of Julio Masito. Marciano Angelico was arrested, tried and given a life sentence in prison, but his sentence was commuted to probation because he had co-operated with the prosecution, and he was suffering from a terminal disease.

The fallout from Cardinal Angelico's testimony was substantial. Joseph Baldone was sentenced to ten years in prison for theft, but on appeal his sentence was reduced to two years. He served one and was released on good behavior.

Howard Liebermann was arrested, tried, and was serving time on death row, at least until his appeals expired, and his capital punishment could be carried out.

Father Seeley received a light sentence, but was also defrocked and ex-communicated by the Church.

The Pope and President James Harrison Woodrow escaped prosecution. They both died of natural causes during the five year span.

ᙏᙏᙏ

Betsy, Katrina and Mary became the closest of friends through the tragic deaths of their husbands. They moved to Flagstaff, Arizona, and watched Julian and Amelia Masito grow up in the Hopi Way. Their lives made apparent the everlasting spirit of communion that their father had described before his death .

There were various stories and books written about Julio. The impact he had made on the world was dramatic, turning humanity away from the precipice of self-destruction. Eventually, the United Nations adopted the proposals that Julio had put forward, and the entire world started in a new direction. Followers devoted to Julio's leadership and captivated by his legacy were scattered across the land. They began to organize, and when these believers gathered together, often they shared bean stew and

recited in unison a new statement of faith that became known as
Julio's Creed:

"I believe that God is the individual and collective All. The
human features of God's nature are defined by our individual
and collective actions, giving us true responsibility. Our
recognition of this responsibility gives us purpose.

"I also believe that the essence of divinity can be discovered
by entering a state of communion with All. Some call this
state of communion the kingdom of God, although it is
known by many names. It is within this state of
communion that I hope to dwell, forever.

Amen."

BIBLIOGRAPHY

The author wishes to acknowledge certain research material which held the story together. A debt of gratitude is owed to the authors of these works, but especially to Joseph B. Tyson, my favorite professor, who still teaches at Southern Methodist University.

Boissiere, Robert. *Meditations With The Hopi*. Santa Fe: Bear & Company, Inc., 1986

James, Harry C. *Pages From Hopi History*. Tuscon: The University of Arizona Press., 1974

John Paul II, Pope. *Crossing The Threshold Of Hope*. New York: Alfred A. Knopf, 1994

Hawking, Stephen W. *A Brief History Of Time*. Toronto; New York: Bantam Books, 1988

Lemonick, Michael D. Article in *Time Magazine* entitled *Life, The Universe and Everything*. New York: Time Inc., February 22, 1993

Microsoft Encarta. Microsoft Corporation, 1993

Ostling, Richard N. Article in *Time Magazine* entitled *Is Jesus In The Dead Sea Scrolls?* New York: Time, Inc., September 21, 1992

Pagels, Elaine H. *The Gnostic Gospels*. New York: Random House, 1979

Remnick, David. Article in *New Yorker Magazine* entitled *The Devil Problem*. New York: The New Yorker Magazine, Inc., April 3, 1995

Smith, Huston. *The Religions of Man*. New York: Harper & Row, Publishers. 1958

Tyson, Joseph B. *A Study of Early Christianity*. New York: The Macmillan Company. 1973

Wright, Robert. Article in *Time Magazine* entitled *Science, God and Man*. New York: Time, Inc. December 28, 1992